DYING FOR YOU

Praise for Jenny Frame

Longing for You

"Jenny Frame knocks it out of the park once again with this fantastic sequel to *Hunger For You*. She can keep the pages turning with a delicious mix of intrigue and romance."—*Rainbow Literary Society*

Hunger for You

"I loved this book. Paranormal stuff like vampires and werewolves are my go-to sins. This book had literally everything I needed: chemistry between the leads, hot love scenes (phew), drama, angst, romance (oh my, the romance) and strong supporting characters."—*The Reading Doc*

The Duchess and the Dreamer

"We thoroughly enjoyed the whole romance-the-disbelieving-duchess with gallantry, unwavering care, and grand gestures. Since this is very firmly in the butch-femme zone, it appealed to that part of our traditionally-conditioned-typecasting mindset that all the wooing and work is done by Evan without throwing even a small fit at any point. We liked the fact that Clementine has layers and depth. She has her own personal and personality hurdles that make her behaviour understandable and create the right opportunities for Evan to play the romantic knight convincingly…We definitely recommend this one to anyone looking for a feel-good mushy romance."—*Best Lesfic Reviews*

"There are a whole range of things I like about Jenny Frame's aristocratic heroines: they have plausible histories to account for them holding titles in their own right; they're in touch with reality and not necessarily super-rich, certainly not through inheritance; and they find themselves paired with perfectly contrasting co-heroines…Clementine and Evan are excellently depicted, and I love the butch:femme dynamic they have going on, as well as their individual abilities to stick to their principles but also to compromise with each other when necessary."
—*The Good, The Bad and The Unread*

Still Not Over You

"*Still Not Over You* is a wonderful second-chance romance anthology that makes you believe in love again. And you would certainly be missing out if you have not read *My Forever Girl*, because it truly is everything."—*SymRoute*

Someone to Love

"One of the author's best works to date—both Trent and Wendy were so well developed they came alive. I could really picture them and they jumped off the pages. They had fantastic chemistry, and their sexual dynamic was deliciously well written. The supporting characters and the storyline about Alice's trauma was also sensitively written and well handled."—*Melina Bickard, Librarian, Waterloo Library (UK)*

Wooing the Farmer

"The chemistry between the two MCs had us hooked right away. We also absolutely loved the seemingly ditzy femme with an ambition of steel but really a vulnerable girl. The sex scenes are great. Definitely recommended."—*Reviewer@large*

"This is the book we Axedale fanatics have been waiting for…Jenny Frame writes the most amazing characters and this whole series is a masterpiece. But where she excels is in writing butch lesbians. Every time I read a Jenny Frame book I think it's the best ever, but time and again she surprises me. She has surpassed herself with *Wooing the Farmer*."—*Kitty Kat's Book Review Blog*

Royal Court

"The author creates two very relatable characters…Quincy's quietude and mental torture are offset by Holly's openness and lust for life. Holly's determination and tenacity in trying to reach Quincy are total wish-fulfilment of a person like that. The chemistry and attraction is excellently built."—*Best Lesbian Erotica*

"[A] butch/femme romance that packs a punch."—*Les Rêveur*

"There were unbelievably hot sex scenes as I have come to expect and look forward to in Jenny Frame's books. Passions slowly rise until you feel the characters may burst!…Royal Court is wonderful and I highly recommend it."—*Kitty Kat's Book Review Blog*

Royal Court "was a fun, light-hearted book with a very endearing romance."—*Leanne Chew, Librarian, Parnell Library (Auckland, NZ)*

Charming the Vicar

"Chances are, you've never read or become captivated by a romance like *Charming the Vicar*. While books featuring people of the cloth aren't unusual, Bridget is no ordinary vicar—a lesbian with a history of kink…Surrounded by mostly supportive villagers, Bridget and Finn balance love and faith in a story that affirms both can exist for anyone, regardless of sexual identity."—*RT Book Reviews*

"The sex scenes were some of the sexiest, most intimate and quite frankly, sensual I have read in a while. Jenny Frame had me hooked and I reread a few scenes because I felt like I needed to experience the intense intimacy between Finn and Bridget again. The devotion they showed to one another during these sex scenes but also in the intimate moments was gripping and for lack of a better word, carnal."—*Les Rêveur*

"The sexual chemistry between [Finn and Bridge] is unbelievably hot. It is sexy, lustful and with more than a hint of kink. The scenes between them are highly erotic—and not just the sex scenes. The tension is ramped up so well that I felt the characters would explode if they did not get relief!…An excellent book set in the most wonderful village—a place I hope to return to very soon!"—*Kitty Kat's Book Reviews*

"This is Frame's best character work to date. They are layered and flawed and yet relatable…Frame really pushed herself with *Charming the Vicar* and it totally paid off…I also appreciate that even though she regularly writes butch/femme characters, no two pairings are the same."—*The Lesbian Review*

Unexpected

"If you enjoy contemporary romances, *Unexpected* is a great choice. The character work is excellent, the plotting and pacing are well done, and it's just a sweet, warm read…Definitely pick this book up when you're looking for your next comfort read, because it's sure to put a smile on your face by the time you get to that happy ending."—*Curve*

"*Unexpected* by Jenny Frame is a charming butch/femme romance that is perfect for anyone who wants to feel the magic of overcoming adversity and finding true love. I love the way Jenny Frame writes.

I have yet to discover an author who writes like her. Her voice is strong and unique and gives a freshness to the lesbian fiction sector."
—*The Lesbian Review*

Royal Rebel

"Frame's stories are easy to follow and really engaging. She stands head and shoulders above a number of the romance authors and it's easy to see why she is quickly making a name for herself in lesfic romance."—*The Lesbian Review*

Courting the Countess

"I love Frame's romances. They are well paced, filled with beautiful character moments and a wonderful set of side characters who ultimately end up winning your heart...I love Jenny Frame's butch/femme dynamic; she gets it so right for a romance."—*The Lesbian Review*

"I loved, loved, loved this book. I didn't expect to get so involved in the story but I couldn't help but fall in love with Annie and Harry...The love scenes were beautifully written and very sexy. I found the whole book romantic and ultimately joyful and I had a lump in my throat on more than one occasion. A wonderful book that certainly stirred my emotions."—*Kitty Kat's Book Reviews*

"*Courting The Countess* has an historical feel in a present day world, a thought provoking tale filled with raw emotions throughout. [Frame] has a magical way of pulling you in, making you feel every emotion her characters experience."—*Lunar Rainbow Reviewz*

"I didn't want to put the book down and I didn't. Harry and Annie are two amazingly written characters that bring life to the pages as they find love and adventures in Harry's home. This is a great read, and you will enjoy it immensely if you give it a try!"—*Fantastic Book Reviews*

A Royal Romance

"*A Royal Romance* was a guilty pleasure read for me. It was just fun to see the relationship develop between George and Bea, to see George's life as queen and Bea's as a commoner. It was also refreshing to see that both of their families were encouraging, even when Bea doubted that things could work between them because of their class differences...*A Royal Romance* left me wanting a sequel, and romances don't usually do that to me."—*Leeanna.ME Mostly a Book Blog*

By the Author

A Royal Romance

Courting the Countess

Dapper

Royal Rebel

Unexpected

Charming the Vicar

Royal Court

Wooing the Farmer

Someone to Love

The Duchess and the Dreamer

Royal Family

Home Is Where the Heart Is

Sweet Surprise

Wild for You

Hunger for You

Longing for You

Dying for You

Wolfgang County Series

Heart of the Pack

Soul of the Pack

Blood of the Pack

Visit us at www.boldstrokesbooks.com

DYING FOR YOU

by
Jenny Frame

2022

ISBN 13: 978-1-63679-073-2

This Trade Paperback Original Is Published By
Bold Strokes Books, Inc.
P.O. Box 249
Valley Falls, NY 12185

First Edition: March 2022

CREDITS
EDITOR: RUTH STERNGLANTZ
PRODUCTION DESIGN: STACIA SEAMAN
COVER DESIGN BY TAMMY SEIDICK

Acknowledgments

Thank you to all the BSB staff for their tireless hard work. Thank you to Ruth for always helping my books be the best they can be, and thanks to my family for their support and encouragement.

Lou and Barney, I wish we could spend forever together. I know for certain I'd never get bored, and you two would make me laugh every day.

To Lou, My Immortal Love.

CHAPTER ONE

Smoke billowed from the raging torches being held by the cloaked and hooded figures beneath the arches of the replica Acropolis. The heavy beat of the drums rang out like a heartbeat, a steady rhythm that coursed through the veins of all who gathered to take part in this ancient Beltane Fire Festival.

"Daisy?"

Daisy MacDougall moved through the dancing and singing crowds atop Calton Hill in Edinburgh to find the best spot to watch the players in the festival. The smell of the smoke from fires and the torches lit everywhere around gave her a sense of what the festival would have been like two thousand years ago.

It was only when she bumped into a group of teenagers who were waving glowing light sticks that she came back to the present day with a bang.

"Daisy? Can you hear me?"

She turned around and saw her friend Skye. "Sorry, what?" The shouts as well as the singing and drumming didn't make communication easy.

"This looks like a good spot," Skye said.

Daisy walked over to Skye and her other friends, Zane and Pierce. Together, Daisy and her friends were Monster Hunters, a team they formed at university to explore all things paranormal. Their vlogs and website were essential watching and reading for all those who were interested in finding out if the myths and legends of paranormal beings had some substance to them.

Of course, since meeting and befriending Amelia Debrek and

Byron, the Principe of the Debrek vampire clan, she knew the truth about the paranormal world. It was all real, but she could tell no one, as she had promised Amelia and Byron.

But even though she knew the truth, Daisy still felt her friends' goal to document different mythical legends and sightings was worthwhile—plus she liked spending time with her friends.

"Okay, let's set up," Daisy said. Zane, their camera guy, came up close and tried to take off the scarf she wore around her neck. She tensed and took a step back. "Don't, Zane."

"We need to see more of you. It's a warm spring night."

"Just get ready to record, Zane. It's up to me what I wear," Daisy said.

He pursed his lips in anger but then backed off. It was a warm May evening, but she had to wear this warm scarf to cover the bite she had received from Victorija Dred. Victorija was the leader and Principe of the Dred vampire clan—a clever and remorseless killer, and enemy to the Debrek clan.

Much to Daisy's horror, she and Victorija Dred were now blood bonded. The night Victorija attacked Amelia Debrek at The Sanctuary, a club where paranormals and humans mingled, Daisy protected her friend, and Victorija had tried to drain her blood at her neck. But instead of killing her, Victorija recoiled at the first taste, and they'd shared a moment in time that Daisy still didn't understand.

Afterwards, when the bite mark didn't heal as it should have done, Daisy came to understand that her DNA was compatible with Victorija's, and she had become blood bonded to her, just like Amelia was to Byron Debrek.

Byron explained that Victorija now needed Daisy's blood to survive, just like Byron needed Amelia's, or she would plunge into madness. Of course, Byron and Amelia loved each other and gladly accepted their bond.

Victorija was a homicidal killer and she would only use and abuse Daisy for blood. Daisy had been keeping a low profile at Byron's insistence for a few months, but she couldn't miss going to the Beltane Fire Festival in Edinburgh. It was one of the best nights for paranormal events in the calendar, and one where Monster Hunters had to be.

So together with her team and the two guards, Owen and Trista, whom Byron insisted watch over her, she travelled from London to

Edinburgh yesterday. Pierce, their sound man, walked up to her and said, "Zane takes every opportunity, doesn't he."

"To touch me? To get too close? Yes," Daisy said with frustration.

"I'll talk to him. He's besotted with you, has been ever since we met at uni."

"Would you, please? When he's filming me, I feel like he's undressing me with the camera lens," Daisy said.

"Don't worry, honey. I will. Who are these weird Men in Black who're following us?"

Owen and Trista stood behind Skye and Zane, to protect her from Victorija, because she would be out there somewhere, plotting to get Daisy and use her as a blood bank.

Daisy couldn't tell Pierce the truth, so she said, "Byron got some threats from…some terrorist group, and she thought because I'm so close to Amelia, I should be protected"—she had to distract Pierce from her wafer-thin explanation—"and they're not in the way, are they?"

Pierce looked back at them and grinned. "No, especially the big guy that looks like a rugby player, what's his name?"

"Owen, and the woman is Trista. Maybe you could do your best to distract him so he's not breathing down my neck all the bloody time."

Pierce waggled his eyebrows. "I'll gladly distract him anyway."

Skye, the team's director, said, "Let's start filming now—the main players are just a minute away."

"Okay."

"Good luck, babe," Pierce said.

Both Pierce and Zane were ready with their equipment. Daisy closed her eyes and let the beat of the drums get her into the right headspace. She ran over a few of the lines she had written for her piece to camera, but with her eyes still closed, she felt someone's breath on her neck and in her ear.

She jumped and looked around for anyone who could have done it, but the groups of people around her hadn't moved. The bite Victorija gave her started to tingle, and she felt the urge to give herself to her blood bond. It was a feeling that had dogged her ever since that night at The Sanctuary. Sometimes it was light like now, and sometimes overwhelming. Daisy assumed that it was the same for Victorija.

"Daisy? You okay?" Skye shouted.

"Yeah, let's do it." Daisy tried to shake off the feeling.

"In ten, then," Skye said and started counting down.

Daisy put on her bright smiling face, and began, "Hi, monster hunters. We are lucky enough to be at the Beltane Fire Festival in Edinburgh. It's April the thirtieth and a very important time of year on the Celtic calendar. It's said that the veil between our world and the land of the gods, the dead, and the monsters is thin and allows them to visit our world."

She turned around and indicated to the large crowds. "Adults and children all come to see this display, a reinterpretation of an ancient Iron Age Celtic festival. Beltane means *bright fire*, and the Celts would come together to celebrate the return of spring. It marked the turning of the wheel of the year, fertility, and hope."

Daisy walked up close to the camera and beckoned their audience closer, then whispered, "And rumours are that the paranormal and monsters that we search for come out to play on Beltane night and mix unnoticed with the painted players and reenactors of this festival. Let me introduce you to some of the actors in this drama."

"Cut," Skye said. "Brill, Daisy. Perfect as usual. The actors will be here in a sec."

Something made Daisy look around, and she caught a flash of blond hair, but then it was gone. Her heart beat faster, and her bite mark tingled.

Owen and Trista must have noticed because they came up to her, and Trista said, "Did you see something?"

Daisy felt something when she saw that flash of blond. Blond like the hair of her blood bond, Victorija.

"No, nothing. Just a loud bang of the drum."

"Daisy, they're here," Skye shouted.

She looked and saw the entourages of the two main players coming towards them, dancing and singing. People covered in red or white body paint interacted with the crowd as they went.

"Okay, start filming, Skye."

Zane brought the camera up closer, and Daisy began, "The red characters are creatures of chaos and misrule and represent the Horned God. The people in white dresses and white body paint are the court of the May Queen. Let's follow them."

The group followed the crowds and the procession down to a stage area. The May Queen, a woman in white with an elaborate headdress, got up on stage followed by a man in green body paint, the Horned God.

Daisy nodded to Zane to begin filming again. "The May Queen embodies purity, strength, and potential for growth. The Horned God sees the May Queen, and he realizes that to be with the woman he loves, he will need to undergo a huge change. He surrenders his life to her. Then the May Queen gives him life energy and brings about his new spring form, the Green Man. He represents the life that grows on earth. They cannot exist without each other."

The shouts and chants were building up to a crescendo. Then the crowd surged, and Daisy found herself carried along by the crowd away from her friends. She began to panic as she felt crushed in the throng, but she managed to push her way into some space.

Daisy leaned over, putting her hands against her knees, and tried to get her breath back. She was claustrophobic at the best of times, but that was horrible. Then she felt someone brush past her, and they set her whole body tingling. This was what her friends lovingly called her spidey sense.

Whenever Monster Hunters were to meet someone claiming to be a paranormal being, in their quest for the truth, they knew if the person didn't set off Daisy's spidey sense, then they weren't the real deal.

It was an intuition she'd had from birth, and she had been ridiculed mercilessly as a child for talking about it. She'd learned to keep it to herself until she met her Monster Hunter friends, because they were open to that kind of thing.

Daisy stood up quickly and saw another flash of blond hair, and someone in a gothic black jacket carrying a cane. "Victorija? It can't be." But her bite mark was telling a different story. She got a sharp pain and a longing, deep inside, to present herself to Victorija, if it was her. She looked around and saw none of her friends, and no Owen or Trista. They'd be furious with her for it, and Byron would be too, but she had to get to Victorija, had to understand this bond and if there was no way to break it.

Daisy saw the blond figure stop, but they kept their back to her. Daisy broke into a jog and made her way towards the blonde, pushing past the people who got in her way. But just as she got within ten yards, a group of drummers got in her way, and by the time they cleared the path, the figure was gone.

She jumped when she felt a hand on her shoulder and turned around. It was Trista, with Owen coming behind her.

"Are you okay?" Trista said.

"Yeah, yeah, I'm fine. Just got caught up with the crowd."

"Follow us back to your friends," Owen said.

As she walked back, the pain in her bite got fainter. *Was that you, Victorija?* Why didn't Victorija grab her and run? She could have done.

❖

The bedroom was dark, but the moon outside the window was glowing light through the open curtains. Victorija Dred sat in a basket chair across from Daisy's bed.

It was insanity coming here. But Victorija just had to see Daisy in the flesh again, no matter how hard it was.

Now that they were blood bonded, Victorija could only be satisfied with Daisy's blood, and if she didn't drink from Daisy, she would slowly slip into madness. Every impulse she had was demanding she drink from her.

Normally she wouldn't have given it a second thought, would have taken what she needed, but Daisy MacDougall was different, she was special. When Victorija first felt the effects of the blood bond, she needed to know why she was unable to take Daisy's blood.

Victorija found out Daisy was a descendent of the Brassard family, and her whole world came crashing down. Angele Brassard was the one woman she had loved in her life. They were star-crossed lovers, the Brassards being French vampire hunters, and the Dreds, a royal clan made up of born vampires.

She heard Angele's voice in her head. *Promise me, you will never hurt or drink the blood of my descendants without consent.*

She remembered the words she'd said in return. *I swear on my life. It'll be the only vow I ever keep. I swear, Angele.*

And that vow was now coming back to haunt her. She felt her hands start to shake with the knowing hunger inside of her. Victorija quickly pulled out a hip flask, containing whisky mixed with a potion given to her by Anka, a dark witch who was aligned with the Dreds.

It helped with the symptoms, helped her bear the pain of not drinking the blood of her bonded soul. As she put the lid back on the flask, she saw the other physical symptom of her body's rebellion. The blue veins in her wrist had been changing slowly to green, inch by inch. This wasn't another symptom of the blood sickness. Her father had been cursed with blood sickness, too, and she'd never noticed this happening to him. She had told no one about this. Not her Duca—her second in command—Drasas, nor the witch Anka who made her potion.

She was showing enough weakness as it was. If her clan saw she was further compromised, then they would be less fearful, and less willing to follow. Victorija had already heard whispered wonderings about her continuing state of poor health. They weren't stupid. And it wasn't just the blood bond that was turning her life upside down. She was dealing with the cascade of her formerly repressed emotions that were released just before she murdered her grandmother, the Grand Duchess Lucia, the matriarch of the Debrek clan.

The Dreds were once part of the Debrek clan, until Victorija's father, Gilbert, would not accept the Debreks' sacred vow of only taking blood by consent. In response, Gilbert set up the Dred clan and took Victorija and his wife with him. He emotionally and physically abused them, and Victorija felt abandoned. She blamed her former family, especially her grandmother, for failing to protect her and her mother.

But just before Victorija killed her grandmother, the former matriarch had apologized for not being there for her and touched her cheek. When she did, Victorija was swamped by emotions, by memories of the loving, happy times that she'd spent with Lucia and her Debrek family in Venice. But still Victorija's anger and need for revenge overcame her, and she ripped her grandmother's heart out.

Lucia said that a small part of Victorija's soul had a chink of light still there. Of course Victorija didn't believe that, but when she killed her grandmother, some of the walls that she had erected to prevent her abuse from destroying her started to crumble. That and the new blood bond were destroying all the certainties she had about herself.

Every fibre in her being was telling her to drink from Daisy, but she couldn't escape the vow she'd made to Angele. Victorija was in utter torment. She had loved Angele, and the pain she suffered now proved how wrong love was.

Victorija got up and walked across the room and looked down at Daisy. She was different from Angele in many ways, but she recognized Angele in Daisy's bone structure.

She had spent many days as a seventeen-year-old vampire lying with Angele in a grassy field, away from the bother of their families, and memorizing every inch of her. Her nose, her eyes, everything, and now looking at Daisy, as much as she was different—Daisy's hair was dark, while Angele's had been a strawberry-blond—there were similarities, especially her little nose.

But she wasn't her Angele and never would be. Victorija hungered, and to make matters worse, Daisy moved in her sleep and bared her neck. Victorija's mouth watered, and the fangs in her mouth ached.

Victorija reached a shaking hand towards the neck of Daisy's nightie. She had a silver chain around her neck, and when Victorija pulled the collar of Daisy's nightie down slightly, she saw the same familiar necklace that had stopped her in her tracks when she had bitten her when they encountered one another in The Sanctuary bar.

Angele had worn it. It was a Brassard heirloom, one that protected the wearer from a vampire's compulsion. Angele had always worn it, apart from one fateful day when her life changed. Gilbert had caught Angele early one morning without the necklace. He compelled her to go to Victorija, and he slit her throat in front of her.

The incident destroyed Victorija, and her heart and soul turned dark with no light still remaining within her, or so she believed.

Victorija stroked Daisy's hair softly. "I've got no way out, Daisy MacDougall. I need your blood."

But even as she contemplated sinking her teeth into Daisy, she could hear Angele's words echoing in her ears.

Please don't do this, Torija.

She closed her hand tightly and brought it firmly against her forehead in frustration.

"I need to do it, Angele."

Victorija used every ounce of her will to turn around. She urged herself to think, just think, and take a deep breath. She had never been taught to resist her urge for blood. Victorija learned from her father that she could take whatever she wanted, whenever she wanted. The last time in her life when she had denied any kind of physical impulse was when she was falling in love with Angele.

Angele brought light to her soul, and Victorija was happy to let her lead the pace of their relationship. And here she was, generations later, trying to talk herself out of draining her descendant of blood.

Victorija ran her tongue over her fang and said, "I can't do this."

She was just about to turn around and take what she needed when she spotted something that looked familiar on Daisy's dressing table. She walked over and recognized two things she hadn't seen for a very long time. A beautiful gold hand mirror and brush, which she had gifted Angele for her birthday. It was quite a shock to see them again after all these years, and she was surprised that they were still in the Brassard family.

Victorija reached out and touched them, then closed her eyes. In her mind's eye she saw Angele and she said clearly, *This is my family, Torija. Don't hurt her.*

She opened her eyes and, without taking her hand off the mirror, looked over at the sleeping figure of Daisy. Before she could change her mind, Victorija sped out the way she'd come in, through the open window.

Daisy woke with a gasp. She looked over at the basket chair and was relieved to find it empty. She covered her face with her hands. "My God."

She'd had the most vivid, terrifying dream that Victorija was in her bedroom, about to drain her blood. Daisy could have been killed in her sleep and never woken up.

She tried to calm her breathing and reason this out. Victorija needed to keep her alive, to be a blood servant to her. But Byron had explained that the longer a vampire went without their bonded's blood, the more their mental health started to break down.

Who knew what a starving, desperate Victorija would do?

Daisy slipped out of bed and put on her slippers. She needed coffee. Daisy shivered now that she was out of the warmth of her bed. She looked around. The window was open, and a feeling of uneasiness spread through her.

She was certain that she never left the window open last night, especially after her experience at the festival. Daisy hurried over and closed it quickly.

Daisy tried to convince herself—she must have gotten up to go to the bathroom during the night and opened it.

She shook it off and walked towards her bedroom door. As she passed her dressing table, she realized her brush and her hand mirror had been moved, and she felt uneasy. They were antiques, purely decorative. Her granny kept them here in her old room, on her dressing table. They'd been passed down to her from the French side of her family.

She used to be fascinated by the brush and mirror as a child and remembered playing with them when she watched her mum get ready for her work trips. Her mum and dad quite often went away on business. Daisy missed them a lot, but she enjoyed staying with her granny while they were away, until the day they didn't come home.

She brought her hands to her eyes. *No, don't go there.* Daisy could be caught up in her grief so easily, and the hurt was too much to bear. She touched the mirror and brought it up to her face.

Her eyes looked red as she tried to hold back her tears. Daisy gazed at her neck. The wound was red and angry this morning. Some days, the wound seemed to be receding, but on other days it flared painfully.

Daisy gazed at her reflection and touched her fingertips to her wound. A waft of cold air made her shiver and she saw a shadow. Then, as clear as day, she heard a voice whisper, "Help her."

She jumped around and looked behind her. There was nothing there, and nowhere the blast of cold air could have come from. "Bloody hell."

Her heart hammered in her chest, and she dropped the mirror back onto the dressing table. Daisy was an expert at paranormal situations. With Monster Hunters, she had spent nights in haunted houses, gone into graveyards after dark, met people who claimed to have poltergeists in their homes, and interviewed individuals who claimed to be anything from a werewolf to a necromancer. But nothing made her as scared as she was at that moment.

"It's just this bite freaking you out," Daisy told herself.

She quickly left the bedroom and hurried downstairs. Daisy slowed when she heard her granny on the phone, sounding worried.

Daisy crept along the hall and stopped outside the kitchen and just listened.

"I knew this day would come, Sybil."

Sybil. That name rang a bell with Daisy, but she couldn't place it. It was an unusual name nowadays.

"She tried to say the mark was from an accident at work, but I know a vampire bite when I see one, and one of them was here last night," her granny sighed.

Daisy was shocked. Granny knew? How did she know about the existence of vampires, and how did she know what a bite looked like? Her grandmother had always discouraged Daisy from her interest in the paranormal and laughed because Daisy actually believed in it.

Then it hit her. Her dream was real. Victorija had been here, in her bedroom.

If it was real, why hadn't Victorija taken her? Victorija needed her as a permanent blood dispenser. There must be something else going on.

Her grandmother continued, "I can't lose her, Sybil. I've lost too much already." She took a big breath. "I know, I know. Fate is a hard monster to fight. I better go—she'll be up soon. Bye, Sybil."

Daisy felt frozen to the spot. It felt as if a locked door in her life was starting to creak open. Her granny obviously knew what was going on with her. Granny sounded scared, and that was unusual. Daisy came from a long line of strong women, and Margaret Brassard, her granny, was one of them. Did she really believe in the paranormal world?

She cleared her throat, alerting her granny she was there. Daisy walked into the kitchen just in time to see her nearly drop a plate.

"Morning, wee Daisy-bell," her grandmother said nervously.

"Morning, Granny."

Margaret Brassard was as far away from the image of an old granny as you could possibly get. She had a short modern hairstyle and wore clothes that belied her sixty years. She had worked in the Ministry of Defence straight after university, just like her mum before her. But when her daughter, Daisy's mother, died, her grandmother shifted to part-time working, so she could look after Daisy. But since Daisy had left home, Granny was back working for the ministry on a consultancy basis.

"Did you sleep well, sweetheart?"

Daisy slid into the kitchen chair. "I had a really vivid nightmare."

"Oh? What about?"

Daisy lifted the packet of granola and poured some in her bowl. "I dreamed there was a vampire in my room, standing over me."

She could see the tension on her granny's face, and her knuckles went white around the two coffee cups she was holding. "What happened then?"

Her granny knew something.

"She touched my necklace, and then—"

"Then what?" Her grandmother brought both their coffees over and sat down.

Daisy shrugged. "I can't remember after that."

She began to eat her granola as an awkward silence set in. Her grandmother tapped her nails nervously on the side of her cup. "Have you thought any more about coming back home to Scotland?"

If Daisy wasn't suspicious before, she certainly was now. Every time she visited recently, Granny asked this question. "What is this all about? You encouraged me to go to London. I said I would get a job in tailoring up here, but you said go. Go and learn as much as you can, and enjoy the social life in London. Now, since…" Daisy tried to think about when her granny started to change her tune. Then it hit her. She snapped her fingers. "Since Byron Debrek came on the scene and started going out with Amelia, you want me to come home."

"Don't be silly. I just miss you, that's all. Why would I care that your friend is going out with a banking billionaire?"

Daisy shook her head in frustration. "Nah, I don't think so. I mean, I know you miss me—I miss you, too—but you're still busy with work, and when you have free time, you jump on the plane to London to see me."

Her granny looked down at her coffee and sighed.

"It is about Byron, isn't it? You know about them, don't you?"

Her granny looked up sharply. "Know about them? What do you mean?"

Daisy hesitated. She had become used to Amelia's world and talking about vampires like they were completely normal, but saying it to her granny was a whole different thing. "That the Debreks are vampires. I heard you on the phone just now," Daisy said.

The silence was deafening. "Yes."

Daisy shook her head and felt anger course through her. She jumped out of her seat and started to pace. "I can't believe it. All these years you made me feel silly for believing in the paranormal, for wanting to investigate it with my friends, and all the time you knew?"

"I'm sorry. I was trying to protect you."

"Protect me how?" Daisy said angrily.

"To protect you from the same fate that befell your mum—and dad."

Daisy's anger abated, and instead a ball of worry grew in her stomach. She walked back to the seat and sat down. "Dad had a heart attack, and Mum was killed in a car accident."

"I'm sorry, but they weren't. They were killed by a vampire."

Daisy's legs turned to jelly. She grabbed the corner of the table for support and fell back into the chair. She tried to speak, but all she could manage was, "Why?"

"I understand you're angry, but if you let me explain, you'll see I was trying to protect you."

"Tell me," Daisy demanded.

After a few moments, her grandmother said, "Your mum and dad were tracking a vampire when your dad was killed, and then years later the same thing happened to your mum."

"What? Why?" Daisy was completely confused.

"They were vampire hunters."

"Vampire hunters?"

"Yes, it's a calling, a task, handed down through the Brassard side of your family. My grandad was one, my mother was one, I was one, and your mother. A long time ago a witch named Lucia gave us the gift of touch. It's a strange buzzing feeling when you touch a paranormal, which helps us track vampires."

"I have it. I call it my spidey sense," Daisy whispered.

"That's it."

"Wait," Daisy said, "is it the same Lucia that was Byron's great-grandmother?"

"Yes, that's her. A wise woman whose power for love changed the world and turned around the ethos of the Debrek clan. She saved many millions of lives because she loved Byron's ancestor, Cosimo."

Daisy rubbed her forehead. It was all too much to take in. "Was Dad a hunter?"

"Your father didn't have the gifts your mum had, nor the necklace around your neck, but he believed in her cause—to protect humans from vampires who had no care for the life of a human."

Daisy pulled the necklace from under her collar. "This?"

"That necklace stops you from being enthralled by a vampire. It was passed down through the family and helped and protected us in our cause. It was originally one of five necklaces, but they were captured, one by one, until that was the only one remaining."

"Why have you not told me any of this before?" Daisy asked.

"When your parents died, I wanted to protect you. The Brassards had given too much to the cause. I thought if I didn't tell you, then you'd always be safe."

Daisy got up and walked to the kitchen window. She stared out, trying to make sense of all this new information. Her whole world had been turned upside down.

"You should have told me."

"I know that now. I didn't want to lose you, but obviously the power of destiny was too strong. You ended up studying the paranormal with your friends, and now…here we are."

"You did this, too?" Daisy asked.

"Yes, I'm a Brassard, your mother was a Brassard, and now you are."

Then Daisy had a thought. "The work you do at the Ministry of Defence. Was that a cover for you and Mum to hunt vampires?"

Her grandmother joined her at the kitchen window. "No. We—your mother and I—worked for a secret agency within the ministry. One that monitors and protects the public from vampires, werewolves, shapeshifters, dark witches, and many more."

"The government knows about this whole paranormal world?" Daisy asked.

"Not all of it. The agency has a level of secrecy that even the prime minister and their cabinet don't know about."

"Why doesn't the prime minister know? That's who we vote for."

"Their position is only temporary. We can't risk them knowing. They might eventually share their knowledge for political gain or monetary reasons. Besides, would you trust our current incumbent? It would be in the tabloids the next morning."

"And why wouldn't that be a good thing? People deserve the truth. I've searched for the truth with Monster Hunters for a long time, and our followers are hungry for the truth."

Her grandmother turned to face her. "People, countries, would try to use paranormals for their own gain. If a tyrant or a dictator had knowledge of this world, they could gain unquestionable power over everyone else. Not to mention that the public would be so angry this secret had been hidden, and all their beliefs and certainties would come crashing down. There would be civic unrest, and a dark time would be ushered in."

Daisy thought about it. Byron had said pretty much the same to her, about protecting their work. She supposed that some humans would seek to leverage the paranormal world to gain an advantage over others, and life wouldn't be the same.

"So, how did they die?"

"Your dad was killed in Munich while helping your mum with a case. He was a brave man. Your mum was tasked with tracking a particularly vicious vampire who was killing with impunity."

Suddenly the thought came into her head, "It wasn't Victorija Dred, was it?"

Her grandmother shook her head. "No, although she has killed many around these parts. No, we don't believe so. She always gave our family a wide berth for some reason. We really don't know why."

Daisy felt all the air sucked from her lungs. Victorija'd had a reaction to her that night in The Sanctuary. If only Daisy had known then what she knew now, she could have…Well, she didn't know what, but she'd have done something.

"I need to know everything about this, Granny. It's my destiny."

"I know that now. I will tell you, but you must tell me everything you know, too."

CHAPTER TWO

Drasas, Victorija's Duca, strode into the throne room of the French castle which served as the clan headquarters of the Dreds. She was followed by her next in command, Leo, and a group of elite guards. Since Victorija had gone to Scotland to seek out Daisy MacDougall, she had free rein over the day-to-day business of the clan and the castle. She liked it and revelled in the power it gave her.

All their vampires and human servants were hers for the moment, but she wanted more than a moment—she was hungry for more, and thanks to her alliance with Anka, she was determined she would get a whole lot more.

"I have a report on our Principe, Duca," Leo said in a somewhat hushed voice.

Leo was loyal to her, and she could rely on him for whatever came next, but to talk this way could be deemed treasonous. Drasas thought she had garnered the support of the elite guard, but Victorija still struck fear in them all, despite the big mess of oncoming madness she was experiencing.

Drasas stopped at the throne that sat on a dais and hesitated. She so wanted that throne. Drasas was hungry for it. Ever since she had been turned by Victorija, she'd wanted power. Before she was turned, she'd been living on the streets since she was sixteen. Drasas felt powerless as she sat on the pavement being passed by human after human, some throwing her some coins, some spitting on her, others assaulting her.

But from her first taste of blood, after the first kill, Drasas knew she would no longer be the victim—she would be the predator. She vowed to punish the humans, to hurt and terrify them as she had been.

As Drasas eyed the throne, which only Victorija and her father, Gilbert, had sat on, her hunger for that throne and the power that Victorija had intensified. Drasas might be a vampire with super speed, strength, the ability to enthral others, and near immortality, but Victorija was on another level.

Victorija was a born vampire, who descended from a royal house of vampires and a witch, while she was merely a turned vampire.

Leo said, "Sit, Duca. You are in charge of the clan just now. The Principe is not here and is becoming weak without the blood of her bonded."

Leo was right. This was her place. She sat down slowly, and those vampires that were in the room turned to look at her in silence.

Would they turn on her? Leo stood at her side, holding the back of the throne in a symbol of support. The elite guards also showed support by lining up at the bottom of the stairs that led up to the throne. When the other vampires saw that, they turned back to their own conversations.

Drasas had made it. Some time ago she had instructed Leo to peddle the idea that Victorija's blood sickness for Daisy MacDougall was making her weak, mentally and physically.

She gripped the arms of the throne and felt the rush of power that Victorija must feel. It was intoxicating.

"So, your report, Leo?"

"Yes, Duca. Victorija arrived in Britain a few days ago. She travelled up to Scotland, where the human, Daisy MacDougall, is staying with her grandmother, Margaret. Turns out MacDougall's family has a long history with the vampire world."

"Why?" Drasas asked.

"The grandmother and Daisy are descended from the Brassard family."

Drasas wasn't easily shocked or surprised, but she was when she heard that name. "Brassard? The vampire hunters?"

"Exactly. The very ones," Leo said.

Drasas couldn't help but laugh at the twist of fate that had chosen a Brassard, a vampire hunter, to be the blood bond of one of the most powerful vampires on the planet. "Amazing."

Victorija had only one rule after she turned Drasas. None of the Dred clan was to kill or turn any member of the Brassard family. Drasas could never understand why. Victorija was ruthless. Why would she protect vampire hunters? It made no sense, then or now. In fact, years ago, when Drasas was being tracked by a vampire hunter, a Brassard, Drasas killed her and her male companion, and never told her Principe. Could they have been Daisy's relatives?

"So, has she got Daisy yet?"

"No. The guards I sent to follow her watched her go into Daisy's bedroom and leave without her," Leo said.

"Did she feed on her?" Drasas asked.

"I don't believe so. The guards reported her hands shaking, and that she was drinking greedily from the potion Anka made for her."

Anka wanted to keep Victorija as calm as she could, and her blood sickness under control, until she got her blood bond where she wanted her. Once Victorija was drinking from Daisy, then she would have her full control and powers back. And Anka would steal them. Anka had been building her power for a long time now, draining it from the world's most powerful paranormals.

Anka had reported that the last one she had drained was Dante Wolfgang, Alpha of the Wolfgang pack. Now she needed a powerful born vampire. Byron Debrek was the most powerful vampire in the world but would be too difficult for Anka to get to, whereas Victorija would now be easier, in her weakened state.

Drasas was promised that, in return for her assistance, Anka would make her the strongest vampire on earth, and that was just too good to turn down, even after all that Victorija had done for her. It was survival of the fittest.

"What do you want us to do?" Leo asked.

"Send our best guards, pick up Daisy MacDougall, and bring her back here. The Principe needs her, and she's going to get her."

Just at that, the large oak doors of the throne room burst open, and Victorija came striding in.

"Getting comfortable, Drasas?" Victorija sneered.

Drasas jumped up quickly. Victorija might be compromised by her sickness, but she could still end Drasas's existence. "Sorry, Principe. We were just talking about you. We were concerned. Have you brought Daisy MacDougall back with you?"

Victorija's eyes were bloodshot, giving her a frightening and unpredictable look.

"No, I couldn't find her."

Why was Victorija lying, and why did it look like she was struggling?

"Shall I send some of the guards to pick her up?"

"No," Victorija barked, bringing silence to the whole room. "I want some time to think. Nobody is to touch her for the moment, understand?"

"Yes, Principe."

Victorija turned to walk away but then turned back and grasped Drasas by the back of the neck and looked down at the throne. "Mind your place next time, Duca."

Drasas's jaw tightened and then she managed to say softly, "Yes, Principe."

Once Victorija was away upstairs, far into the castle, Drasas finally spoke. She'd waited because otherwise Victorija would have heard them with her excellent vampire hearing.

"We need to find out what this is all about, Leo," Drasas said.

"You're right, Duca. There is something stopping the Principe from pursuing her blood bond. Should I send guards to pick up Daisy?"

"Yes, the elite guard only. I don't want this getting out."

Drasas watched as Leo talked to the guards at the bottom of the dais. She was going to give this present to Victorija wrapped up with a bow, whether she liked it or not.

Daisy followed her granny up the old staircase that led to a floored attic. They climbed the last level by a wooden ladder and emerged into a large room, filled with keepsakes, books, and paintings on the wall.

"All of the old papers are up here," her grandmother said.

"So our family has a long history with Victorija?"

Granny walked over to a pile of boxes, and Daisy followed. "You could say that." She lifted a few boxes off the pile in front of her, and below was an old-looking trunk. "This is it."

"What is it?" Daisy asked.

"Our history with the Dred clan or, more specifically, Victorija Dred."

"We have a…history?"

"Yes, it's saved us many times. The Dreds kept their distance from us. But I should have known it would come to a head one day." Her granny pointed to the wound on her neck. "She's going to come for you, Daisy. I know I wanted you here, but maybe you would be safer under Byron's roof."

Daisy agreed she would be. "I have to find a way to erase this bond."

"I know, and if there are any answers, you'll find them in these papers. There's a notebook in there, but it doesn't open. It seems some sort of charm is on the lock." She stood up and brushed down her shoulders. "Just promise this."

"What, Granny?" Daisy asked.

Her granny pointed to her necklace. "Don't take that off. Without that, you are defenceless."

"I won't. I promise."

Once her granny left, Daisy opened the chest and found labelled folders, neatly stacked. She flicked through some quickly and saw they were on all the different vampire cases her family had worked on. Then she came across an old paper folder labelled *Victorija Dred*. The folder looked tattered and tired but was tied up with red ribbon. She untied it and found mostly papers, but on top there was a notebook and some very old-looking letters.

She put the notebook to the side and opened the first letter. It was to an Angele Brassard. She scanned the letter quickly until she found a signature. It said, *My only love, Torija.*

"Torija? That couldn't be Victorija, could it?"

She had heard tales of her French Brassard side of the family. That they were wealthy, and travelled Europe, helping and protecting those they encountered. Bringing peace to the land, was how her granny put it.

Daisy had never asked *how* they brought peace, but now it seemed clear. They were vampire hunters. But how if they were vampire hunters did Victorija become involved with a Brassard? Did Victorija just seduce the young woman? She began to read.

Angele, the first time I saw you in the market, I truly saw
an angel, someone shining with goodness and self-sacrifice,

and one who is kind. You did not fear me when I spoke to you,
something that I treasured. I do not wish to be feared the way
my father is. I wish to have love—I hunger for it the way my
father hungers for fear.

You give me that love, even though I don't deserve it.
Angele, I wish we didn't have to sneak around to meet in
private, but maybe soon we can leave. We could go to Venice.
I have family there. Tell me my hopes are not in vain.

Yours faithfully,
Torija

"This is insane. There is no way this is the bloodthirsty Victorija Dred talking." Daisy leafed through some of the other letters, and the loving words continued between Angele and Victorija. She found a notebook in her mother's handwriting and opened it up. She ran her fingers over her mum's sentences, trying to connect with the woman who wrote them.

Daisy was seven when her dad died, and eleven when her mum died. She wished she could remember more about them. She guarded jealously any new information she found about them. The notebook seemed to be her mum's research into their family.

She spotted an entry marked: *Angele Brassard, aged 17— everything changed!*

Everything changed? What did her mother mean by that?

Daisy put the letters to the side and picked up the notebook again. It was elaborately decorated gold filigree on a duck-egg blue background, with tropical birds on top. The clasp that held it securely closed was gold.

Even though her granny said no one could open it, there was no lock. Just to satisfy her curiosity, Daisy put her thumb under the clasp and pushed. It opened easily.

"It opened," Daisy said with surprise.

Her heart began to pound and her spidey sense tingled all over her body. She opened to the first page and saw the name *Angele Brassard*.

"Angele? That name again."

She turned to the next page and got to the first entry. It was in French. She'd never studied French longer than a few years at school, so she didn't have a clue what was written there. Like she had with her mother's words, she traced her finger over the letters. As she did, Daisy was hit with a myriad of images and sounds, confusing and coming all at once.

A marketplace, a blond-haired young woman, blood dripping from a knife, a scream, and sobbing. Daisy closed the diary quickly, and the sounds and images stopped. She tried to catch her breath. Her heart was hammering like she'd done a ten-mile run.

"What is going on?"

No one else could open the notebook, apparently, but Daisy could, and she'd been assaulted by sounds and images she couldn't understand.

Daisy felt a breeze across the back of her neck, as she had in her bedroom, and then a whisper in her ear said, "Look at her through my eyes. Save her."

"Save her? Victorija? Victorija doesn't need saving. People need to be saved from her," Daisy said to the apparently empty room.

The breeze returned and flipped open the notebook to the first entry. Was Daisy brave enough to pick it up again?

She turned her eyes back to the open pages, and what she saw shocked her. The once-unreadable French was now in English. Daisy's stomach dropped to her toes. The notebook must be enchanted. She could read the title of the first entry in the notebook: *Monsters are made, not born.*

Surely Angele couldn't be talking about Victorija? From what she'd heard about her from the Debreks and others, Victorija was a cruel vampire who revelled in terror. Angele clearly wanted her to read this notebook, but she had to think.

She heard her granny shout from downstairs, "Are you okay? I heard talking."

"I'm just coming down, Granny."

Daisy put the notebook back in the chest with the other letters and carried it from the room. She might be hesitating now, but Daisy knew she had to read that notebook.

Later.

❖

Victorija strode into her castle apartment and pulled her jacket off. That wasn't enough, so she ripped open the buttons of her white shirt. She felt hot all over and like ants were crawling under her skin.

She caught sight of herself in the mirror across the room. What had happened to her? Victorija always prided herself on her dapper appearance, but now she looked like an unkempt wild animal. Eyes red, clothes ripped open, her blond hair wild and messy.

Victorija walked over to the mirror and looked at herself silently. She was disgusted at the state she had let herself get into.

"All you had to do was take her blood."

But she saw Angele so clearly inside her head. No matter how hard she tried, Victorija couldn't block out the memory of her only love. She picked up the freestanding mirror and threw it across the room so hard that it embedded in the wall.

Her hands shook—in fact, her whole body was shaking apart. She needed her tonic, and her last bottle was in her desk drawer. Victorija sped over to the desk and took it out. It didn't feel full, and when she went to drink, she only got one mouthful out of it.

She was going through it a lot more quickly now that her sickness was progressing. Anka's potion didn't take her constant hunger away, but it made it slightly more bearable.

Victorija saw her pile of letters from Angele, tied up with a red bow. She untied it and picked one letter from the pile randomly. Victorija opened it and began to read. It was the letter that Angele had penned before she died.

> *I will leave your life today, my love, but I don't want you to get lost in anger and resentment. I want you to remember me by being the best person you can be. I know you dread becoming like your father. It's all in your hands, Torija. Remember—monsters are made, not born. You have everything in your hands to be the woman you want to be.*
>
> *Don't get lost in hate because of my death. You love me, I know, but you have an even greater destiny ahead of you. Remember the oath you made to me? Please don't harm, or feed from, without permission, any of my family or descendants. I beg of you. Don't give in to it.*

Your love,
Angele

Victorija slammed the letter on the desk. "You ask too much of me, Angele." Surely Angele couldn't have imagined this situation. Angele wouldn't have wanted her to slip into madness and eventual death?

It was ironic that the one person who probably could have helped her, the most powerful witch in the world, Victorija had just recently killed in great anger—her grandmother, Lucia Debrek.

She hadn't felt regret about killing anyone in generations, but for Lucia she did. When she ripped Lucia's heart out of her body, Victorija was hit with memories she had repressed, lots of wonderful memories about spending time with Lucia as a child, and the relief she'd felt being with her grandmother, and not fearing her father.

Her father had never been violent to her or her mother when Lucia was around. It had given them a small break from Gilbert's sadistic tendencies.

Victorija looked up at the ceiling, tears forming in her eyes, and said, "I'm so sorry."

"Victorija Dred, sorry? What could one of the most powerful born vampires be sorry for?"

Victorija jumped up and spun around. The dark witch Anka was sitting in the chair.

"How did you get in here?"

Anka just smiled. "What does it matter? I'm here now."

Drasas trusted this woman. Victorija, on the other hand, was highly suspicious of her. Anyone with Anka's dark abilities was a threat to Victorija, but she had to put up with that at the moment, because Anka brewed the medicine that kept Victorija off the edge of starvation.

But after she found a solution for her plight, Victorija would kill her. Anka was too confident in herself around Victorija. Plus, the witch seemed to be giving Drasas more confidence than she should have.

She couldn't have imagined catching Drasas sitting on her throne, holding court. If Victorija wasn't as sick as she was, she'd probably have broken her neck as a warning to everyone. But not now. Victorija had too many things to occupy her mind, like dying a slow death.

"What do you want, Anka?"

"Two things. One, to find out about your search for your blood bond, and two…" Anka pulled out a fresh, full bottle of medicine. When Victorija saw it, her mouth started to water.

"How did you know I needed one?"

"I know everything about you, Principe." That overconfidence irked Victorija. She sped over to Anka like lightning to grab the bottle, but Anka pulled it out of her way. "No, no. Not yet, Principe."

Victorija was so hungry she tried to grab it again. "Give me it!"

"Once you calm and answer my questions," Anka said.

Victorija felt powerless in that moment, as she had done around her father years before. "What?"

"Did you find your little blood donor, Daisy MacDougall?"

Victorija looked directly into Anka's eyes and lied. "No, she's gone to ground. The Debreks are probably behind it."

"Perhaps." Anka didn't look as if she was accepting her story.

"Why do you care so much about me getting better, Anka?"

Anka sighed. "I've told you before—if we are to have an alliance that will take down the Debreks and others in the paranormal world who don't want to join us and subdue the human population, I need power on my side, and a fully fit born vampire." She then handed Victorija the bottle. "You need to find this Daisy MacDougall because this tonic will not work as well, as time goes on, and you will slip into madness."

"I'll find her," Victorija said firmly.

"Good, I'll leave you to it, then."

After Anka left, Victorija said, "I have no choice, Angele. I hope you'll be able to forgive me."

She looked over at the pile of letters on her desk, picked up one from the pile and read the first line. *Do you remember the day we met?*

"I'll never forget."

CHAPTER THREE

Amelia Debrek went around the room, lighting candles and incense burners. Part of her redecoration of the Debreks' London home was to create a room where she could practise and develop the magic skills that her mentor Magda was teaching her.

Everything was set up exactly how she needed it to be to practise her daily mediation and connection with the ancestors, which gave her power. It was a difficult job to learn the craft from scratch as an adult. Normally knowledge was passed down from generation to generation, starting in childhood. But since Amelia didn't learn she was a witch until sometime after she'd met Byron, Amelia was playing catch-up. She breathed in deeply, and the scent of the essence started to take her to that calm place where she communed with the other side.

Her casting circle was drawn on the floor. It had symbols to help create the enchantment that was needed to make the connection to the spirit world. When Amelia stepped into the circle, she felt a pleasant burr of what felt like electrical current on her skin but was actually magical energy.

In the middle was a cushion to sit on and make things a little more comfortable now that she was pregnant. Having a baby wasn't something she and Byron had planned, it just sort of happened, but after their initial shock subsided, they were both delighted.

Amelia sat cross-legged on the pillow, trying to get into a more comfortable position. The baby had raised all sorts of worries and questions. Sybil, the woman who saved Amelia as a baby and the last remaining member of the cunning folk witch coven, had told her that she was one of the descendants, two people who would unite the paranormal world and save the world from the darkness ahead.

Who the other descendent was and how she was capable of fighting evil while pregnant, or as a beginner to magic, Amelia didn't know. One thing was for certain, though—her pregnancy helped her communicate with her witch ancestors on the other side.

Magda explained that every witch opens themselves up to their ancestors in a different way, and Amelia discovered hers was through her love and passion for Byron. They were a very tactile and passionate couple, and concentrating on that passion and love for Byron took her to a place where she could open a door to the other side.

Now that she was carrying the evidence of that love and passion, Amelia found it a lot easier to open to her ancestors. She put her hands on her slight baby bulge and closed her eyes. The love for Byron and the baby filled her from her head to her toes.

At first, she heard only garbled noises and chatter from the other side. As Magda had taught her to do in her daily practice, she imagined an old-fashioned radio, and when she had it clear in her mind, Amelia began to tune the dials, separating the voices from each other.

Every time she did, a part of her hoped her birth mother would step forward, so she could talk with her and learn all about her, but she never had so far. Magda said she was confident she would one day when the time was right.

Once the many voices spoke as one, Amelia opened her eyes and held there for a moment to make sure her connection was strong.

We are here to help you, the voices said. At the other side of the circle was a row of different-sized stones. Concentrating on the biggest stone first, and with the strength of the countless witches that came before her, she lifted the stone and moved it through the air and placed it on one of the symbols drawn within the casting circle.

Amelia was getting faster at this and tuning in more easily. The more she practised, the more second nature it would become, Magda told her, and she was right. She lifted the next couple of rocks to their places with ease.

She felt so calm and at peace with the world when she took part in her practice. Amelia delivered the next couple to their places, and when she brought her eyes front again, she saw a pair of legs and a walking stick.

Amelia gasped in fright and looked up. It was the Grand Duchess standing in front of her. "Lucia?"

Lucia smiled. "You're getting good at this. Very good progress, just concentrate a bit more, or you won't keep me here."

Amelia took some deep breaths. She wanted to keep the Grand Duchess here. "Why—"

"Am I here? I check in on you and Byron often. Congratulations on baby Debrek."

Amelia smiled. "It was a surprise."

"Nothing is truly a surprise. Things generally turn out how they are meant to, as long as there is no interference from darker forces. But you, Amelia? You are everything I thought you would be. You are the life force of the Debreks, and between you and Sera I hope we will have many more Debreks."

"I think there are too many women out there for Sera to settle down," Amelia joked.

Lucia raised her eyebrow. "You think so? There's a lid for every pot, Amelia."

Amelia touched her stomach. "Is everything all right?"

"Yes, of course."

Lucia stamped her walking stick onto the floor. "Now, to business. We need you to be the voice of reason in the coming weeks and months."

"What do you mean?"

"Life always gives you a chance to do better, no matter who you are, and for some it takes something extraordinary for that to happen."

Amelia knew who she was talking about immediately. "You mean Victorija, don't you? The letter you left for Byron."

Lucia smiled. "Just remember, things aren't usually black and white. There are many shades of grey and many reasons why we turn out how we do."

Amelia blinked and Lucia was gone. "Lucia? Lucia? What about my mother? Will she ever…"

But Lucia was gone and Amelia was talking to an empty room.

❖

That night, after dinner with her granny, Daisy made her excuses about being tired and ran upstairs to her bedroom. She was desperate to learn everything she could from her ancestor's notebook.

She changed into her nightie and jumped into bed. Daisy touched the fiery vampire bite on her neck. It was really calling her today. She had a deep, primal urge to go to Victorija and let her feed. That was dangerous. There must be another way to break this curse. Maybe Angele's words would help her.

Daisy opened the notebook to the first entry and read the title as she had earlier. *Monsters are made, not born.*

Daisy didn't know if she really believed that. She couldn't imagine a time when Victorija wasn't cruel and vindictive. As it had earlier, the French writing started to morph into English.

She touched the words, and with a whoosh, Daisy was pulled into a memory, Angele's memory. Daisy looked around in shock. "What is happening?"

The still memory of a village market suddenly came to life. The noise and hustle and bustle of the market was everywhere. Stallholders tried to sell their wares, customers were haggling over prices, and horses and riders walked through the marketplace.

It appeared to be a very long time ago, going by the clothing, road, and market stalls. She looked down and saw she was still wearing her nightie, but no one batted an eyelid. She must be invisible.

She heard a voice near her say, "Thank you, Mademoiselle Angele."

Daisy turned her head quickly and saw a young beautiful blond woman. "You must be Angele."

To Daisy's surprise, the woman turned and smiled. "Yes, thank you for coming here. She needs you."

"Who?"

"Your destiny."

"My destiny?" Daisy repeated with confusion.

Angele pointed to the other side of the market. She saw a tall, lanky blond-haired...boy? Girl? She wasn't sure.

Angele turned to the market stall vendor and said, "Who's that? Do you know?"

"I know all right. That's Victorija Dred. Her family live in the castle up on the hill. I wouldn't get too close. Everyone says the family are vampires. You probably won't believe in them, but people go missing around here, and it always comes back to them."

To Daisy's surprise, Angele's thoughts on the scene she was watching sounded clearly.

Little did he know, I was brought up to believe in vampires. My family, the Brassards, are vampire hunters, and my father brought us here to find the Dreds and discover what threat they posed.

Angele turned to Daisy and said, "I'd never normally approach a vampire without my parents, but something about her…It pulled me in." *I saw her flinch as people backed away from her in fear, and then she gave up and walked away from the market.*

Angele started to jog as quickly as she could in her dress, trying to catch up with Victorija. Daisy followed suit and watched as Angele shouted for Victorija to stop. When Victorija turned around, Daisy saw a young face that appeared to be battered down by life, both mentally and physically.

She had bruises on her face, and Daisy spotted more on her arm. This confused Daisy. Why would a vampire have bruises? Surely any injuries would heal. Daisy knew that both the Debreks and the Dreds weren't vampires turned by other vampires. They were born vampires, the only two clans in the world that could have children.

Perhaps the younger vampires didn't have the same powers of recovery?

Victorija said to Angele, "You don't want to talk to me—no one around here does."

"Why is that?" Angele asked.

"They say my family are vampires."

Victorija looked puzzled when Angele didn't turn and run at that information. Instead, she smiled and said, "Well, I'm from a family of vampire hunters, so that doesn't bother me."

Victorija stood in silence, totally perplexed.

Daisy was astonished at how different Victorija looked. She walked up close to her and studied her. It wasn't just her youthful appearance. Her face showed painful bruises, some fresh, some yellowing as they healed, but Daisy could also see mental anguish in Victorija's eyes and the way she held herself.

The Victorija she knew was brash, vicious, uncaring, and unfeeling. It was surreal to see her like this.

Angele said, "May I walk along with you for a while?"

Victorija looked shocked and in fact stood still while Angele walked ahead, but she soon ran to catch up.

"Who are you, Victorija?" Daisy said.

Chapter Four

Anka's limousine turned in to a leafy Parisian suburb. Mothers and fathers with prams strolled along the pavement, while others walked their dogs. It was truly nauseating, but if Asha was right about the house he had found, it would all be truly worth it.

The car slowed to a halt. Anka saw Asha waiting on the steps of a pleasant mansion. One of her werewolf guards opened the car door, and Asha walked down to offer Anka a hand out.

"Welcome, Madam. I hope you will be pleased with this house I have found you."

Anka looked around the mature gardens at the front and said, "Tell me about it."

Asha led her up the stairs and said, "It's a fifteenth-century house once owned by an Italian nobleman with a keen interest in the occult."

"I see. Interesting."

Asha led her into the entrance hall. There were guards standing at attention at the stairs and the doors. The walls had centuries-old paintings, and tapestries hung from the walls. Despite being an ancient being, Anka's taste never ran to reminders of the past. She was a forward-looking person who enjoyed the latest technologies and the trappings of whatever century she was in.

"I hope there is more than these dusty old relics, Asha."

Asha smiled. "Much more, Madam. Follow me."

Asha led her down a long hallway.

"Was this place empty?" Anka asked.

"Not quite, Madam, but the owner was persuaded to sign the house over to you."

Persuaded conjured up so many powerful images that made Anka smile.

They arrived at a locked door in the hall. Asha used his key and opened the door. This revealed a padlocked metal door.

"Down here is what makes this place special, Madam."

"Show me," Anka said. She followed Asha down the stairs to another door, and that opened into tunnels lit by torches on the wall. This was starting to look up.

Asha started to fill Anka in on the history of the place. "The first owner had the house built here because of this cave system. He was fascinated with the occult and had many friends come down here to take part in rituals and dark magic."

Anka could feel the dark energy seeping out of the very walls. The death, the destruction, the endless delicious pain. The tunnel led them into a big open room, and Anka felt a current of electrical energy course through her body, meaning her lord and master was not too far away.

The room was set up almost like a church, with seats to watch and take part in ceremonies, and at the head of the room was a stone altar with candles lit all around it. Behind the altar, human bones were embedded into the wall.

"This looks perfect, Asha."

"There's a lot more. The owner used to have occult meetings, orgies, talks, and dinner parties."

"Humans playing with the darkness?" Anka asked.

"Yes, Madam."

Anka walked up to the altar and found the freshly killed body of a man on top of it. His throat was slit from his chest down to his lower stomach, and his face was frozen in the terror of his final moments.

The stone altar had a trough around the sides, so the blood seeping from the victim dripped into the wells and down into four stone collecting cups underneath.

"I can see the original owner liked to dabble in the black arts."

"Yes, he was known to the locals as a devil worshiper," Asha said.

"Devil worship?" Anka chuckled. "Humans and their little tales of terror." She pointed to two iron gates on either side of the skulls and bones. "What is beyond these gates?"

"These are what makes this place so perfect for you, Madam. These gates give you access to the entire Paris catacomb system."

Anka grinned. The ancient quarries underneath Paris were shored up by six million skulls and bones, taken from the nearby overflowing graveyard, after cave-ins started to happen in the late 1700s. She shivered slightly as she thought of all that energy coming from the dead, disturbed from their original resting places.

"This is perfect, Asha. You have outdone yourself."

Asha bowed his head. "Now you have the perfect place to commune with our master."

"Indeed I will."

The next morning Daisy woke up with a banging sore head and an equally sore bite mark. She wandered to the bathroom and got two painkillers from the bathroom cabinet. Daisy poured a glass of water and swallowed them down quickly.

She wetted a facecloth and held it to her bite mark. Daisy hissed as the cold water met the angry, fiery hot wound. She looked at herself in the mirror and saw how tired she looked.

"You look awful."

Daisy couldn't remember falling asleep. The notebook extract that she had witnessed just morphed into her dreams. So when she did wake up, it was like she'd been in an emotional wringer.

All Daisy could think about was going to Victorija. But was that because of the deep biological need their blood bond had given her, or because of her ancestor's plea for her to help Victorija? How she could help a bloodthirsty vampire, she didn't know. Daisy got dressed and went downstairs for breakfast with her granny.

After the meal, Daisy asked if they could go for a walk together. There was a beautiful wooded area not far from the house. Daisy wanted to talk to her granny. She needed to make sense of what was happing to her.

Twigs crunched underfoot as they walked arm in arm in the forest. Daisy's Debrek minders, Owen and Trista, were not too far behind them.

"I wish you didn't have to go home today," her granny said.

"I know." Daisy sighed. "But I have to get back to work at the tailor's. Amelia was good enough to let me have time off to film at the Fire Festival. I'm meeting my friends to get the train after lunch."

Her grandmother squeezed her arm. "I'm going to be worried about you the whole time. Will you phone me at every point in your journey?"

"Yes, Granny, but I'll be fine. I'll have my friends and my two vampy bodyguards back there."

"Not your friends nor even your vampire bodyguards could keep you safe from a born vampire like Victorija Dred."

For some reason, Daisy felt in her gut that Victorija wasn't coming for her. If she was, then why hadn't she taken her away in her room the other night? There was something strange going on. Why wouldn't Victorija come and get her, satisfy her hunger, and end her torment?

There was something more going on here, and she was sure it was connected to Angele.

"Granny, what's the difference between a born vampire like the Debreks and Victorija, and a normal turned vampire?"

"Well, the story goes that the powerful witch Lucia begged her coven for a chance to have children with her Debrek vampire husband."

"Normally vamps can't have children?"

"Exactly. You can't create life from death, and when you are a vampire, you are essentially dead," her granny explained. "Lucia's coven weren't exactly happy about an alliance with the Debreks, but according to reports I've read in the department, they felt since Lucia was the most powerful witch alive, she might have a good influence in the vampire community. So they helped."

"When they're born, are the children true vampires?" Daisy asked.

"No, they inherit excellent strength, dexterity, and speed, but they are not immortal. The Grand Duchess Lucia and her coven built consent into the system. The Debreks had to pledge to get consent from those that they fed from or turned to vampirism. That also extended to their children."

Daisy stopped by a bench in the woods and sat down. Her granny followed, and Owen and Trista both took positions either side of the bench but gave them some space.

"How do they give consent?"

"At eighteen, every vampire child makes a decision whether to follow their parents and become a full born vampire, or stay as an enhanced but still very mortal human."

"Wow, have any ever chosen not to?"

"I believe some, going by the department's intelligence reports, but the majority turn."

"And how does that happen?"

"A ceremony on their birthday. Their parents kill them by breaking their neck. They wake up, feed, and are then born vampires."

Daisy couldn't believe it. She couldn't imagine anyone's parents wanting to kill them like that. Immortality must really change your outlook on life. The memory she had seen last night must have been before Victorija was turned—that's why she had bruises. Daisy was desperate to learn more about Victorija and find out who gave her those bruises and who gave her the mental scars that were evident on her face.

"Amelia is pregnant. I don't know how she'll deal with that in the future," Daisy said.

"She probably hasn't even thought that far ahead. Vampires might have immortality, but that doesn't mean they are happy for their immortal lives, in fact, mostly the opposite."

One thing was certain, Victorija hadn't been happy for her immortal life.

"We better get back. I'll be leaving for the train soon."

Daisy wanted some more time with the notebook, and soon.

CHAPTER FIVE

It was harder than expected for Daisy to get some time to read, with all her friends around her on the train. Especially Zane, who had managed to engineer a way to sit right next to her.

He spoke the whole time, and she felt him getting more and more in her space. Skye was straight across from her, and Daisy gave her pleading looks.

"Zane," Skye said, "why don't you and Pierce go and get us some lunch from the shop. It's just two carriages along."

"Yeah, we could do that," Pierce said. "Are you coming, Zane?"

"No. I think I'll stay here and keep Daisy company," Zane said.

As he said it, Daisy felt him push his leg tightly against hers, and his hand sneak onto her thigh. Daisy jumped.

"I'll just go to the bathroom. Can I get past you, Zane?"

Zane reluctantly moved.

"Are you okay?" Skye asked.

"Yeah, I'll be fine now."

When Owen and Trista saw her on the move, they got up from their seats in the next booth.

"It's okay, you two. I'm just going to the bathroom, right there."

They nodded and sat back down.

Thank goodness, Daisy thought. She needed space to read her notebook. When she walked along to the end of the carriage, instead of going into the bathroom, she walked straight onto the next carriage and got a seat on her own. She brought out the notebook and opened it at the next entry. Daisy touched her fingertips to the words and was sucked into a new memory. She wasn't in a marketplace this time—she was in a wheat field.

Daisy heard Angele say, "We began to meet every day, in secret. Neither of our families would be happy about it. Vampire hunters making friends with vampires, it just isn't done. In fact, if our families found out, it could be extremely dangerous."

Daisy heard laughter and voices a few yards away, so she followed the sound and found Victorija and Angele, lying on the grass side by side. This was a Victorija she never expected to see.

Daisy kneeled beside them so she could eavesdrop on their conversation.

"I'm going to tell him, Angele."

"Tell him what?"

"That I don't want to become a born vampire. I want to remain as human as I can be, for you and me."

"I appreciate you feel like that, but you'd need to leave here. Imagine what he'd do to you. Look what he already does to you, Torija." Angele caressed Victorija's cheekbone, which was bruised black and blue.

Daisy couldn't believe it. Victorija's father abused her, and she also didn't want to be a vampire?

"I've got great anger and darkness inside me, Angele. I'm frightened that I'll become like Gilbert, my so-called father, descending into madness, abusing my wife, and keeping her locked in the dungeon for her blood."

"You won't—"

"Don't say I won't because you don't know the extreme emotions you get when you turn."

"I'll support anything you want to do," Angele said, "but if you did go down that path of darkness, you would always be able to return, because there will always be light inside you. I can see it."

"You have such faith in me. I don't deserve it."

Angele pulled Victorija to her and whispered, "You do because I love you."

"I love you," Victorija replied, and then their lips came together in a kiss.

Daisy couldn't help the tears that came to her eyes then. The simple, youthful love between these two was remarkable. To think, Victorija Dred was capable of this—it was incredible.

Victorija had obviously lived through abuse and witnessed the horrible fate of her mother locked away in the dungeon. Was this torment what changed her character so much?

Victorija pulled back and said, "I want to take you and my mother away from all this. I'm planning to get my mother and run somewhere safe. I hope my grandmother Lucia will take us in. Will you come with me?"

The scene suddenly changed. She saw Angele running through the field. She hurried to catch up with her. Eventually they found Victorija sitting on the ground, sobbing her heart out.

"I got your message, Torija. What happened?"

"I told him I didn't want to become a born vampire, but his Duca had found out my plans to rescue Mother and run away with you."

"Did he hurt you?" Angele asked.

Victorija jumped up and roared in anger. "He had mother brought up and he…he beheaded her in front of me, then burned her heart in a fire on the dais."

Angele pulled Victorija to her, and Victorija clung to her, sobbing. "He's killed everyone I've ever cared about, and I'm afraid he'll come for you. We can't see each other any more."

Angele pushed her love back and said, "That's my decision. I love you, and I'm not giving up on you, not ever."

"I can't risk you being hurt. It would destroy me. He's going to make me turn, Angele. I'm scared of what I'll become. There would be no coming back."

"I told you, there will always be some light in you. I see it, and anyone else who takes the time to look hard enough will see it."

"Would you be my blood bond?" Victorija asked.

"If that's what fate decides."

Angele turned and checked out of the scene she was playing for Daisy's benefit.

"She needs you, Daisy. It's your destiny. It was always meant to be you."

"What? Why?"

"I was there to support her when she needed it, but you were always meant to be the one who brings her terror to an end."

"She's a vicious monster, Angele. Have you seen what she's done?"

"Of course I have. Why do you think I wrote *Monsters are made, not born*? Gilbert thought he'd destroyed all the light in her, but it's there. I see it, Lucia her grandmother saw it, and you have to find it, Daisy."

"She doesn't deserve a second chance."

"Does the May Queen forgive the Horned God? He changes into the Green Man."

Suddenly Daisy was pulled from her vision. Skye and Trista were standing above her.

"Are you okay, Daisy? We were worried about you," Skye said.

Daisy scrunched her eyes shut then opened them again. It was hard to go from the vision back to the real world so quickly.

"Yeah, sorry. I just wanted to be away from Zane. He touched my thigh and pushed his body into mine at the table."

"He did what?" Skye's face went red with anger.

Uh-oh. Skye was going to go mental at him. Trista, behind her, didn't look too happy about it either.

"It's okay, Skye. Don't make a fuss."

"Don't make a fuss? Women have been saying that for generations. No, he's gone too far. We've all made so many excuses for him, but this is too much. Come on, Trista. You can back me up."

As they stormed off, Daisy sighed and shook her head. Zane had to sit with them for hours till they got back to London.

The words Angele had said echoed through her mind. *Does the May Queen forgive the Horned God?* That was a big part of the Fire Festival. In her research she learned that the Celts believed that the May Queen forgave the Horned God for his sins, and he became the Green Man, ushering in a new season, a new start. Was that what Angele meant?

She gave it ten minutes and went back through to the carriage, clutching her precious notebook. Daisy found Zane, sitting, arms folded, a few booths away, clearly unhappy, next to Owen and Trista. Skye patted the seat next to her and said, "It's all sorted. Sit with me and Pierce. Owen and Trista are keeping an eye on Zane."

"He wasn't too upset, was he?" Daisy asked.

"It doesn't matter if he was. You're being too soft on him," Pierce said.

"We've still got to work together as Monster Hunters."

Skye pursed her lips. "I've a feeling he'll be resigning from our group."

Daisy rubbed her forehead. She felt like she'd left half her mind back in her vision. "Can we manage as a three?"

"Of course we can," Pierce said, "Think about it, Daisy. We film in pitch blackness in some very scary places. How could Skye or I leave you alone with that obsessed freak? He's gone too far."

"You're right, you're right."

The hours passed slowly, but Daisy made sure she texted her granny often, just to keep her mind at ease. Daisy looked at her watch. They should be at Kings Cross in twenty minutes, so Daisy stood and got her holdall from the shelf above.

"I don't know about you two," Pierce said, "but I'm going home to a takeaway and my bed."

"I promised I'd stay the night at the Debreks'. They wanted to make sure everything went all right when I was away."

Skye narrowed her eyes. "I suppose a banking billionaire has lots of enemies, but ones who would attack their friends?"

Daisy was getting caught up in lie after lie, and she hated it. "So they tell me."

Luckily Pierce changed the subject. "What's Amelia's house like?"

A safe subject. This was good. "It's stunning, now that Amelia has decorated. I mean, before it looked like your classic haunted house."

"Oh, has your spidey sense detected any paranormal activity?" Pierce asked.

More lies. "Not that I've noticed. Anyway, when Amelia decorated the house it became a warm family home. Beautiful white walls with gold trim, and cornices, chandeliers. She's really brought the house back to what it would have looked like a century ago, but with some nice modern touches. There's a cinema room, and Amelia has her own meditation room. Gorgeous."

Skye smiled. "It must be fun spending a billionaire's money."

"You're not wrong," Pierce said. "I need to find myself a billionaire. I could be a wonderful trophy husband."

Daisy laughed. "Shut up, you numpty."

"Oh, I do love your quaint Scottish words."

"Shall I hit him?" Skye asked jokingly.

"Please do," Daisy replied.

Thankfully the train was finally pulling into the station. It was a long journey, but she had learned so much from Angele's notebook. She really wished she could go home and immerse herself in it again, but Amelia wanted to have the night together, to catch up, and Byron and Alexis wanted to debrief Owen and Trista.

The train pulled in, and her two guards took the bags out of her hands.

"Hey, you don't have to—" But they were off, out the train door.

Syke nudged her. "Don't knock it, babe. I'd love to have two strapping people like that to look after me."

Daisy felt a little guilty. Syke, Pierce, and Zane had joined her to find out the truth about paranormal stories, but little did they know that two vampires were on this trip with them the whole time. It felt like lying to her friends, but she was doing it to protect Amelia and Byron, and their world.

As she waited her turn to exit the train, Daisy noticed an advertising screen. It had an image of the Celtic Green Man and the May Queen. That image seemed to be following her around.

Why were those two faces on an advertising screen? There were no words, no other indications of what it was about. She closed her eyes tightly, and when she opened them, there was just an advert for the train service.

Weird. Daisy shook it off.

"Whose idea was it to play Scrabble?" Bhal said.

"Mine, as well you know," Serenity said.

Amelia looked over to the card table and smiled. Bhal and Serenity had been bickering all night. Byron had told her sister to travel home from her US stay, due to the threat of the Dreds, and forbidden her from going out. Serenity was a party girl, so that didn't go down well. But each night Bhal, Serenity, Alexis, Katie, Amelia, and sometimes Byron would gather to play games to pass the evenings together.

"I've got one," Sera said and then started placing tiles on the board. *"W-A-N-K-E-R."*

"Very funny, Sera," Bhal said. "What would your mother think if she walked in right now?"

"She'd think it was funny because she has a sense of humour, unlike you, warrior."

Amelia was reading a book recommended by Magda, her witch teacher. She didn't feel like games this evening. Byron was in her office taking care of some business.

She became aware of a tapping noise and looked up to find Alexis tapping her booted foot on the floor while Sera and Bhal bickered. Alexis kept looking up and locking eyes with Katie, who was holding a Scrabble tile and tapping it insistently.

Amelia smiled. This was still so new for them—a blood bond, a marriage, and true hunger for one another. Katie was coping so well with her change to vampirism, which had happened quite by accident. Not only were the vampire needs and feelings new for Katie, but love and a bond were something Alexis hadn't felt for centuries.

Katie's and Alexis's looks got more intense until Katie jumped and said, "Um, I need to check...check on something in the kitchen."

After Katie left the room, the atmosphere was still tense. Alexis tried to appear cool and calm but failed miserably. "Sorry, Bhal, Sera, I need to check on the blood rota for tomorrow." And with that, she sped out of the room.

Sera sighed, knocked over her remaining tiles. "That's that, then." She got up, leaving Bhal to put away the board and collect all the tiles in the bag. Sera flopped down on the couch beside Amelia. "You have to talk to Byron for me, Amelia. I'm going stir crazy, staying in night after night with bossy over there and the walking vampire hormones, Katie and Alexis."

Amelia laughed at Sera's vivid description. "It's not that bad, is it?"

Sera squeezed Amelia's hand. "It's not bad in that way. I love my family and love my new sister-in-law, as you well know."

"Well, yes, I'm pretty loveable," Amelia said with a wink.

Sera laughed. "Yes, so true, but I'm a people person, a party girl.

I love to meet new people, see new things, hear new music, and learn new things. I was having a great time staying with Angelo in New York, before Byron told me I had to come home."

"I suppose the city that never sleeps is perfect for a vampire that likes to party?" Amelia said.

"You are not wrong. Although my cousin was pretty annoying, having guards follow me all the time. I'd spend the day going to museums and art galleries and nights going from bar to bar, club to club, and the women—"

Bhal interrupted them by clearing her throat. "Excuse me, Principessa, I'm going back to my room now. If you need anything, just send an attendant for me."

"I will. Thank you."

Amelia saw tension etched on Bhal's face.

"Goodnight, grumpy," Sera said.

Bhal's jaw tightened, but she simply turned and walked away.

"Poor Bhal, you always give her a hard time."

"Poor Bhal nothing." Sera snorted. "She thinks she's the boss of me. Anyway, less about Bhal. I was having a great time in New York. Angelo is a lot more chilled than my stuffy big sister."

Amelia giggled. "She is not stuffy—she is lovely."

"Maybe to you, but to her I'm still seventeen and not been through my ascension ceremony yet."

"She's on edge. We found out about the baby, my role as this descendent thing, the upcoming darkness that Anka is supposed to bring. Byron loves you and just wants to keep you safe. If the darkness is on its way, she wanted you with us, and I agree."

"You are no help," Sera joked. "So, how's my little niece or nephew?"

"Doing well. Making me hungry all the time." Amelia rubbed her stomach.

"For food or for sex?" Sera winked at Amelia.

"Sera!" Amelia felt her cheeks burn.

"Oh, you're so human about these things. Sex is a celebration, and I know you two can't keep your hands off each other. Just like Alexis and Katie. Of course *I'm* not allowed to go out, so I'm stuck with Scrabble and grumpy Bhal."

They sat in silence for a few minutes and watched the flames dance in the fireplace.

"You know, you really make my sister happy, Amelia. I've never seen her so content and fulfilled in life," Sera said.

Just as Amelia was about to reply, the drawing room doors opened, and Byron strode in. Amelia got that surge of excitement and love she always got when she saw her partner.

"Sera, my darling wife, what have I missed?" Byron rubbed her palms together.

"Sex and my lack of it."

Byron immediately looked uncomfortable. "Wonderful. That's exactly what you want to hear your baby sister talking about."

Amelia and Sera started to laugh, and then Sera stood and gave her sister a kiss on the cheek. "Well, you needn't feel weird. I'll leave you two lovebirds to it. I'm going to watch some TV in my room since I'm not allowed out."

As Sera walked to the door, Byron said, "It won't be forever."

"Hmm," Sera replied, "let's just hope that I can hear the TV over the noise of Alexis and Katie."

Katie pulled off Alexis's T-shirt frantically as her blouse lay ripped open. In their haste to feel each other, the blouse had become a casualty. Katie had her legs around Alexis's waist as Alexis carried Katie across the room.

"Oh God, Alex, I've been waiting for this all night. Touch me." Katie grasped Alexis's hand and pushed it up inside her bra.

Alexis moaned, and she pushed her tongue deeply into Katie's mouth while she palmed Katie's breast.

Alexis appeared to lose all sense of direction. Instead of speeding to the bed, she banged them both into the writing bureau. A few of the chairs and pictures on the wall had already become casualties to their passion as they crashed around the room.

"I need to taste your blood, Alex. Take us to the bed."

To prove her point, Katie bit Alexis's lower lip and sucked on the blood that flowed from it.

Alexis growled and ripped off Katie's bra before racing them over to the bed. Katie laughed. "Where's the growling coming from? Are you a werewolf or a vampire?"

"You bring out the animal in me." Alexis grinned. Alexis made some more animalistic growls as she sucked Katie's nipple into her mouth and grazed her fangs along it, just like Katie loved.

Katie pulled at Alexis's trousers. "Take these off. I want your fingers inside me and your teeth in my neck."

"I'll give you exactly what you need." Alex shrugged off her trousers and underwear and then turned on her back to unzip Katie's skirt. "I can't concentrate when you wear these skirts every day."

"I'm glad I can keep you interested," Katie said.

Alexis was mesmerized by Katie's fleshy buttocks. "I need to have one taste of you first." Alexis drew her fangs along one buttock and then bit down. Katie squealed slightly and then grasped the pillow above her. The taste of Katie's blood was always pure bliss, but this was one special place that Alexis loved to drink from, especially when she felt Katie's hips start to undulate along with her, sharing the pleasure. Alexis went with her instincts and slipped two fingers inside her wife while she drank.

"Yes, Alex, just like that," Katie said as she thrust herself back onto Alexis's fingers. Katie hugged her pillow while her hips rocked back and forth with more pace.

Alexis could feel Katie's sex start to flutter, and her own orgasm was starting to build without much stimulation.

"Let me drink while we both come," Katie said.

Alexis wanted that badly. As much as she loved drinking from Katie, there was nothing more intimate than when they both fed off each other. She hadn't done this with any other vampire. It was a special thing between them.

She turned Katie over and positioned her sex over Katie's thigh. Katie reached up and wiped a drop of her blood from Alexis's mouth and sucked it herself. There was no more erotic sight.

Katie pulled her down into a kiss while Alexis pushed two fingers back inside her wife. They began to thrust together, slowly at first, savouring every feeling, but then they were soon sinking their teeth into each other's neck.

They drank and fed, surrounded in love, until their hips sped up, and Alexis felt the flutter around her fingers. She gripped as Katie came with her fingers deep inside her. Alexis followed a few seconds later, throwing her head back and thrusting hard, while she groaned in release.

"I love you, Katie."

"I'll love you forever," Katie replied breathily.

Victorija thrust onto the writhing vampire beneath her. Her vampire lover had already come twice, but not Victorija. Nothing was working, and she was becoming more and more frustrated.

Her blond lover had gone down on her, but nothing, she felt nothing. Then she put on her favourite strap-on, and nothing. She always came so easily with that, but not today. So she got rid of it and began thrusting against her lover's thigh—again, nothing.

What was wrong with her? Sexual release was always so easy for her, but it felt like she was dead from the waist down. Victorija needed to come so badly, something to make the constant hunger for her blood bond more bearable.

Giving it one last shot, she sank her fangs deep into her lover. In normal times the taste of blood would be enough to bring her to the edge of orgasm, but now it tasted like nothing, and it did nothing.

Her frustration built to anger. She rolled off her lover and said, "Get out."

"Principe? Was I not...? Let me give pleasure."

The woman was about to try to go down on her again, but Victorija grabbed her throat. "I said, get out."

The woman looked down in fright at Victorija's hand. "What is wrong with you, Principe?"

The green in her arm had spread from her hand to higher up on her wrist. What was happening to her? "Get out!"

The woman gathered her clothes and bolted from the room. Victorija lay back on the bed and studied her hand and arm. Her whole body wasn't working. Something was clearly poisoning her, and she was dead from the waist down.

She didn't remember her father slipping into blood sickness as quickly as this after he killed her mother. Was she weaker than Gilbert? That's what he always said. She was a disappointment. Why couldn't she have been a son?

If her vampires found out how badly affected she was, she could lose control of her clan. Not that she'd been much involved in clan business for the last while. She had delegated control to her Duca, but she had noticed Drasas getting a bit comfortable in her leadership role.

Maybe she should spend the evening downstairs with her vampires. They hadn't seen her in a long time. Victorija got up, put on her best clothes—with leather gloves to cover her hand, took a big swig of the potion that Anka made her, and forced herself to leave her chambers. This was the last thing she wanted to do. Her hunger was destroying her from the inside.

But she forced herself. When Victorija entered the throne room, her Duca was standing by her throne, muttering to some of her higher-ranking vampires.

"What if she doesn't recover?"

The conversation ended abruptly when they saw Victorija.

"Principe, you're joining us this evening?" her Duca asked.

"Looks like it. Not getting too comfortable on my throne, Drasas?"

Drasas had worry etched on her face. "Of course not, Principe. Please sit. We are happy to have you with us tonight."

I'll just bet you are. She was growing ever more suspicious over Drasas and Anka's relationship. Drasas seemed besotted by Anka, but would Drasas really be plotting against her? Victorija had rescued her from the streets and gave her power, power that Drasas loved. Maybe Drasas wanted more.

She would have to try to find a way out of this. This blood bond, this poisoning. There had to be a way, or she would lose everything that she had taken from her father.

CHAPTER SIX

Daisy sat on Amelia's couch with an ice pack on her neck. Her bite mark had been burning hot since she'd arrived back to the Debreks' house. Every fibre of her being was telling her to find Victorija. But she couldn't. How was she going to beat this? To be truthful, she wanted to go to bed and spend some more time with Victorija. *Did I just think that?* She had to remember that young, sweet Torija was gone. All that was left was a bloodthirsty vampire, although Angele would have her believe the light was still inside her. Maybe at one time, but not any more. Victorija was too dark now.

"Are you okay?" Amelia asked.

Amelia was sitting on the couch in her nightdress and dressing gown. When Daisy arrived at the house, she would have been happy to go straight to bed, but Amelia was sitting on her own, reading. Byron had gone to get Amelia some food from a late-night takeaway.

They had lots of staff to do that kind of thing, but Byron saw it as taking care of her pregnant wife, Amelia explained.

"How is it?" Amelia pointed to her neck.

"It's calming down," Daisy said.

Amelia took her hand. "I know how hard it is. Remember, I carried Byron's bite when we weren't together. It physically hurts not to go to them, doesn't it?"

Daisy nodded. "I don't know why this had to happen to me. Why did nature, mother earth, the gods above, *whoever* decide that Daisy MacDougall should be bonded by blood to the most notorious vampire in the world?"

"I don't know, but Byron says there's always a reason. Remember I told you about the Grand Duchess Lucia?"

"Byron's great-grandmother? The one Victorija killed?"

Amelia nodded and rested her hand on her small baby bump. "She left a letter for Byron, asking her to bring Victorija back to the light, to the family."

"She thought she could be saved? That was before Victorija killed her, though," Daisy said.

"Lucia was a very powerful woman, is still, over on the other side. Her power, along with my ancestors', gives me the Debrek life force and my magic."

"What are you saying?"

"When we were under attack from Victorija, at the castle in Scotland, Lucia walked out of the castle, knowing she was going to her death. Lucia was so powerful that she could have stopped Victorija at any time, but she didn't."

"Why?"

"From what I've gathered since, she felt she failed Victorija."

"Failed her how?"

"Victorija's father Gilbert was an angry, resentful, jealous vampire. He wanted to be Principe of the Debreks and rejected the family's new oath to only take blood by consent. Victorija and her mother were innocents. Lucia felt that she should have tried to get Victorija and her mum back, if they wanted to. It seems Victorija was angry that the family didn't, and Lucia thought her anger was just. But right to her last moments, she thought there was good in Victorija."

Just like Angele said. It was so strange. The image of the evil, sadistic Victorija was falling away, bit by bit.

"Monsters are made, not born," Daisy said.

"Exactly what Lucia said in her letter to Byron. Where did you hear that phrase?"

"Oh, I can't remember." Daisy felt bad, but she wanted to keep the notebook to herself for the time being. Amelia and Byron might make a fuss about the whole thing.

Their conversation was interrupted by loud voices approaching the drawing room doors.

"Sounds like food," Amelia said with glee.

❖

Anka was standing in the pouring rain, thunderclaps crashing overhead. The scene looked like London on a dreary grey day. Luckily Anka had an umbrella, which she held over her head while she waited at this bus stop.

After a minute or so, a red bus came to a halt, and she calmly and without questioning the scene got on board. She shook out her umbrella and walked past seat after seat. Each one was filled by one or two people, faces deadpan, and Anka could feel they were filled with darkness.

She stopped at the first double empty seat, and the bus took off. The rain was even heavier outside now, battering the window and the people walking outside. They had the same expressions as the people on board. She truly was in her patron god's realm.

The bus slowed and stopped at the next stop. A steady stream of people came on board, but she didn't pay too close attention until one tall man dressed in black, with a goatee, sat down beside her.

"Are you the one I was told to expect?" Anka asked without turning and looking at him.

"Yes, I am your god Balor's emissary."

"Pleasure to meet you. I am Anka."

"Your reputation goes before you, Anka. I know what a powerful woman you are. Together we can make the darkness return."

"We will," Anka replied.

"Is the ring charged with power? Did you get the born vampire?" the emissary asked.

"I am very close. I should have Victorija Dred's power very soon."

"Balor has seen a complication."

"What complication?"

"The descendants," the emissary replied.

"We know of Amelia Debrek, but the second one is unclear, and they are not powerful enough to take on Balor like the prophecy shows," Anka said.

"Not any more."

"You know who it is?"

"Daisy MacDougall."

As soon as he said the name, the bus, the dreary people, and the dreary streets of London fell like a pack of cards, and Anka was left kneeling in front of her altar, gasping. The dead man was still lying on the altar, but his blood wasn't dripping any more. Together with the skulls and bones of the dead, this new temple, as she would call it, brought her closer to the dark side than she'd ever been before.

Anka gasped and forced herself to her feet. "Asha! Asha!"

He came striding into the underground temple. "Yes, Madam."

"I know who the other descendant is. Daisy MacDougall. Call Drasas. We need Victorija to drink from her blood bond as soon as possible."

❖

Victorija's vision was blurry. She was drinking from the wrist of the vampire standing beside her while holding a bottle of whisky in her other hand. One new symptom of her blood sickness was an inability to handle alcohol.

Victorija couldn't remember feeling as awful as this before. All she wanted to do was go to her room and pass out, because if she passed out, she couldn't feel the torment any more. She pulled her teeth from the wrist of her vampire and stumbled to her feet.

"Principe? Are you okay?"

Victorija heard but ignored the woman. She made her way on unsteady feet over to the stairway and began lumbering slowly up the stairs, feeling extremely woozy. It was amazing she was still on her feet.

She got to her rooms at last and walked over to her bedside. Victorija fell to the floor and began to feel a cold, icy atmosphere encircle her, and the unmistakable sound of heavy rain. She opened her eyes, and although she had a drink-addled brain, she could see a circle of ghostly figures standing around her.

She jumped in fright and tried to scramble backward towards the wall but then noticed the ghostly people were at her back, too.

"Face us," the spirits said loudly.

She was sure that she recognized a few faces from somewhere. Then from the circle, a blond woman walked forward. It couldn't be.

"Angele?"

Angele crouched down. "Yes, it's me."

Utter shame spread all through Victorija. "Don't look at me."

"Why?"

"Because I've become everything I hated in my father. I'm a monster."

"You can change your life, Torija. You still have light in you."

"There is nothing but darkness in my soul. No light, no love, only pain. I have blood sickness. I can't keep my vow to you any more, Angele. I'm going insane. Why is she my blood bond? It should have been you."

"I was your beginning, Torija. Daisy is your end. I know you will keep your vow."

"I won't. I'm going to find her and rip her throat out," Victorija screamed.

Angele got up and started to back away. "All you have to do is face what you've done."

The circle of ghostly figures stepped forward, and Victorija began to recognize more faces amongst the crowd. They were people she'd killed or ordered dead. Pain, guilt, and despair tortured her.

"No, leave me alone."

Then she spotted one face that particularly stood out. It was Alexis's lover who had been killed on a raid on the Debreks' London home. Victorija wasn't used to feeling shame, or any such emotion. She had switched off any emotional response apart from hate and anger a long time ago.

But her grandmother had kicked the door of her emotions open a crack, and blood sickness and her mental health were pushing it open further, inch by torturous inch.

"Face us, face us," the souls shouted, louder and louder.

Victorija covered her ears and screamed, "No!" as the feelings of guilt, remorse, and shame stabbed her in the chest and guts, like heavy spears.

The ghostly figures' words turned to horrible screams and wails, and the sound of the rain became deafening. They got so close the screams were right next to her ears. The sound was unbearably painful.

"No, no, no!"

❖

"It's okay, Daisy. We're nearly there," Byron said.

Byron carried Daisy upstairs. She was followed by Amelia, and in a second Alexis and Katie were by their sides.

Daisy was writhing in pain, calling for Victorija. Byron had just arrived back with Amelia's food and was having a drink in the drawing room when Daisy collapsed.

"What happened?" Alexis asked.

"She just fell. I think it's the blood sickness."

As they got to the top of the stairs, Sera came running towards them.

"Alexis, get the door."

Alexis opened the door, and Byron placed Daisy on the bed while Amelia explained what happened to Sera.

"What will we do? She's getting worse," Amelia said in a panic.

"Should we call the doctor?" Katie asked.

Byron pulled Amelia into a hug. "There's nothing a human doctor can do for blood sickness. She'll keep feeling Victorija's pain."

Sera kneeled by the side of the bed and held Daisy's hand. "What about Sybil, or Magda? Do they have any ideas on how to deal with this?"

Amelia rubbed her baby bump. "I asked Magda, and she said she would consult some of her books and friends."

Bhal came running into the room. "Is Daisy well?"

"She doesn't look it, does she, Bhal?" Sera said sarcastically.

Bhal sighed and turned to Byron. "Principe?"

Byron kissed Amelia and said, "You settle Daisy with Katie and Sera while I talk to Alexis and Bhal."

The three stepped outside and shut the door.

"What can we do, Principe?" Bhal said. "She's going to come for Daisy—in fact, I'm surprised she hasn't already."

Alexis hissed. "Just let her try. I'll rip her head off."

Byron held up her hand. "I know how much you hate her. Her vampires killed Anna, but to beat Victorija and protect Daisy, we need to keep clear heads, especially as Victorija gets less clear-headed with blood sickness."

Bhal nodded. "There's something badly wrong at the centre of the Dred clan. My sources say Anka is involved, and if she is, we and the world are in trouble."

"You've met her?" Alexis asked.

Bhal nodded. "A long time ago, and the devastation she caused to the human population was vast. She made humans distrust any of us who had paranormal skills. It took a lot to trap her."

"Now it seems she's found her way out," Byron said. "She feeds on power, the power of other paranormals. It's not beyond the realm of possibility that she is using Victorija for her power."

"What's our next move, Principe?" Alexis asked.

"I think we need the combined knowledge and power of Sybil and Magda to find our way through this. I'll call Sybil in the morning and ask if she'll come. Alexis, send someone to bring her here, and Bhal, send Wilder to pick up Magda."

"Yes, Principe," Alexis and Bhal said in unison.

As they started to walk away, Bhal stopped and said, "Byron, if Anka is involved with the Dreds, we're headed towards great darkness."

Byron's stomach twisted at the thought of Amelia, now pregnant, being expected to help fight this darkness. "We will not let Daisy and the Principessa be hurt in any way."

"Aye," Bhal said. "We'll protect them with our lives and our souls."

CHAPTER SEVEN

Daisy awakened slowly. Her head was pounding, but the terrible pain in her stomach had eased. She saw a bottle of water on the bedside table, with a packet of painkillers. Exactly what she needed.

She swallowed them quickly and went to get her phone from her bag. When she saw Angele's notebook, she couldn't resist taking it back to bed. The whole night, while she was socializing with her friends, all she wanted was to get upstairs and read more about Victorija and Angele, but was that wise now? After such a bad reaction to Victorija's hunger?

But there was only one answer—she had to know. It was driven by this new hunger inside her to know and understand the woman who could have sparked such devotion in her ancestor Angele.

Daisy sat cross-legged on the bed and opened the notebook. She had a bookmark on the last page that she had been reading and turned to the next, but it was blank. She turned to the next, and the next, but there were no more entries in the book.

"This can't be right."

She felt panic and sadness about not being able to connect with Angele and Victorija. Daisy placed her hand on the blank pages and said, "I need to know more, please?"

In an instant, she was pulled into the vision of the notebook. She was in an elaborate walled garden this time, and Angele wasn't anywhere to be seen. Daisy heard a voice behind her.

"I wondered when you'd arrive."

She turned and saw a petite slightly grand-looking woman with a walking stick.

"Who are you?" Daisy asked.

"I'm the Grand Duchess Lucia, of the Debrek clan."

She looked just how Daisy had imagined. "You're Byron's great-grandmother?"

"And Victorija's grandmother. Shall we sit?" Lucia indicated a bench beside them.

"Where is Angele?" Daisy said.

"She didn't make any more entries, Daisy."

"God, that means—"

Lucia tapped her stick on the ground and nodded. "That is why I'm here to guide you through this memory, Daisy. Today Victorija becomes a born vampire."

Daisy held her head in her hands. "No, she didn't kill her, please, no. She loved Angele so much, and she didn't want to become a born vampire."

"She didn't have much choice with Gilbert as a father. He was my son, but I could find no redeeming features," Lucia said.

"Why do you want me to watch this? It's too heartbreaking. To kill the only woman you've ever loved?"

"Daisy, I need you to know everything that made Victorija the woman she is today. Her crimes are awful, but I should have gotten her out of there. The Debreks failed her, and monsters are—"

"Made, not born," Daisy finished.

"Exactly. Just watch and listen."

Victorija appeared in the middle of the lawn. She was pacing up and down. Victorija was mumbling, "I can't do this, I don't want to do this."

Daisy felt sick. Victorija clearly had to kill Angele. Was it her father who forced her? She didn't want to watch this. Young Victorija was so in love with Angele that it was going to break Daisy's heart to watch Victorija kill the one person she'd ever loved.

Daisy had the sudden urge to pull Victorija into her arms and beg her not to go down this path. She was capable of great love. She didn't have to make the rest of her life full of death and destruction and, as Daisy now understood, lots of pain.

Victorija continued to mutter, "I don't want to transition. I need to get away."

Daisy walked up closer to young Victorija and said, "You don't have to. Turn your back on this." Logically, Daisy knew this had already happened and the future was written, but she couldn't help but say it.

Victorija stopped pacing and looked up. She and Daisy saw Angele walking towards her in a white dress.

"Angele, don't," Daisy shouted, but of course she couldn't hear her. "Please don't do this, Victorija," Daisy pleaded.

"Angele? Why are you here? I told you never to come here. It's not safe with my father around."

Daisy noticed that Angele was walking stiffly, like a robot, and her face was expressionless. No, something was badly wrong here.

"Angele, go. Father is trying to make me transition today."

When she got up closer, Angele said in a monotone, "Promise me, you will never hurt or drink the blood of my descendants without consent."

"It'll be the only vow I ever keep. I swear, Angele. Where is your necklace?"

Daisy grasped the necklace that she wore all the time, exactly like Angele's. It protected her from vampire compulsion. And Angele didn't have hers on.

Daisy's eyes flicked down to Angele's side and saw a knife. "No, no."

But it was too late. Angele lifted the knife to her throat and said, "I love you, Torija."

"No!" Victorija screamed.

But it was too late. Angele slit her own throat and slumped onto the grass. Victorija dropped to her knees and pulled Angele into her lap as she bled out.

"Why, Angele, why did you take your necklace off?"

Victorija kissed Angele's face, while Angele could only gurgle as her blood seeped into her white dress. She then screamed and roared into the sky above her.

So Victorija didn't kill her. Angele was compelled to kill herself in front of Victorija, to cause her the most pain. Daisy held her hand to her mouth. It was so distressing to watch.

Victorija's tears were streaming down her face, and all Daisy wanted to do was hold her.

She heard laughter and looked up to see a man approaching with a woman. It must be Gilbert, the only one that would want to hurt his daughter so much.

"You," Victorija screamed. "You had Angele under your compulsion and told her to kill herself."

"Yes, it was rather a good plan. Are you ready to become a born vampire now?"

Victorija roared and launched herself at her father. He easily dodged with his superspeed.

They stalked around, circling each other.

"You have killed every person I've ever been close to. I loved Angele. She was the most pure, innocent thing in my life, and you've destroyed it."

"You're pathetic, Victorija. Just like your mother. There is no love for us, especially from those that belong to a vampire hunter's family. They live to kill people like me and like who you will be."

"Maybe that's a good idea," Victorija shouted. She went for her father again, but he leaped over Victorija's head and grasped her by the head from behind.

"You may be a disappointment to me, Victorija, but you will become a born vampire as you are destined to be."

"You might kill me, but I'll never drink blood and complete the transition," Victorija pledged.

Gilbert laughed and said, "You won't say that when you feel the blood hunger." At that he snapped Victorija's neck, and she fell to the ground.

"No, no," Daisy cried. This was heartbreaking to watch.

After a minute or so, Victorija lifted her head. Her eyes were red, and her vampire teeth were protruding from her gums. She clambered over to the body of Angele and held her close.

Then Gilbert pulled the woman he brought with him over and used his fangs to rip open her wrist. The blood dripped down onto the ground.

"No," Victorija said, "I don't want to turn. I want to die with my Angele."

Daisy was praying for Victorija not to turn, even though she knew it was futile. This moment changed the course of thousands of lives, and it didn't have to be like this.

Gilbert licked up the woman's arm and gave an exaggerated hum. "You want this. You're a Dred."

"I'm a Debrek. I was born a Debrek," Victorija insisted.

"You'll never be one of them. You're too much like me. You have a dark soul. Drink."

In an instant, Victorija charged over to the woman, knocked her to the ground, and began to drink feverishly from her neck.

Then all the players in this tragedy disappeared. Daisy fell to her knees on the grass. Tears streamed down her face. "Why did you show me this?"

Lucia said. "Because I need you, we need you. Come and sit."

Daisy was traumatized by what she had just seen, and she was angry. She turned to Lucia and said, "Why did you all not do anything to help Victorija? She was a sensitive, tortured soul, and you Debreks just left her with that monster Gilbert, and he created another monster."

"Your anger is justified, Daisy. That's why I want to help her. Gilbert was my son, and he was always a jealous, dark soul, but I never thought he'd kill his bonded wife, or force his daughter to turn."

Daisy shook her head. "You should have helped her."

It was so strange to feel empathy and sorrow for someone like Victorija.

"My only excuse is that I didn't know this incident happened, Daisy. I didn't know till shortly before I died. Angele came to me, much like you, and showed me the light."

"Amelia said you walked willingly to your death. That you knew Victorija would kill you, and you could have stopped it," Daisy said.

"I did walk willingly—that is the only way you can get forgiveness. I'd lived an extremely long and privileged life. I'd passed on the Debrek clan to Byron and Amelia. Sera, I knew, would have Byron and Bhaltair to take care of her, but my biggest regret was Victorija. In the months before I died, Angele came to me and begged me to bring Victorija's pain to an end. She showed me what happened here, how Victorija's love was killed and Victorija forcibly turned. I vowed to Angele I would help Victorija find you and give her a chance to change her life."

"Just because she has reasons why the darkness overtook her, she still made those decisions and killed those people. You can't just be forgiven." Daisy wiped away her tears.

"You have to face what you have done, and then your forgiveness is in the hands of those you have wronged," Lucia explained.

"Why me?"

"There was no one else. Angele told me that she was Victorija's beginning, and you would be her end."

"What? Like, kill her? I don't think—"

"No—well, in a way. Kill the Victorija that is, and bring back to life the Torija that Angele loved," Lucia said.

"I don't know how I could possibly do that."

Lucia pushed herself up with her stick and stood by Daisy. "There is a dark time coming, Daisy, and you and Amelia are the two people that will bring the paranormal world together and keep them together like glue."

"I don't understand," Daisy said.

A golden light appeared, and Lucia started to walk towards it. Daisy's mind was reeling from what she had seen. A question popped into her head. "Lucia? How do you love a monster?"

The Grand Duchess, who was almost at the light, stopped and turned around. With a small smile she replied simply, "You take off their mask."

In an instant Lucia disappeared, and Daisy was back on her bed in the Debrek house. She was breathing heavily and feeling queasy. Everything she had learned was almost too much to process.

But then a thought as clear as day came into her mind. She knew what she had to do.

Byron walked from the bathroom into their bedroom. Amelia was already in bed, facing away from her. Byron got in beside her and hugged her from behind. "Are you well, mia cara?"

Amelia sighed. "I'm just worried about Daisy. I don't see that there's any way out for her."

"We will find a way."

"You didn't when you were bonded to me," Amelia noted.

"Maybe I didn't want to find a cure."

Amelia reached her hand back and pulled Byron's head to her neck. "And I'm so thankful you didn't. It's time to feed from me."

Byron ran her hand over Amelia's slightly rounded stomach and thigh. "Are you sure you're up to it?"

"Will you please stop asking me that every time you feed? I'm not going to break."

Byron kissed her neck and then whispered in Amelia's ear, "I never thought I'd have a wife and a baby on the way. Forgive me if I'm a little careful."

"I need you, Byron. I need to feed you and for you to touch me."

"But you are worried," Byron reminded her.

"I need to feel safe." Amelia took Byron's hand and pushed it into the back of her underwear. "And you make me feel safe."

Byron grasped the tender flesh of her wife's buttock and squeezed. "Anything you wish, mia cara." She ran her teeth over Amelia's pulse point and felt her shiver. "Do you want me to go inside?"

Amelia answered with an, "Uh-huh," and pushed back against Byron's groin.

"Your wish is my command." Byron pushed her hand down Amelia fleshy buttock and into her wetness. "You do want this, don't you?"

"Yes, inside."

Byron pushed into Amelia's wetness and heard her gasp. She quickly followed that up by biting into her wife's neck. Byron moaned as she did every time she fed on Amelia. It was like pure Elysium. No other human she had fed on tasted and felt like this.

Amelia's hips began to thrust back against her fingers, and Byron pulled her closer. Byron usually would have been inside her wife with her strap-on, but she wanted this to be gentle, and to bring Amelia tenderly to her orgasm. Byron matched Amelia's thrusts as she got faster, and it didn't take long before Amelia's groans grew, and then she grasped her arm around Byron's waist and went rigid, as she fell in her orgasm.

Amelia panted as she tried to get her breath back. Byron pulled her fangs from Amelia's neck and lapped the remaining blood from Amelia's wound before it began to heal fast—one of the perks of being blood bonded to a born vampire and inheriting the Grand Duchess's ring, which made Amelia the life force of the Debrek clan.

"Thank you," Byron said.

"Don't ever thank me for feeding you, especially when you make me feel so loved," Amelia said.

Amelia went to turn around, but Byron stopped her. "No, mia cara. Just fall asleep in my arms. That's all I want."

"Okay. I love you, sweetheart."

"I love you, and don't worry. We'll find a way out of this and keep Daisy safe. Somehow."

"Byron?"

Byron wrapped her arm around Amelia's waist. "What is it?"

"In my morning practice, when I was connecting to the ancestors…"

"Yes?"

"Lucia came to talk to me."

Byron sat up, leaning on her elbow. "Really? What did she want?"

"She said she wanted me to be the voice of reason in the coming weeks and months."

"About what?"

"Victorija."

CHAPTER EIGHT

Daisy crept to the bedroom door and looked out the keyhole. There was someone there guarding the door, not to keep her in, but to try to keep the Dreds out. It would have to be the window.

She hated heights but was just going to have to force herself. Daisy walked to the window and opened it. Luckily there was a porch roof just below that she could drop onto. She got out onto the windowsill, and her knees turned to jelly.

"Why am I doing this for a murdering arsehole?" Byron and Amelia would kill her, but after what she'd seen, Daisy couldn't do anything else. Plus, her bite was making it so hard not to go to Victorija.

Clambering down from height was made all the more difficult by Daisy's jelly legs, and her intense fear. But she made it down. Daisy quickly dived behind a stone pillar at the back of the house when she saw some of Bhal's warriors patrolling the garden.

Okay. Just get out of the garden, and the Dreds will get me.

They had probably been watching all the time since she'd left Scotland. She must be insane to throw herself into their clutches, but it felt like destiny. If Victorija had any part of the younger Torija still in her, she owed it to Angele to try and find it.

Once the warriors had passed, Daisy ran to the garden gate and left the garden. She ran the opposite way from the Debrek front door and came out on a busy street. It was late, but London was never asleep.

She walked down the street for a few minutes, and nobody approached her. It probably wasn't quiet enough for the Dreds to grab her. Daisy flagged down a taxi and got in.

"Where to, miss?"

"London Bridge, please."

The bridge seemed like a good open space for the Dreds to pick her up, and it was likely to be quiet at this time of night.

Before long they had arrived. Daisy paid the driver and walked to the middle of the bridge. She leaned on the railing and realized she probably looked like a jumper. Daisy just prayed this would work. She was crazy, allowing herself to get captured and taken to the lion's den, but if you wanted to help the lion, then you must go to their den.

Daisy heard a car stop behind her and the sound of car doors opening and shutting. Her heart started to pound, and her spidey sense was pinging.

Why did I do this?

"Daisy MacDougall?"

Daisy shut her eyes and tried to gather her courage. She slowly turned around and saw a blacked-out Jeep and five or six vampires, she presumed, standing in front of her. One stepped forward and said, "Hello, Daisy, my name is Leo. It's pointless to run—we are faster and stronger than you."

Daisy surprised them, she thought, by being calm, cool, and collected on the outside. "Yes, I know." She walked to the car and said, "Shall we get going, Vamp?"

Leo furrowed his brow. "Yes, please."

"Not a bother." Daisy felt far from calm on the inside, but it was amusing to see the looks on the Dred vampires' faces.

Anka thrust herself up and down on the male body underneath her. This was when Anka enjoyed her powers the most, drawing the energy from another person, and she was doing that just now.

"Anka, please?" the man said.

She didn't even remember the man's name, but that was no matter. Anka grasped his chin and said sharply, "That's Madam Anka to you."

"Madam Anka, may I come inside you."

"Don't be ridiculous. Only the very special are allowed to do that, and it's not you." Anka insisted on using condoms. There was only one person with whom she didn't.

Her denial only seemed to excite him more. "Sorry. I need—"

"I know what you need," Anka said. Her own orgasm was so close, and she wanted to make it powerful. She sat up straighter as she undulated her hips and held her hand above him. He was close to coming, too, she could tell. Anka moved her thumb and forefinger towards each other and stopped with them a few inches apart.

The man grasped his throat in panic.

"Don't fight it, you are going to go out on the ride of your life." Anka thrust faster and pinched her fingers closer together, slowly choking him. She didn't take her eyes from his face, which showed an intoxicating mixture of pleasure and panic. Anka fed off it, her orgasm fed off it, and as she got closer to her own peak, she closed over the man's throat.

She could tell he'd come while perishing beneath her. Anka's full body shook with exquisite pleasure and power. She growled and then groaned before the feeling started to dissipate.

Anka quickly climbed off him and put on her silk dressing gown. There was a knock at her bedroom door. Anka loved the house that Asha had found her. It was pleasant and had beautifully decorated rooms, but the best thing was the access to the Paris catacombs where she worshipped her power benefactor.

"Come?"

Asha walked in. "Drasas is here to see you, Madam."

"Is she? I hope she has some good news about Daisy MacDougall. Lead on, Asha. My little puppet vampire is waiting for me. Oh, and get rid of that." Anka pointed at the body on the bed.

"Yes, Madam."

Anka didn't dress. She thought she would have more of an impact on Drasas simply dressed in her silk dressing gown. She'd give Drasas a tantalizing glimpse of what she could have.

She wasn't particular about the gender of her sex partners—Anka just loved sex, and she knew she could have so much fun using Drasas's body. By the time she walked downstairs and was near the sitting room, she could feel Drasas's pent-up sexual energy and excitement.

This was so easy.

Anka walked into the room, and Drasas said, "Madam Anka, I have her. Just like you said."

She feigned indifference and sat on a chair across from Drasas. "Who?"

"Daisy MacDougall, Victorija's blood bond," Drasas said.

Anka crossed her legs seductively and watched Drasas's eyes follow intently.

"About time. Where is she now?"

"Just about to board a private aircraft to come to Paris."

"I suppose you think you deserve a reward?" Anka said with disdain.

Drasas shook her head. "My only reward is pleasing you."

Anka gave her a grin. "Good answer." She held up her hand and moved it up and down her body. Anka knew the warm glow felt like a touch was caressing Drasas's body. Drasas closed her eyes and started to moan. Then Anka abruptly shut off her power.

Drasas opened her eyes. "Please, Anka."

How pathetic these Dred vampires were, but this little puppet would serve her purposes well. "Get on your knees, Drasas," Anka ordered.

Drasas hesitated. She knew Drasas hated to feel weak, but that make her subservience more delicious.

"Knees, Drasas," Anka said with a honeyed voice.

Drasas groaned and fell to her knees. "Yes, Anka."

"Madam Anka," she reprimanded her. "Crawl to me, and I'll tell you exactly what I want you to do."

Drasas obeyed and crawled on her hands and knees across to Anka.

Anka leaned forward and grasped Drasas lightly by the hair. "I want you to make sure Victorija drinks regularly from Daisy MacDougall. I need to have her back to full power as quickly as possible."

"But if she is, how am I to go up against her, Madam? She's a born vampire—I couldn't hope to match her," Drasas said.

"You don't, and you won't. Once she is back to full power, I will drain every last bit of power she has and make you the most powerful vampire the world has ever known. You will stand at my right-hand side as the Principe of the Dreds. We will lead the rest of the dark forces out into the world that is rightly ours."

Drasas smiled. "Yes, Madam Anka. I will do anything for that."

Anka smiled. "I know you will." She untied her dressing gown and let her legs fall open. "Kiss me, and make me come."

Drasas grinned.

❖

Victorija came to slowly. Her head was pounding from a mixture of the alcohol she'd consumed and the blood hunger. Hangovers were never something she needed to concern herself with when she was at full strength, but now that her vampire body was refusing to work properly, this hangover was all too real.

She sat up against the wall where she had fallen. Victorija thanked the gods the dead that Angele had brought were gone. At one time she could have looked them all in the eye and laughed. Not now.

Was it really Angele or just a symptom of the blood sickness? Whatever it was, Victorija felt true shame when Angele looked at her. She didn't want to face all the harm she had caused in Angele's presence.

Victorija looked down at her wrist, at the green colour climbing inch by inch through her veins. It was higher than yesterday, by a small amount. It was then that she noticed a new bottle of Anka's potion beside her. That meant Drasas and her other vampires had seen their Principe, passed out and weak.

If she didn't get better and quick, they were going to start questioning her leadership. Victorija grasped the bottle, unscrewed the top quickly, and drank it down. She pulled her legs up against her chest and tremored. She felt pathetic and weak. It was horrifying that her time as a powerful born vampire had come to this. But she couldn't do it. There was no other way out. She would have to break her vow and drink Daisy's blood. It was too much of Angele to ask.

It was either that or lingering death. She would instruct Drasas to send some of her vampires to find Daisy. At least she wouldn't be getting her hands dirty. Victorija pushed herself up. She would need to make herself look a bit more presentable before going down to talk to Drasas.

She staggered towards the bathroom. Once there, Victorija ripped off her shirt and doused her face in water. She looked up at her image in the mirror and saw a pale, sickly image staring back at her.

Was this the vampire that came up with the elaborate plan to kill her father, slice off his head, and burn his heart, in revenge for her mother's and Angele's deaths?

No, but she needed to get back to that Victorija soon. There was a knock at the door of her chambers.

"Come." Victorija grabbed a towel and patted her face dry as she walked into the main living area.

The doors opened and Leo, her third in command, came in. "Principe. Drasas would appreciate it if you would come down to the dungeon."

"Why?" Victorija was suspicious.

Leo grinned and said, "Drasas has a surprise for you."

"I'll be down in a moment. I just need to dress."

"Yes, Principe." Leo bowed his head and left her.

Victorija felt uneasy about this. What if it was some plot to oust her? "You're still a born vampire. Start thinking like one," she chastised herself.

Victorija put on a fresh shirt and ran a comb through her unruly hair. Unruly was never a word anyone would have associated with Victorija before the blood sickness. She was always well-dressed, often elaborately dressed, almost a dandy. Now she was no dandy.

She put on her longer-sleeved ruffled shirt so the cuffs would mostly cover the green veins traveling up her wrist and started walking downstairs to the basement where the dungeons were. As she approached, she heard some raised voices. One was Drasas, but the other she didn't know. Victorija nodded to the two vampires stationed outside the dungeon doors and walked in.

She wasn't prepared for the sight that waited for her on the other side of the door. Daisy MacDougall was strapped to the chair her father used for her mother, to extract her blood.

Victorija had a flashback to finding her mother there as a youngster. She was drugged out of her mind to make her more compliant, but she remembered running to her mum and hugging her tightly, while she cried.

Despite the drugs coursing through her body, her mother managed to whisper to a young Victorija: *Run, Victorija. Run as far away as you can, or Gilbert will end up destroying you.*

"Principe?" Drasas said.

Victorija shook herself from her memory. "Excuse me, Drasas."

Drasas was full of smiles. "I hope you like my surprise present?"

• 86 •

Daisy's presence had totally caught her by surprise. She couldn't show Drasas that Daisy's presence was anything other than a good surprise.

"You did very well, Drasas. Thank you. Could you leave us now?"

"Of course, Principe. Enjoy her."

Daisy piped up and said, "I'd rather be drained of my blood than listen to one more word of you, Vamp."

Drasas grasped Daisy by the neck, and without even thinking, Victorija sped over and pulled Drasas from Daisy and said angrily, "No, she's my blood bond."

Drasas stood back and held up her hands. "Sorry, Principe. We'll leave and let you feed. I think it'll take you some days of the human's blood before you feel quite yourself again. We'll set up a blood collection after that, and then you can feed wherever you are."

The gnawing hunger was painful in her stomach, now that she was face to face with her blood bond. She could see the effect of her hunger on Daisy. She was struggling against her bonds, and her face was contorted.

"Thank you, Drasas."

Daisy felt her bite mark burn intensely. Victorija was clearly struggling. When the guards left, she would be able to tell how seriously she was going to take her vow to Angele. She knew she was taking a big risk coming here.

Victorija was suffering with blood sickness. Her control would be wavering, and she might just kill her, but Daisy had to have confidence in Angele and Lucia, and pray she got a chance to see if Torija was still in there. As soon as the door was shut, she would find out.

Drasas and the guards walked out, and as soon as the door clicked shut, Victorija sped over to the chair in an instant. She grasped her arms that were strapped down. "How did you get captured by my vampires? You've had Debrek guards with you everywhere you go. What is Byron playing at?"

Victorija was furious, and that wasn't one of the reactions she was expecting.

"Byron doesn't know I'm here. No one does. I walked to London Bridge, then just waited for your vampires."

"Are you insane?" Victorija started to pace in a panicked fashion. "Why? You stood up to me and tried to save Amelia in the club. Now you give yourself to vampires?"

Daisy was sure now that Victorija was conflicted because of her vow. She had to play this right. "I'm here to save you."

Victorija stopped pacing and burst out laughing. "You, Daisy MacDougall, are here to save me? Save me from what, cherie?"

"From yourself."

"Myself?"

"Yes, to find that light inside you."

Victorija grasped her chin and said menacingly, "Victorija Dred does not have any light inside her."

Quick as a flash, Daisy replied, "No, but Torija does."

Victorija almost fell as she staggered back in shock. "Where did you hear that name?"

"Angele Brassard's journal, and your grandmother Lucia. Her notebook and some of her things were passed down through the family. MacDougall is my dad's family name, but my mum was a Brassard— but you knew that, didn't you? You knew when you tasted my blood in the club, you knew when you came to my bedroom in Scotland."

Victorija turned away and clutched at her hair. "No, no, why did you do this to me, Angele?" She took a deep breath, and when she turned back around, the cool Victorija was back. "There is no Torija. She died the day I became a born vampire."

"I don't believe that, Torija. You've just forgotten her."

"You are deluded, Daisy MacDougall." Victorija stalked around the back of the chair and pulled down the side of her top, exposing more of her neck. Daisy gasped when she felt Victorija's nose and lips on her neck. "Do you know how much I've been fantasizing about this neck?"

The feel of Victorija's lips against her neck made her tremble, and her sex started to throb. It was intoxicating, and all she wanted to do was offer herself to Victorija. It was what the blood bond demanded, but she had to stay strong.

It was even harder to stay strong when she felt the tips of Victorija's fangs. "I want you so much."

Daisy's body wanted Victorija, too, but her brain wasn't going to let that happen. "You don't even know me."

"I don't need to. I know your blood, and I need it desperately," Victorija said huskily.

Daisy took a breath, trying to control her body's reaction to Victorija. "I do not consent."

Victorija hissed and put her arm around Daisy's throat, choking her slightly. "Why do you think your consent means anything to me?"

"Because I'm a Brassard, and you swore an oath to Angele never to take blood without consent from a Brassard."

Victorija was silent for a moment and loosened her grip on Daisy's throat. "I don't know who told you about that, but it was just something to pacify Angele. She's long dead, and it meant nothing."

It was then that Daisy noticed the green in Victorija's veins, climbing up her wrist and forearm.

"I saw how she asked you to vow, I saw how she killed herself, and I saw how you cried over her body while your father laughed."

Victorija grabbed the back of Daisy's hair painfully and pulled her head back. Her eyes were blood red and wild. Daisy was frightened, her heart was beating hard, but she remembered the young Torija in pain, crying over both her mother and Angele. She now believed she could save—was destined to save—Victorija, so she stayed as strong as she could.

"How could you see my past?" Victorija asked.

"The notebook she left. No one in my family has been able to open it. It opened for me, easily. Angele showed me her days with you. I got to know the real you."

"You know nothing about me." Victorija bared her teeth.

"You won't feed from me, Torija. I do not consent."

Victorija let go suddenly and roared as she fought with her want and desire for Daisy's blood. She ran for the wall of the dungeon and punched, leaving a crumbling hole. She bent over, gasping for breath, then took out a hip flask, before downing it.

This Victorija was a very different creature than the one who had taken Amelia out for dinner, charmed her, and then tried to abduct her. When Daisy tried to stop Victorija from taking Amelia in the bathroom of The Sanctuary Club, she was full of anger, hate, and injustice, all the negative emotions that if you don't fight them, will take over your soul.

Now she saw a mentally scarred, sad vampire that was trying to come to terms with emotions again, the emotions that their blood bond and Lucia helped to bring out.

This was more like Torija. She wasn't dead, she was just buried so deep inside Victorija's soul. It took Victorija's deteriorating mental health to open the door for Torija to take a tentative step out that door.

Victorija scrubbed her face with her hands, then walked back towards her. She pulled off the arm restraints and said, "I am not my father."

"What does that mean?"

"My mother was kept in this chair and drained of her blood when he needed it."

Daisy rubbed her wrists. "What are you going to do?"

"I need time to think." Victorija pulled a knife from her pocket. "Cut yourself on my bite wound with this."

"Why would I do that?"

Victorija leaned over said, "Out beyond that door, my vampires all need to believe that I am feeding on you, or I will lose control of this clan. They already think I'm weakened. If I lose control, I can't protect you."

Daisy smiled. "I knew Torija was still inside you."

Victorija grasped Daisy's chin. "Then you're a fool. I'm going to find a way to break this bond and keep my vow to Angele. You are just an old debt."

"Keep telling yourself that, Vamp. I know what's inside you."

Victorija turned slowly and said, "If that's the case, then consent to giving me your blood, and I'll give you safe passage out of here."

Daisy couldn't do that. She had to coax Torija out of this vampire—she couldn't just give her what she wanted.

When Daisy stayed silent, Victorija held up her hands and smirked. "You see? No one loves the monster, no one cares about the monster, no one trusts the monster. Oh, and cherie, don't take that necklace off if you don't want me or any of my vampires to just take what they want."

"Don't worry, I won't," Daisy said sarcastically, "and don't call me cherie. I'm nobody's sweetheart."

"And if I can't find a way to break this bond, you will be breakfast, lunch, and dinner, believe me."

"I don't, Torija," Daisy said.

It was crazy to have such surety in a vampire that she previously thought was an evil sociopath, but Daisy knew when she watched Torija cry over Angele's body that she wouldn't harm her.

❖

"Thanks, Uncle Jaunty," Amelia said.

She ended her call and walked quickly back to the grand dining room, where she found Byron pacing backward and forward, while Alexis, Sera, Bhal, Wilder, and her most trusted lieutenants were sitting around the dining table, some working on tablets, trying to gather information.

"Byron," Amelia said, "Uncle Jaunty's sending his assistant manager next door to run the outfitters for me."

Amelia's uncle owned gentlemen's outfitters on the famous Savile Row in London. Amelia's dream had always been to make a similarly welcoming place for women to come be fitted for suits and other clothes that had traditionally been the preserve of men.

"Excellent. I want you with me."

Byron held out a chair for Amelia and made sure she was sitting comfortably. "I've just come off a call with Sybil."

"What did she say?" Amelia asked.

Just then Katie led Magda and her granddaughter, Piper, into the dining room. Byron greeted her. "Thank you for coming, Magda. I'm sure it doesn't make you popular in your coven to come into a vampire's lair."

Piper, who seemed to have a permanent scowl on her face, said, "Especially when said vampire got one of your coven's best witches killed."

"Piper, sit down," Magda said. "The Debreks are an honourable vampire clan. I'm sorry, Byron."

"Not at all. There have been historical reasons behind the mistrust between our two kinds, but I assure you we only have the best intentions."

Piper sat next to Wilder with a heavy sigh. Katie shut the doors and sat beside Alexis.

Magda said to Amelia, "How are you feeling?"

"I'm feeling good, thanks."

"Good, you, Byron, and your child will hopefully bring the witches and the vampires together as the Grand Duchess Lucia and Cosimo Debrek did. We all need each other."

"I hope so, Magda. I think we all want peace. Sybil said she wouldn't come here, that she knew where she must be. Do you know why?" Byron said.

"I do, but show me the letter Daisy left." Amelia handed Magda the letter, and she gazed over it. "Yes, as I thought. The time has come."

"What time?" Byron asked.

"Sybil isn't coming here because she is at Daisy's grandmother's house in Scotland," Magda said.

Amelia wasn't expecting that answer. "What? Why?"

"She feels Daisy might go there if she escapes the Dred castle. Daisy's grandmother, Margaret, is familiar with Sybil. They have crossed paths many times over the years."

"She has?" Byron said with surprise.

"Margaret *Brassard* is her full name."

"Brassard?" Byron said.

"You recognize it, Byron?"

Byron looked at Alexis, and Alexis replied, "We both do."

Amelia hated being in the dark like this. "Byron, what is this about? How do you know the name Brassard?"

Byron sat down beside Amelia and said, "The Brassards are, and have always been, vampire hunters."

Amelia gasped and looked at Magda. "Is this true?"

"Yes, indeed it is. The Brassards have always been vampire hunters, and the calling has been passed down through the generations, along with the ability to sense when they are with a paranormal."

"Her spidey sense, as Daisy calls it," Amelia said.

"Yes," Magda said. "Daisy's father was a MacDougall, that's why she doesn't carry the family name, but the calling to be a vampire hunter…yes."

Katie piped up, "Does Daisy know?"

"She does now, but not until very recently. Margaret kept the knowledge of the family business a secret. The calling had already gotten Daisy's mother and father killed, and she couldn't bear to lose Daisy, too."

"And yet Daisy found her way to this secret life anyway, starting with her Monster Hunters YouTube channel."

"Indeed," Magda said, "that's why it is a calling and not a job. Margaret works for a government agency based in Edinburgh that protects the public from paranormals with ill intent. Daisy's mother worked there, too."

Amelia was shocked. She turned to Byron and said, "You never told me about that."

"The department? They got those of us who wanted to help with the war effort involved in World War Two."

Amelia shook her head. "Every time I think I know something about this world, it turns out I don't."

"How will she get away from the Dred castle on her own?" Byron asked.

"There is only so much I know. Sybil knows more."

"Alexis, Bhal, we're going to rescue her. Daisy is one of us, and she's obviously important for more than one reason."

Amelia squeezed Byron's hand. "Thank you, sweetheart."

"Oh, and one more thing?" Magda said. "Amelia is one descendant, prophesied to bring the paranormal world together, and the second is Daisy."

Everyone in the meeting room gasped.

"Daisy?" Byron said.

"Yes. She is as vital as Amelia. If Anka and Victorija find out, it will destroy our fight against them. They will kill her," Magda warned.

Victorija walked down the hallway with as much energy as she could muster. She had to show her vampires that there was a marked improvement in her condition, and just give herself time to think.

Leo came towards her and said, "Feeling better, Principe?"

"Indeed I am. Thank you for bringing Daisy to me."

"You're welcome. Can I be of service to you, Principe?" Leo said.

"No, in fact I feel so much better, I'm going to take a ride out on one of the horses."

Leo looked surprised and tense. "Very good, Principe. Have a good ride."

When Victorija got around the corner, her shoulders slumped, and she was sure the pain of the blood sickness was etched on her face. She just needed time, but time was not on her side.

As Victorija gathered her breath, her exceptional hearing picked up several voices.

"Excuse me, Duca," Leo said.

"One moment, Leo, I'm on the phone…Yes, Madam Anka. The plan is in place. She's feeding from Daisy MacDougall now."

"Make sure she is fit and healthy for me. I need the strength of a born vampire, and if I don't have it, I can't give it to you, Drasas, and I know how much you want to be Principe."

Victorija couldn't believe her ears. Her own protégée was plotting against her?

"Yes, I do. I will give you anything."

Treacherous little fuck.

"Are you sure this will go well?" Drasas continued. "She is a born vampire, too strong for me."

Always will be, you gutter trash.

"Believe me, you will soon have more power than Victorija can dream of. Then you will take her head and burn her heart to dust," Anka said.

Drasas had been sleeping on the street, sickly, starving, and with no hope when Victorija met her. How could she?

"What shall we do with Daisy MacDougall once Victorija is dead?"

"Kill her."

That remark made her snarl. Daisy might be a human with delusions of grandeur, but she was her Daisy, and her Brassard, and she would make sure she kept Daisy alive, if only for Angele's sake. But Victorija wanted to live. There had to be some way to break this bond. There was always a way. She had to think.

As Victorija walked, she thought, *I gave Drasas everything.*

She followed her instinct to get out of the castle and go for a ride. She approached the stable block and saw one of her stablehands brushing down her favourite horse, Angel.

The lad was seventeen and had worked in the castle stables since he was a young boy. His father was her dresser, and they were two of the humans that she could be accused of being fond of and were off limits to her vampires.

"Jacque, I'd like to take Angel out for a ride."

"Yes, Principe, I'll get her ready for you."

As she was waiting for her horse to be saddled, she saw Drasas running out the door to meet her. Victorija stood a little straighter and tried to appear as well as possible. "Drasas?"

"Principe, Leo said you had fed from Daisy. How are you feeling?"

"Excellent, Drasas. I think after a few more days, I will be back to full strength, the born vampire that I always was."

Drasas looked uneasy. "Wonderful, Principe. I was thinking, since you're feeling better, why don't we have one of those grand balls we used to have? We could invite Anka and her witches, toast our new alliance?"

Although she had already overheard Drasas's plans, hearing it now whilst looking her right in the eye cut even deeper. She forced a smile and said, "What a wonderful idea, Drasas. Set it up."

"Yes, Principe."

When Drasas walked away, Victorija said, "Oh, Duca?"

Drasas turned around. "Yes?"

"I will pay you back for your loyalty to me as Duca. Where would I be without you?"

Drasas looked slightly unsure but then walked away.

Once she was out of earshot, Victorija said to Jacque, "Stick around. I want to talk to you when I get back."

Plans were already formulating in Victorija's brain. They were giving her much needed energy, and the adrenaline was helping with the blood sickness.

She was going to defeat both Drasas's premeditated attack and the blood sickness, and save Daisy for Angele.

CHAPTER NINE

Daisy lay on the uncomfortable bed in the dungeon, wondering why she had done this. She could be at home now or at the Debreks'—but no, she had to listen to some weird visions. If she'd interviewed someone like herself for Monster Hunters, even she wouldn't have believed.

"I'm here to save Victorija Dred's soul. Bloody nuts."

If Skye and the guys knew where she'd gone—not to mention, her granny—they'd go crazy.

She jumped when the dungeon door opened and a confident-looking Victorija walked in, but as soon as the door was shut, her whole demeanour changed. She slumped, and pain was etched on her face.

Daisy jumped up and was about to speak when Victorija put her finger to her lips. Daisy didn't say a word and watched Victorija carefully. She pointed to her ear and then pointed towards the door. Victorija was clearly worried about being heard by the guards at the door.

"I'm here to feed," Victorija said.

"Please don't."

"Do you think I care what you say, human?"

As Victorija got closer, Daisy saw her pull an envelope from her waistband. She handed it to her, and Daisy broke the seal.

The first line said, *Don't say a word. They'll be able to hear.*

Daisy looked up to Victorija and saw her clutching her midriff in pain. Victorija must have loved Angele so much to be working this hard to keep her vow.

She began to read the letter.

In two days, Drasas is holding a ball to celebrate our new alliance with Anka and her followers. That's when you will make your getaway. This is the plan. My trusted human servant Jacque will guide you to a place where I can meet you, and then I'll get you out of here.

Wow. Victorija really had changed, a bit anyway. This was Daisy's chance to get through to the light in her soul. Daisy gave her a thumbs-up. Victorija nodded and pointed at Daisy's neck. She had to feign the bite again.

Daisy brought out the small penknife in her pocket and screwed up her eyes as she cut into the wound. It stung really badly, and she made sure she made lots of painful noise. She watched as Victorija's eyes went red and her fangs popped out at the sight of her blood flowing freely now.

"No," Daisy cried out, "you've had enough, stop."

Victorija covered her face with her hands and sped out.

The night of the Dred ball had arrived. It was a day long awaited by Anka. She would bring to fruition her master's plan for the dark time to take over the earth once again.

She was sitting in her casting circle, set deep in the catacomb system in the basement of her house. Her attendant Asha carefully placed candles, a skull, and other dark totems she had collected over her long life.

Anka sat cross-legged and closed her eyes. "Step forward, dark ones."

In her mind's eye, she saw the dark souls of witches who had pledged themselves to her lord, Balor. He was sitting on a high throne behind them. She bowed her head and said, "Balor, we are ready. Once we have the born vampire, then we'll be able to bring your emissary back to the world."

There was a figure obscured by the darkness and the sound of rain in the background. He stepped forward but still was obscured.

"This will be over tonight, and I will bring you back to the world. I promise you that."

❖

Each time Victorija came into the dungeon, she looked worse. She kept it together until the dungeon door shut, and then she let go, holding her stomach in pain, feeling dizzy, sick. The night of the celebration ball was the worst so far. When the door shut, Victorija fell to one knee. Daisy was over to her in a second to offer help. Victorija stood up without taking Daisy's hand.

"I don't need your help."

"Stubborn, aren't you?" Daisy said.

Instead of answering, Victorija brushed the dust and mess from her suit. Daisy stood back and looked Victorija up and down. She was wearing a black suit with a white shirt, ruffled at the collar and cuffs.

"Well, you look—nice. Going for the Regency dandy look, Torija?"

"Stop calling me *Torija*. I don't answer to that name."

Daisy crossed her arms and smirked. "Stubborn and sensitive."

"Is that so, cherie?"

Before she was even aware it was happening, Victorija grabbed her, and she found herself pushed against the dungeon wall, held by her T-shirt. Victorija's eyes were red, and her fangs were protruding with a snarl.

Daisy's heart was pounding hard, but she tried not to show it.

Victorija was just a few inches from her face and terrifying. "Do you understand what I'm doing here, the torture I'm going through hour to hour, minute by minute, having my blood bond here and not drinking from her? And all because I made a vow to someone I loved, and who you just happen to be related to." Victorija released her grip on Daisy's T-shirt and drew her nail down Daisy's bite mark. "Don't push me."

Instead of being frightened at that gesture, Daisy's heart was beating from attraction and not fear. In that moment she would have begged Victorija to kiss her. The pull of their blood bond was great, but it was more than that. She felt something more for this evil, scary vamp, but she tried to remember what Angele and Lucia had said—*Monsters are made, not born.*

Torija was in there, somewhere.

Catching Victorija by surprise, Daisy said, "You're right. I apologize. That's not fair when you're fighting your instincts."

Victorija stepped back, her eyes returned to normal, and her fangs receded.

"Well, thank you," Victorija said.

Daisy straightened her T-shirt. "You do still look like a dandy."

Victorija gave her a half smile. "I *was* a Regency dandy. I've lived through many ages, and I like to take the best from each age and keep it alive. I've only recently stopped wearing a top hat."

Daisy laughed at Victorija's joke, and the tension of a few moments ago had gone. "You look nice. I would be happy to dance with you at a grand ball," Daisy said.

"You know the plan?" Victorija said seriously.

Daisy nodded.

"Good. I'll see you on the other side, then, and if not—"

"I'll know you tried your best, Torija," Daisy said.

Victorija nodded and walked out the door. As was her practice, every time Victorija left the dungeon, Daisy used the penknife Victorija had given her to cut her bite mark and let the blood flow.

Just like clockwork, the dungeon guards looked through the shutter in the door to see the evidence that Victorija had fed. The blood ran down her neck, and they were satisfied everything was in order and shut the hatch again.

It was so clear to see Victorija's clan were working against her. If she could just get Victorija away from the influence of the clan, Daisy was sure she could save her.

The Debrek household was tense with worry, but busy with staff preparing clothes and supplies for the three seniors in the Debrek clan— Byron, Alexis, and Bhal—leaving for Paris, to try to rescue Daisy.

Byron, Alexis, and Bhal were standing in the entrance hall while their bags were taken out. The family were waiting in the drawing room to say goodbye.

"Just about ready, Principe," Alexis said.

Byron sighed and looked at her warrior, Bhal. "Maybe I should leave you here, Bhal. Sera may not be ready to—"

A split second later, her sister Sera arrived at speed from the drawing room. She looked furious. "I want to talk to you, Byron."

Byron looked at Bhal and Alexis and indicated for them to go to the drawing room.

Once they were away, Sera said, "What is Sera not ready to do? Lead and defend our family? Don't you have any faith in me?"

"Sera, this is not a slight against you. But you haven't been in the position to lead my vampires and Bhal's warriors before."

"Only because you won't ever let me. When I went to America, you had our cousin never let me out of her sight. I'm not a child, and I think you sometimes forget I'm a born vampire, too. Do you think I'd put Amelia and my niece or nephew in danger?"

"Of course I don't."

Sera folded her arms defensively. "Then trust me. Let me do this. You, Mum, Dad, Bhal—you all always treat me like an airhead child. I'm not."

"I never intended to make you feel that way, Sera, but you can be impulsive. Remember what happened in Monaco?"

Sera rolled her eyes and then shook her head. When Amelia and Byron were first dating, they went on a trip to the Debrek Monaco house. And against Byron's instructions, Sera took Amelia out to a club, and the Dreds nearly captured Amelia.

"I've apologized for that, like, a million times. I can do this. Trust me?"

Byron smiled then kissed Sera on the cheek. "Of course. Let me say my goodbyes. Come on."

Sera was smiling widely now. Byron was worried and had her reservations, but she wouldn't show Sera that. It was going to be so hard leaving Amelia. She was a capable woman, but she was only just learning about her powers, and they had a baby to protect.

When they entered the drawing room, Sera sat beside Amelia and Katie on the couch. Everyone else was circled around the couch or sitting on chairs.

Byron stood in front the fireplace, and the chatter quieted down. "Alexis, Bhal, and I are about to leave for France. It's imperative that we rescue our friend Daisy from the Dred clan, and Victorija. Daisy is not only our friend, but she is a descendant, and along with Amelia, her destiny is to bring the paranormal world together against the darkness that is approaching. Sera will be in charge of our vampires while we are away, with Wilder helping."

Wilder nodded. "Yes, Principe."

"Thankfully, Magda helped Amelia cast a circle of protection around the house, so that will keep Anka and the Dreds out, but keep on your toes."

Amelia looked intensely worried. Byron said, "Could I have a moment with the Principessa, please?" As everyone filed out, Amelia made her way over to Byron's arms. Byron heard her sniffle. "Hey, don't cry."

Amelia wiped away her tears. "I'm sorry. I want you to save Daisy, but at the same time I don't want you to go."

"You have nothing to be sorry for. I feel the same." Byron put her hand on Amelia's baby bump. "Everything in my being is telling me to stay with you, to protect you, but I know duty and friendship mean I have no choice but to go. Daisy is too important."

Amelia straightened Byron's tie. "I know. She is my sister-in-arms, as Magda put it. Go and bring her back quickly."

Byron kissed Amelia deeply and then rested her forehead against hers. "I will think of you every minute. Walk me to the door?"

Amelia smiled and took her hand, and they walked out into the hallway. She saw Alexis and Katie kissing each other goodbye. It was the first time the newlyweds were going to be parted for an extended period.

In contrast, Bhal was with Sera, giving her a list of dos and don'ts for while she was away, and Sera was getting increasingly angry, and started bickering.

Sera snapped, "Look, Bhal, I know this. I'm not an idiot. Just go, will you?"

Bhal said, "Fine. You know everything." She stomped out the front door. Those two always clashed, but when push came to shove, Byron knew Bhal would die for her sister.

Alexis gave Katie one last kiss and joined Byron. Before she walked out the door, Byron addressed everyone, both staff and family, who were seeing them off.

"Look after each other, and make sure the Principessa is safe." Byron looked at Amelia and winked. Then she turned to everyone and spoke the Debrek motto and vow: "*Et sanguinem familiae*—blood and family."

Everyone repeated the motto, and Byron forced herself to turn her back and walk away from her wife. It was so hard.

Bhal was holding the car door open for her, and she slipped in. "Thank you, Bhal."

Once everyone was in the car, Byron said to Alexis, "Is the Debrek plane ready at the airfield?"

"All fuelled and read to go. We'll be in Paris in no time."

"Let's go and find Daisy then."

CHAPTER TEN

It was taking every bit of Victorija's will and strength to look as if she was well and strong, thanks to Daisy's blood. She made her way up the throne room, where the ball was taking place, and noticed the uneasy looks of her turned vampires at her presence.

Oh, Drasas, what have you done?

"Principe," Drasas called from the dais. She was certainly getting very used to the dais where the throne was. Victorija climbed up the steps to meet her Duca. "You look strong and well, Principe."

"I feel it, Duca." Victorija looked out at the room of guests, some dancing, some partaking of blood, but all having a good time.

Drasas snapped her fingers at a server with a tray of drinks. "Would you like champagne, or blood? I know it's not your blood bond's but—"

"Blood, Duca. It may not be the perfect blood for me, but I can still indulge."

Victorija wasn't going to drink anything, but simply hold her goblet, as there might be something in it to weaken her. She pretended to take a sip, and the other corner of the dais caught her eye. The ritual fire had been lit. The one where Gilbert had burned her mother's heart, and where Victorija had burned his. Her fate was clear

She was meant to die this night, but Victorija was determined that was not going to happen. If she died, so did Daisy, and she was not going to let that happen, for Angele's sake.

"Thank you for such a wonderful party, Drasas."

Drasas smiled. "You are welcome, Principe." Victorija walked down the steps and into the crowd. A worried-sounding Drasas said, "Anka will be here soon."

"A dance and some fun are all I want, Drasas. There will be time for Anka."

Victorija handed her goblet to an attendant and pulled a vampire towards her. They began to dance sensually, and then Victorija kissed her. She acted her way through the kiss, but again, she felt nothing. The only time she felt her body come alive was when she was close to Daisy.

Victorija took the vampire's hand and pulled her out of the group of dancers. She kissed her again and compelled her to calmly follow her.

Victorija looked up to Drasas and said, "I'll be back."

"But Anka—"

"Ten minutes and I'll be back with you."

Victorija guided the vampire she'd picked down the corridor and into an empty room. There she looked into her eyes and said, "You won't remember our dance, or me bringing you here. You will wake up with no idea how it happened."

"Yes, Principe."

Victorija quickly snapped her neck, and she fell, knowing the vampire would wake once her body had healed itself. "So far, so good." She felt a sharp stab in her guts that nearly made her throw up, but she forced herself to calm. She did and made her way to a door on the other side of the room. She took a couple of deep breaths. It was adrenaline that was keeping her going at this point.

This door led to corridors and stairs used by the staff, where she was less likely to be challenged.

She just hoped Daisy was ready.

Daisy paced back and forth in the dungeon. She thought every noise she heard coming from outside the jail door was either Jacque, or Drasas coming to kill her, if Victorija's plan went wrong.

How ridiculous it seemed to her to be rooting for Victorija, when not long ago she would have been running from her. The time she'd spent in here had confirmed to her that their blood bond deserved a chance, her one chance to do the right thing.

From what she'd heard and had seen of Victorija, she didn't have much discipline for her impulse for blood, so stopping herself from feeding on her was a big gesture. Angele must have really made a big impact on her.

Finally, she heard keys in the lock. She held her breath, and the door opened slowly.

She let out a long breath when she saw a young man smile at her and say in a thick French accent, "Mademoiselle Daisy?"

"Jacque?"

"That is me. Come, please."

She followed him out the door and was unnerved when the two beefy guards didn't even look at them or react to any sound they made. Compulsion was an extremely powerful gift. Daisy held her necklace that protected her from compulsion, and thanked God she had it.

"Come quickly, please," Jacque encouraged her.

He led her down some very quiet corridors. They only passed a couple of staff on the way. He opened a door to what looked like an old armoury room. There were swords and spears adorning the wall, and some suits of armour that appeared to be for decorative purposes, but it was a big room, and she was sure it would have been full of guards back in its prime.

Jacque pointed over to a huge double door on the other side of the room. "We go out here." He stood by the door and put his finger to his lips, then listened for any activity outside. When he was apparently satisfied, Jacque slid open a couple of bolts and opened one of the huge doors.

She followed him, and they were out at the east wall of the house.

"Come this way," Jacque said. Down at the corner of the house a honey-coloured horse waited. "You wait for the Principe here, okay?"

"A horse? We're making our escape on a horse?"

"The Principe asked me to have everything ready. We wait for her."

Daisy thought this was probably the worst idea ever. How were they going to outrun the Dreds on a horse? She heard movement up above her. Daisy looked up but couldn't see beyond a window ledge in the dark.

Before she knew it, Victorija landed in a crouch beside her with a thump. She stood up slowly, trying to not show her pain.

"You organized a horse for our getaway? I know you lived through the medieval period, but there are quicker conveyances than horses, nowadays."

Victorija held her stomach, clearly in pain, but then straightened herself up and pulled herself together. "Horses can go places motor vehicles cannot." She walked over to the horse and stroked her neck. "We can get lost in the forest on her and buy us more time. Besides, this horse is special."

"Why?"

Victorija rubbed its muzzle and said, "This is Angel."

The penny dropped and Daisy said, "Angel is going to carry us, carry you, to freedom."

Victorija didn't respond, but that was clearly what was happening here. She turned to Jacque. "Is everything I asked for in the saddle-bags?"

"Yes, Principe."

She patted him on the shoulder and went into her pocket. "Thank you for your faithful service, Jacque. I wish I could say goodbye to your father, but alas, we must go. Tell him I will miss him." She handed him a set of keys. "Take your father and mother and get far away from here. These are for two safety deposit boxes at my bank. There's money, and jewellery you can sell. It'll be more than enough to start a new life, Jacque."

Jacque looked really touched. Daisy's heart ached unexpectedly. Was this the bloodthirsty vampire who, Amelia said, referred to humans as *lunch*? Or was this Torija, the vampire who Lucia had helped unlock those long-buried emotions?

Angele was right, Daisy thought. Victorija did have a chance. She could be redeemed.

"Thank you, Principe. You are kind."

Then Victorija handed him a bottle and started to speak rapidly in French. Jacque nodded in understanding.

What did Victorija not want me to hear, Daisy wondered.

Victorija jumped onto the horse easily and offered Daisy her hand. "Come on. We don't have much time."

"Jump? I'm not a bloody vamp—I can't just jump," Daisy said with exasperation.

"Take my hand."

As soon as Daisy grasped Victorija's hand, she was on the horse. "Thank you, Jacque. Good luck."

"The same to you, Principe."

Daisy felt terrified. The horse was a very long way off the ground. "Is this a good time to tell you I've never been on a horse before?"

"Just hold on tightly to me. I'll take care of everything."

Daisy felt a warm glow in her stomach, and without fear she wrapped her arms around Victorija's middle.

"Let's go, Angel. We have a Brassard to save."

With that they were off at a canter. Daisy closed her eyes and held on as tightly as she could.

If only Byron and Amelia could see her now.

Drasas was getting nervous. Victorija had been away for a while, and Anka was due any minute. She had promised to produce a healthy born vampire in Victorija, and for that she would be rewarded.

"Leo, go and find the Principe."

"Yes, Duca."

Almost as soon as Leo went to find their Principe, the doors to the throne room opened, and in walked Anka in a gorgeous ballgown, her aide Asha, and a large group of her followers. Drasas gulped in fear. Not only was Anka herself extremely powerful, but she was also backed up by a mixture of dark witches, vampires, werewolves, fae, and other paranormals.

The Dred vampires that were dancing and having a good time stopped and parted to allow Anka and her group through. There was a tension in the room—Drasas felt it most acutely. She had to deliver Victorija.

"Drasas, this looks like a wonderful celebration of our new alliance. Where is your Principe?"

Drasas gulped. "Leo has just gone to fetch her. She was otherwise engaged with a female."

Anka smiled. "Ah, I see. What a wonderful way to celebrate her return to health."

Leo came out of nowhere with speed to arrive at Drasas's side.

She clearly wasn't expecting to see Anka already there, as his worried look showed. "Duca? A word in private, please?"

Anka walked up the steps to the dais and said, "You will speak in front of me."

Drasas nodded when Leo looked for permission. "The female is recovering from a broken neck. She has no idea how she got there."

Drasas started to panic. She raced off to check the dungeon on a hunch. Leo followed her. Drasas opened the door and found it empty. She screamed in frustration and grabbed one of the guards at the door. "Where is our prisoner?"

"In there? No one's passed us."

"Compulsion." Drasas snapped his neck in anger.

Anka arrived by her side. "Where is Daisy MacDougall?"

"Gone." Drasas was terrified of Anka's reaction.

"Everyone leave us," Anka said firmly.

Drasas's rarely beating heart was pounding like a human's. This must be how humans felt when faced with her. When everyone had gone, Anka backed her up against a wall. Anka didn't have to say anything to make Drasas fearful—her silent stare into her eyes was enough. In fact, Drasas would probably have preferred screaming and shouting.

Instead Anka gazed over her face, examining her carefully. Then she drew a finger slowly down Drasas's cheek. "You wanted me, Drasas, you wanted power, the power I could give you, and all I asked was that you give me a healthy Victorija, so I could have a born vampire's power, and finally"—Anka stood back and continued—"I needed you to secure Daisy MacDougall. She is a descendant, who, along with Amelia Debrek, are the only two who can stop mine and my master's plans. It is crucial that she is killed. Not only have you lost her, but you have lost my born vampire. How am I to give you the power you yearn for?"

"I can get them back for you. I promise. I don't understand this. Victorija would never choose a woman over her clan, a human woman at that. I don't understand it."

"A blood bond can do strange things to you, Drasas. Follow me."

She followed Anka back to the throne room. Anka's guards stood in formation on either side of the throne, holding weapons that looked like machine guns. Drasas doubted they shot traditional bullets. They must be able to at least subdue a paranormal.

The Dred vampires took a collective intake of breath when Anka sat on the Principe's throne. Drasas felt it, too.

But the sight of Anka on the throne flanked by her guards was a powerful sight and produced such a sense of strength and fear in the Dred vampires. Drasas wanted a piece of that, and if that meant handing over her vampires to Anka, she would do it.

She would do anything for Anka. Her choice was made.

Drasas walked up onto the dais and took her place at the side of the throne. Leo and those selected vampires who knew about tonight's goal joined the guard around the dais. The others looked at each other worriedly.

Anka looked at Drasas, and Drasas knew what she had to do.

She took a step forward. "Vampires, you all know our Principe was suffering with blood sickness. It was making her weak, but still I and Madam Anka tried to help, Madam Anka with medicine to ease her discomfort, and I, her Duca, by bringing her blood bond to her."

Drasas saw and heard one of her guards say to Leo, "Her horse is gone."

"We did everything to serve Victorija Dred, and where did that get us? Tonight our Principe has chosen a human female over her clan. She has helped Daisy MacDougall escape our dungeon and run away into the night. Does that sound like a Principe? A true royal vampire?"

Her vampires shook their heads in disgust and murmured to each other.

"No. That is not a Principe I want to follow. Anka, a powerful witch, has offered to help us. Anka?"

Anka smiled. "Thank you, Drasas." She gripped the armrest of the throne. "I lead a group of paranormals who refuse to be hidden, who refuse to stay in the shadows of human society. This was once our world, a long, long time ago. Humans bowed to us, they prayed to us, they feared us. I offered to help your Principe make the Dreds the most powerful vampire clan in the world, and to take down the Debreks. And she chose a human life over her clan. But we won't accept that. Work with my people to bring on a new dark age, led by me, and your new Principe, Drasas."

Drasas waited for the response which came almost instantaneously. The vampires cheered and shouted for Drasas. She had done it. This was her clan now, and she lapped up the attention.

She went back to Anka's side, and Anka said, "You better find them, Drasas. This can all be taken away from you."

Drasas didn't want to ever give up this feeling of adulation. "I promise we will. We'll start now."

"Take my guard with you. I want Daisy MacDougall dead and Victorija's power, if she hasn't descended into madness by the time we catch her."

"She will be fit and able, Madam. Victorija doesn't have any self-control. She will be feeding on Daisy savagely by now."

Daisy hated this. Victorija ran the horse at full speed without fear. But she was a vampire and could heal herself after a fall, while she could not, and so the ride was terrifying.

Victorija slowed as they got deeper into the forest. She had begun to moan and slump in the saddle.

"Are you all right?"

Victorija didn't answer but slowed right down and slid out of the saddle. She hunched over on her knees, holding her stomach. "I need to feed."

Then Victorija sped off into the trees, leaving Daisy on the horse. It felt even more scary being up here on her own. She had to get off.

Daisy held the saddle tightly and slipped her legs off the side, but she was still some way off the ground. Daisy didn't want to let go.

The horse whinnied and Daisy said, "Angel, please move. I'm trying to help your namesake." She couldn't hold on any more and fell to the ground, hitting her shoulder painfully. "Bloody hell." Daisy stood up and cradled her arm, crying out in pain.

Victorija came running out into the clearing with blood around her mouth. "What happened?"

"I'll tell you what happened—I fell off that bloody horse because you went and left without me," Daisy said.

"I left you on Angel, perfectly safe. How did you manage to fall?"

"I tried to get down," Daisy said while rubbing her shoulder.

"So it wasn't Angel—it was your own clumsiness," Victorija said.

Daisy stomped right up to Victorija. "I was scared, okay?"

Victorija laughed. "You who handed herself in to a group of vampires who want your blood are afraid of a horse?"

"I did that to help you. The least you could do is not abandon me," Daisy shouted.

"Help me? Are you insane? You better be a bit more grateful to me. I turned my back on my clan because of you—I mean, because of my vow to Angele. I do not need any help from you. Oh, and I sped off so I could feed on animals and make sure I didn't rip your throat out."

"You want to kill me now?" Daisy asked.

Victorija gripped her hair in frustration and turned back to Daisy angrily. "Do you have any concept of how hard this is for me?"

Daisy stayed quiet.

"When I look at you, it's like dying of thirst, and you're the only drop of water in the desert. I've never been good at being in control. I see something, I take it. Humans were there to satisfy me, and fate has given me a blood bond with you."

The ache and need in Victorija was so strong. She closed her eyes and heard Angele say, *Don't hurt her, Torija—she'll bring an end to your torture.* Victorija gasped. "My blood bond is the one person on earth who I can't have."

Daisy looked at her with sympathy in her eyes. How could anyone look at the monster with sympathy?

Victorija supposed she deserved this, after all the bad things she had done since Angele left her. It was her fate to go slowly mad and die of starvation. The animal blood wasn't helping a great deal, so she headed over to her horse and took some of Anka's potion. She'd need to ration it.

Just as she was putting the drink container away, she heard the thrashing of bushes and voices. Drasas and her new alliance with Anka were in pursuit. Anka wanted her power, and Victorija wasn't going to give that up until this blood bond was broken and Daisy was safe. By then she would have done her duty to Angele and could face whatever was ahead of her.

"We have to go—we're being chased by my vampires." Victorija started taking the bags off the horse.

"What are you doing? How are we going to get away without the horse?" Daisy asked.

Victorija stroked the horse's nose. "This is where we say goodbye to Angel. This is about you now, keeping you safe."

"Why?" Daisy asked.

"Because that's what Angele wanted." Victorija stroked the horse one last time and said, "Be free, Angel."

The horse neighed and ran off.

"I can't walk or run as fast as you can."

Victorija threw the bags over one shoulder, and Daisy squealed as she was thrown onto the other shoulder, and Victorija ran.

CHAPTER ELEVEN

After landing in Paris, Byron suggested they split up. Alexis wasn't happy about letting Byron go anywhere herself, so Bhal left alone to ask around.

Byron and Alexis thought they would start off at an old French haunt of theirs, the club La Nuit.

A taxi dropped them off around the corner from the club. La Nuit was not as old as The Sanctuary in London and catered to the slightly more shady element of the paranormal world. But it was still an old club, and one that held special significance for Alexis.

"Are you sure you're okay with this, Duca?"

La Nuit was the first bar that Alexis went to after Victorija turned her. One of the camp followers saw the symptoms Alexis was dealing with on the battlefields and brought her here.

"I've been here since, Principe."

"But this is different. We are looking for the woman that brought you here, that changed your life."

"Honestly, it's okay. Life is different now. I'm happy," Alexis said.

Byron smiled. "And I couldn't be happier. Come on."

La Nuit looked like nothing more than a barber's out front, a good way to disguise what was really there. At this time of night, there weren't many in the barbers' chairs. Paranormals came here for grooming as well as the club, and to make sure no humans got in, the shop was by appointment only.

Alexis got the door and held it open for Byron. When they both went in, a woman behind the desk said in French, "Do you have an appointment?"

Byron answered her in perfect French. "Yes, Byron Debrek and Alexis, Duca of the Debrek clan."

The woman's eyes went wide, and the barber cutting hair stopped and looked silently at them. They clearly weren't expecting this tonight.

"Oh, of course, Principe. Enjoy your evening."

She put a security code into the door, and it slid open. Byron entered with Alexis and took a staircase to another door that opened as they approached. The sound of the music hit them first. La Nuit was about cocktails, chatting, and cabaret. The room was big and had a lot of round tables and a stage at the other end of the room. It had the feel of a 1920s club, which Byron enjoyed.

Most of the patrons turned around as they made their way to a table. There was a lot of nudging and whispering going, which was a bit pointless since they were vampires with excellent hearing.

They picked a table by the side of the stage, and a waiter came over for a drinks order. "Whisky, Alexis?"

Alexis nodded.

"Two Wulver malt whiskies, please, with ice."

"Of course."

Byron scanned the crowd. "I wonder if Casimir is still here?"

"Of course I am," a voice said behind her. A man who looked like he was straight out of the 1920s was at their side.

"Casimir?" Byron said. Casimir was tall, thin, and dressed in a dinner suit and a bow tie, with a red flower in his lapel. He was the manager of the club and a fellow vampire. Byron stood and offered her hand. "It's so nice to see you. Sit down."

"Alexis." Casimir shook her hand and sat. "How long has it been? Thirty years?"

"Really, that long?" Byron was surprised.

The drinks arrived, and Casimir said, "Would you get me a vodka martini, Andre?"

"Of course, Casimir."

His eyes undressed the young man as he walked away. "Angelic, isn't he? I'm training him."

Alexis piped up. "Well, he won't be angelic for long."

All three laughed, and when Casimir got his drink, the conversation turned more serious.

"I can guess why you are here, Byron."

"Why?" Byron asked.

"Young people, like Andre there, are getting forcibly turned, all over Paris. There's a sudden influx of werewolves, witches—you name it, they are here, and going to the Dred castle."

Byron took a sip of her whisky, and it burned her throat pleasantly. "I am interested in that, but first of all, we're here looking for a young woman, Daisy MacDougall. We believe the Dreds might have her."

"I'm not familiar with that name, but if she is human, I'm sure she will be in the pile of bodies they are collecting up there."

Byron shot Alexis a worried look. "I know the Dreds were always known for their disregard of human life, but has it gotten worse?"

Casimir stirred his drink with the cherry on the cocktail stick. "Much worse. Andre woke under a pile of bodies, hungry for blood and terrified. He won't even talk about what happened inside the castle. I've taken him under my wing."

"Just like you did for me," Alexis said.

"And you turned out all right." Casimir smiled.

"What about Victorija? She usually comes in here, does she not?"

"She hasn't been in for a long time. Strange, that. No one's even seen her around town. I don't know what's going on with her. Drasas seems to be running the clan now."

"Have you heard the name *Anka* before?"

Casimir suddenly looked like he'd seen a ghost. "Is she involved in this?"

"We believe she is working with the Dreds, yes," Alexis said.

He gulped and stood up quickly. "Well, it was so nice to see you again. I better get back to the bar. Goodbye."

Once he was gone, Byron and Alexis looked at each other.

"He's terrified," Alexis said.

Byron replied, "Anka. She's at the heart of everything. We need to keep looking."

Daisy didn't know if she liked being on the horse or over Victorija's shoulder the best. No, she did. "Let me down, Vamp," she shouted.

And actually this time, Victorija listened. She dropped her to her feet and threw the bags on the stone ground.

"What are you playing at?" Daisy said.

They had arrived in an alley at the side of a shop.

Victorija placed her palms against the wall and gasped for air. "Will you just be quiet."

"Be quiet? No one tells me to be quiet, especially not some vamp."

Victorija groaned. "You know, I've never tried to do a selfless act and save someone before, but I'd imagined they'd be more grateful."

"My shoulder's killing me, and I've just had it bumped for the entire way."

Daisy was pulled from her indignation by Victorija crouching down and vomiting. Daisy hurried over and placed a hand on her back. Victorija flinched. It struck Daisy then that it had been centuries since Victorija had been touched by a caring hand.

Victorija heaved again and brought up a mouthful of blood.

"What's happening?"

"The animal blood, my body is rejecting it. Using my powers is weakening me. Can you go to the bag and bring me one of the blood pouches?"

Daisy hurried to open the bag and found about ten blood pouches, bottles of the potion she'd seen her drinking, and some bottled water. She grabbed the blood and a water and headed back over to Victorija.

Victorija's eyes were ruby red as she quickly sank her teeth into the bag.

"Why were you drinking the animal blood if you had these?"

"Because"—Victorija gasped—"I had to ration them. I doubt you would let me take someone off the street and drink them dry."

"You're dead right, but you can't go on like this." Daisy was going to have to let her feed on her, but she couldn't help but fear what might happen.

"I just need some rest, and we'll move on in the morning," Victorija said.

"Do you even have a plan to stop this blood bond?"

Victorija took the bottle of water and washed the blood from her face. "Yes, there's someone my father consulted. He lives not too far from here. I think he might be able to help. There's a nice hotel just down the street. A night's rest will help me."

"Where are we?"

"Gather the bag up and I'll show you," Victorija said.

Daisy picked up the bag and followed Victorija down the alleyway. She heard the sound of car horns and the chatter of lots of people. "We're in the city?"

They stepped out into the street, "Yes, welcome to the centre of Paris, and the first place I ever saw Angele."

"But you met her in a little village—her notebook showed me the day," Daisy said.

Victorija looked uncomfortable about someone knowing so much about young Torija. "That was a long time ago. The city has expanded since then. This street is the marketplace. You see the bakery, down at the end?"

Daisy nodded.

"I was standing there, and the market stall owner wasn't very friendly. I took off, and Angele caught up with me."

Daisy looked around. She could see it now. "I was standing here with Angle when she showed me that memory."

"I don't know why I made any impression on her. I was weak back then, not even a full born vampire, and a continual disappointment to my father."

"Well, you did, and even after all these years, your happiness still matters to her," Daisy said.

"I don't know what happiness feels like any more, just power. And this, our bond, is making me weak again. Just like I was before."

"Let's go and check into the hotel. Where is it?" Daisy asked.

"There."

Victorija pointed across the street to one of the fanciest hotels she'd seen. There was gold and lights everywhere, and a doorman in a top hat and white gloves.

"This is where you want to hide from a clan of vampires chasing us?"

"I've got to have some standards. I'm still Victorija Dred."

Victorija bowed in the most flamboyant of ways, and it made Daisy laugh. "Of course you are."

Yes, Victorija Dred was making her laugh. No, that wasn't quite true. Torija was making her laugh.

❖

Drasas paced up and down as she waited for Anka to come to the phone. She, Leo, and her vampires were in the forested area behind the Dred castle.

Leo stood a few paces away from her. "What will we do if we can't find her?"

"We will. There's a compound in the medicine bottles that Anka can track. As long as Victorija continues to drink it, Anka can point us in the right direction." She then put her fingers to her lips for quiet and spoke into the phone. "Yes, of course we'll find them. I promise."

When she ended the call, Drasas said, "They are at the one of hotels in Rue Parliet. Let's go."

❖

The bellboy led Daisy and Victorija to the hotel's premier suite. They had no money with them, but they couldn't have used credit cards anyway in case they were tracked. Luckily, the ability of compulsion meant money was often not needed. Victorija asked for a suite, the best in the house, and the night manager of the hotel did as she was told.

When the bellboy opened the door to their suite, Daisy gasped. It was the most luxurious room she'd ever seen. She walked in and saw a huge bed, a coffee table and a couch, and a few doors leading off the main room.

When the bellboy put the bags down, he asked, "Is there anything else I can do for you?"

Daisy knew he was waiting for a tip, and they didn't have cash.

"Torija? Tip?"

"Oh, that." Victorija pulled him towards her and using compulsion said, "My tip is that I didn't rip your throat out, boy."

"You can't say that," Daisy said in rebuke.

Victorija rolled her eyes. "We gave you a tip, not big, not small, but just enough to make you smile."

On cue, the boy smiled and thanked them both.

When he left, Victorija said, "That made me feel sicker than I am."

Daisy said, "You know, I think that compulsion thing is maybe worse than a vampire's bite."

Victorija cradled her stomach and sat down on the bed. "It's a useful gift. If you weren't here, I'd have just killed him."

"No, you wouldn't," Daisy said confidently.

"Have the Debreks not told you about me?"

Daisy brought her over a bottle of water. "That was before."

"Before what?"

"Before Lucia unlocked your memories, and you remembered you had a heart."

Victorija brushed away the bottle and walked carefully over to the complimentary drinks cabinet and poured out a large glass of whisky. "Don't be so disgusting, cherie."

"Should you be drinking?" Daisy asked.

"Probably not, because you're looking more like dinner every time I take a sip."

Daisy walked into the bathroom and saw a gorgeous shower and large bath. "It won't work, you know, Torija."

Victorija came to the bathroom and leaned in the doorway. "Don't call me that."

Daisy ignored her and took one of the complimentary dressing gowns from the packaging.

"What won't work?" Victorija asked.

"Trying to goad me into thinking that you're evil."

"I am. I'm a monster," Victorija said.

Daisy sighed and walked up to Victorija. She put her hand on her chest and pushed. "Well, I'm a monster hunter, and I've caught you. So get out, so I can have a shower."

Victorija was taken aback, not for the first time, by Daisy. She allowed herself to be pushed out the doorway and had the door shut in her face. Victorija heard the shower turn on and felt her body come alive with hunger, for Daisy's life-giving blood, obviously, but more than that—sexual hunger.

It was something that had been lost to her until Daisy came into her life. Victorija's mind was mentally picturing the scene behind the door, Daisy undressing and slipping under the warm water.

She placed her forehead against the door and felt her mouth water. She was sure her eyes would be glowing red. But instead of easily pushing the door open, she forced herself back to the bed.

How Daisy had the confidence to lower her guard and have a shower, Victorija did not know. Being denied what she wanted by someone who had no physical power over her was intoxicating.

Daisy had a power greater than any weapon, any superpower, and it made every cell and nerve in her body thrum with excitement. Then she heard singing coming from the bathroom, a beautiful voice to match a beautiful woman.

"Will this torture ever end?"

Victorija knew it would, one way or another. Either way unhappily. She put her drink down and lay back on the bed. The pains in her stomach grew worse, and she rocked, clutching her head tightly.

"Don't fall asleep, don't fall asleep."

Daisy finished drying her hair with the towel and walked out of the bathroom. She threw the towel down when she saw Victorija asleep but pushed up against the headboard, terrified of whatever she was seeing in her dreams.

"No, no. I don't, I won't—I can't. No, don't scream!" Victorija covered her ears with her hands and screamed and thrashed. "The rain, stop the rain!"

Daisy had to wake her. She shook her, trying to wake her gently. Before Daisy knew it, she was on her back, with Victorija holding her down by the wrists. Her eyes were red and her teeth sharp and scary.

Daisy's heart was pounding, and her bite mark was throbbing, but she could only follow her instincts. "Torija, don't hurt me. I know you won't. Torija, listen to me."

Victorija blinked once, twice, and then the fierce red in her eyes was replaced by clear but tortured eyes. "I can't face them, I can't."

Daisy got the biggest surprise when tears filled Victorija's eyes, and she collapsed onto her shoulder and wept. Daisy was frozen. This was not what she expected, but clearly the walls around Victorija's emotions were coming tumbling down, just as Lucia thought.

Taking a chance, she wrapped her arms around Victorija and just held her tightly. It was probably the first time someone had hugged her in decades, if not centuries. Daisy knew she was taking a huge risk, cuddling one the most vicious vampires close to her neck, but she had to trust that this tormented soul was ready to receive help.

They lay like that for a good ten or fifteen minutes before Victorija rolled to the side, groaning in pain.

"What do you need, tell me?"

"Blood, one of the blood packs, and Anka's potion."

Daisy hurried over to the bag Victorija had packed and fell to her knees. Victorija's bite was calling on her to provide the blood Victorija clearly needed. She took some big breaths and pushed back to her feet. When she turned and saw how much pain Victorija was in, she said, "I can't do this." She kneeled at the side of the bed and said softly, "Torija, Torija?"

Victorija didn't even protest the name this time. She lifted her head, and this time her eyes were red from the tears she had shed. Daisy brushed the messy dark blond hair from her eyes.

"Torija, I want you to feed on me. This can't go on."

"No," Victorija spluttered. "I don't trust myself. If I get one taste, or slightly better, I might harm you, and I'll have broken the only vow I've ever wanted to keep. Give me the blood bag."

Daisy handed it over, and Victorija drank from it, but only managed half.

"Now the potion."

"What is this stuff?" Daisy asked.

"Something Anka made for me. It makes the symptoms more bearable."

"Is there anything else I can get you?" Daisy glanced down at Victorija's arm and saw the green in her veins was now halfway up her forearm. "What is *that*?"

Victorija flexed her arm. "I don't know. It just started to appear. I assumed it was a symptom of the blood sickness, but I don't remember my father having this."

"It's spreading, isn't it."

"Yes, but let's not dwell on that. Come and talk to me, tell me about your life, about Monster Hunters, about what ordinary life is like."

"If you like." Daisy got up and went back to her position on the bed. Victorija turned around and faced her. "You should take my blood, Torija. You're no good to me so ill that we can't travel."

Victorija reached out with a finger and pulled Daisy's necklace from between her breasts. Daisy's nipples hardened at Victorija's touch. This was a great time for her body to be turned on.

"There are some things that might be worse even than death,

Daisy MacDougall. Without this necklace, I could use compulsion on you, and make you my portable lunch box for the rest of time. Until you can take that off with confidence, then no, you can't trust me. I will either kill you or destroy you. So please, tell me about your life and Monster Hunters."

There was a sad truth in that. She wasn't ready to take off this necklace. It was her one protection. "How do you know about Monster Hunters?"

"When I was trying to figure out who you were and why you were my blood bond, I did some research, and I saw a video of you in some haunted house, but first, tell me about you and working for Amelia Debrek."

"I worked with her at her uncle Jaunty's tailoring shop. I was her apprentice, and we became good friends. We all became good friends— Sera, Katie—"

"I'd heard the noble Alexis had turned her girlfriend and gotten married."

"It was by consent—Well, it was complicated, but anyway, they are happy," Daisy said.

Victorija gave a hollow laugh. "I turned Alexis, you know."

"I know. Katie told me. She's always been angry because of that."

"I made a lot of people angry. I found her on a battlefield, dying of her wounds. I thought nothing of it. I thought someone would rather live as a vampire than die, but I'm not so sure of that any more."

"When I came in from the bathroom, you were struggling with something in your sleep. What was it?"

Victorija pinched the bridge of her nose and then rubbed her eyes. "Every time I fall asleep, all the souls that I have killed or had killed by my orders circle me, getting closer and closer. They tell me to face them. I can't. I recognize some, not all. I don't even remember their faces. And the rain, there's always the sound of rain, and it feels like despair. I can't face them because facing them terrifies me. My father was right."

"Right about what?"

"I'm so weak without the vampire in me. Torija was weak, and he made me become the vampire Victorija, so that I would be strong. But now I'm going back to that—weakness, crying on your shoulder. It's pathetic."

"Can you not even see it?" Daisy said. "Your dad was a complete idiot. You were strong, loving one of your family's sworn enemies, and now you're even stronger."

"How could I be?"

"Look how hard you're fighting not to take my blood. Every single cell in your body is telling you to drink from me and make yourself feel better, but you aren't. You're fighting yourself to keep a promise to someone you lost so long ago. That is strength."

Victorija didn't reply and kept silent for a minute or so. Then she changed the subject completely and said, "Tell me about your Monster people then."

"I think I can do better than that. I can show you."

"But we don't have any phones or computers."

Daisy grabbed the remote beside the bed and switched the TV on. "I'm sure this hotel has TVs smart enough to have YouTube." With Victorija's help at reading the French onscreen, she opened her YouTube channel.

Victorija sat up against the headboard and said, "You have a whole channel?"

"Yeah, this is my team." Daisy started playing the welcome video. "That's all the monster hunters, Skye, Pierce, and Zane. We met at art college. Great friends—well, Zane is a bit intense and annoying, but anyway…"

"What is he intense about?" Victorija asked.

"He thinks he's in love with me and gets a bit touchy-feely."

"You think he would enjoy getting touchy-feely, as you put it, with me?" Victorija said that with anger in her voice.

Daisy laughed. "No, I don't think so. Anyway, let me show you some videos. It'll take your mind off things. Oh, this is a good one. This guy said he was a necromancer. You see, I've always had this thing, my friends call it my spidey sense, but when I touch a paranormal, I get this buzz, this warmth that goes all over my body. You remember when I first met you at the tailor's? You were taking Amelia out to dinner."

"How could I forget—you were extremely rude," Victorija said.

"I took your hand and could tell you were a paranormal. I hadn't spoken to Amelia about this gift that I had, I didn't think she'd believe me anyway, but I knew."

"There must have been lots of people you found out weren't…one of us," Victorija said.

"Let me show you." Daisy pressed play and her interview started.

Victorija clutched her stomach and shifted uncomfortably. "I know him—well, I know of him. An untrustworthy man who would sell his soul to the devil, if he had one, but who am I to judge?"

"He was a bit scary, to be honest."

"Why did you, *do* you, do this? I mean, you went to art college, you do men's and women's tailoring—monster hunting doesn't seem to sit naturally with that."

"Well, it's just something I've been passionate about since I was young. I've always believed in this paranormal world. I was drawn to it."

"I suppose being a Brassard, monster hunting is in your DNA."

"You'd think, but I didn't know the Brassard family history until just a few weeks ago. When my mum and dad were killed, my granny decided to stop the family cycle of vampire hunting. To protect me."

Victorija looked at her sincerely and put her hand on her heart. "I swear to you, it was not me or my vampires. I always kept my vow to Angele and made it clear to my vampires that the Brassard line was not to be touched."

"I believe you. My granny said the same, that for some reason in all the family clashes with vampires, the Dreds never bothered us," Daisy said.

"All the time my father was Principe, I made certain all of his foot soldiers knew that. My father was concentrated on other matters, and he never seemed to notice."

Daisy twirled the chain of her necklace around. "What was Angele really like? Was she anything like me?"

"No, not really. She had this pure innocence that just shone from her. You're stubborn, annoying, quite different."

Daisy looked back to the screen. "Oh well. We all can't be perfect like Angele, I suppose."

That was strange. Daisy sounded annoyed at that comment.

CHAPTER TWELVE

Victorija didn't want to sleep. Sleep was painful, and she would never be brave enough to face those souls she had hurt. Daisy had been asleep for about an hour, and Victorija continued to watch video after video on Daisy's YouTube channel. Daisy was brave, if not a bit foolish, seeking to meet vampires and witches, to stay overnight in haunted locations. But she admired her courage.

Daisy turned in her sleep and cuddled up close to Victorija, under her arm. Victorija froze. What should she do? Wake her?

It got even worse when Daisy shifted and placed her arm around Victorija's waist and her head snuggled under her arm. Victorija had no idea how to react. She simply gazed at her, trying to think straight.

The subject of her pain, her discomfort, her torment, was lying in her arms, and yet she hadn't feasted on her blood. It was unthinkable. Victorija could imagine what her father Gilbert would say, that this was a sign of her weakness. But not her mother. Before Gilbert had her confined to the dungeon, she used to have nice times with her mother, Ashkar. She taught Victorija to appreciate beauty, in music, in painting, and in poetry. She would have seen the beauty in Daisy. Victorija stroked Daisy's hair, loving the soft feel of it. Then her fingers wandered down Daisy's cheek and jaw.

Earlier Daisy had taken it as a slight that she was nothing like Angele, but it truly wasn't, and she should have said so. Angele had been sweet, innocent, like a balm to her tortured teenage soul, but Daisy was stubborn, obstinate, brave. She challenged Victorija, shook her already weakening belief in herself. Maybe Angele was right—maybe she had been Victorija's beginning and Daisy was her end, whichever way that end would come.

One thing Victorija knew was that it wouldn't end happily for them both. She had lost the Dred clan without a fight. She had chosen to save Daisy over her long lust for power and control over the Dred clan. There was no going back from that. Her vampires would never accept her, and now that Victorija had come this far, she didn't think she even wanted to go back.

Victorija stroked her finger across Daisy's plump and juicy lip. In her mind's eye she saw Daisy's bright red blood flowing out of her lip, while she kissed and sucked in equal measure.

Stop it. She had to stop thinking. If only she could just sleep and take a break from the aching hunger, but sleep only brought the dead's anguished screams, their demand that she face them, look them in the eye, and the incessant, dreary rain.

Could she hide forever from them? One thing she was certain of—without Daisy's blood, her mind was going to sink into madness if she didn't break this bond. She rested her head back against the wall and closed her eyes. She was tired and weary, and every time her brain threatened to fall into sleep, she heard the distant roll of thunder and the pitter-patter of miserable rain. She opened her eyes quickly each time, but eventually as she closed her eyes, she pictured sucking and kissing Daisy's blood-rich lips. That didn't make her sleepy. It made her body come alive.

Her body ached to touch Daisy and have Daisy touch her, which wasn't the usual way sex went for her. It was quick and hot, and everything was about taking and giving exactly what she wanted, power and control. Not with Daisy.

She was so hungry for Daisy's blood and her body. Victorija's stomach ached, as well as her sex. Then a little voice said in the back of her head, *She said you should take her blood earlier, so it would be okay to do it.* She technically wouldn't be breaking her vow to Angele, would she?

Victorija's eyes opened, and her fangs erupted. *She said I should drink from her. Go on, go on, just once to rebuild your strength.*

She started to lower her head towards Daisy's lips. Just as she was about to lose control, Victorija heard the rumble of the elevator, and the sound of her Duca's voice. They'd found them.

"Daisy, wake up."

Victorija speedily grabbed the bag and was back to the side of the bed before Daisy had even sat up.

"What's the panic?"

"We have to go, now."

"Why?" Daisy asked, still trying to come around from sleep.

"Drasas and my vampires are coming up in the lift. Let's move." Victorija pulled Daisy off the bed.

"You can hear that?"

"Of course I can. I'm a born vampire, cherie. Now, *move*."

"How do we get past them?"

Victorija sped over to the window and opened it.

"I can't jump from here," Daisy said in panic.

Victorija secured the bag over her shoulders. "No, but I can." She moved quickly to lift Daisy up in her arms.

"What are you doing?"

"Saving your life, as I seem to have to do." Victorija jumped out of the eighth-floor window and landed gracefully on her feet.

"Jesus, Torija. Don't do that without warning."

"Thank you for saving my life, Torija," Victorija snarked. It dawned on her that she had referred to herself as *Torija*. But being Torija scared her. It had been the worst time of her long life. "I'm giving you warning now, Daisy—you're going to be staying in my arms, so we can escape quickly."

Alexis left the second bar and sped around the corner to the waiting car. Bhal was behind the wheel after meeting them with backup. She got in the car and said, "Drasas and her people have been in and out of a few pubs and clubs, asking if they've seen Victorija, and nobody has."

Byron sighed. "We have no leads. Where do we go from here?"

Bhal turned around in the driver's seat and said, "Byron, you brought the telephone that Daisy left in her room?"

Byron patted her jacket. "Yes, but what good will that do?"

"What we need is a bloodhound to track her scent. What about Brogan?"

Alexis and Byron looked at each other. She remembered the

last time Brogan and Byron spoke, and it wasn't the most pleasant of conversations.

"Brogan Filtiaran?"

Brogan was a werewolf for hire, a mix of a private investigator and mercenary. Originally hailing from the Irish Filtiaran pack, she'd left pack life a long time ago and become a lone wolf in the truest sense.

At one time Brogan and Byron had been friends but certainly not when they parted company. Alexis knew this wouldn't be comfortable for Byron, but in the end she would do the right thing. Byron always put others first.

"It's our only option, I suppose," Byron said. "Do you think she's still living at her studio?"

"I think she will be," Bhal said. "It was the perfect setup for her."

"Alexis?" Byron asked.

"I think it's our only option at the moment, Principe."

"Take us there then, Bhal."

Brogan Filtiaran was going to get a big surprise when they three arrived at her door, Alexis thought as the car pulled off.

Daisy was feeling sick at the blur of the passing landscape as Victorija went at breakneck speed. Luckily, they came to a stop at last, and Victorija fell to her knees after putting Daisy down gently.

Daisy cupped Victorija's face. Blood was seeping from her mouth. "Are you okay? Talk to me."

"Blood…rejecting. Pass me the potion out of my bag."

Daisy pulled out the bottle, and Victorija said, "I don't know how they keep finding us."

They had stopped for a rest twice, and twice Drasas came running on their tail. Daisy looked at the remaining bottles of potion, picked one up, and on a hunch, closed her eyes and concentrated on the feel of the bottle. She filtered out Victorija's cries for the drink and tried to calm her breathing and centre herself.

Then she felt it. The vibration from her spidey sense. It was the potion—Daisy was certain of it. She took out the remaining bottles and stuffed them in a bin.

"What are you doing?" Victorija shouted through her discomfort. Daisy hurried back to Victorija. "It was the potion. I could feel a vibration from the bottle. That only comes as a warning. Anka is connected to you by that potion—that's why we can't lose Drasas and her vampires. Please trust me, Torija?"

Victorija looked in her eyes and nodded. "Let's get out of here."

"Where can we go?"

Victorija staggered to her feet. Daisy steadied her till she got her balance. "I have a house not too far from here."

Daisy held out her hand. "Then let's go, the old-fashioned way. On our own two feet, because you need a rest from fast vampy travel."

Victorija stared at her hand as if she was thinking hard about it, then grasped Daisy's hand tightly. "Let's go. This way," Victorija said. Victorija took them to an old-looking apartment building.

"This is where Angele lived?" Daisy said as she helped Victorija to the door.

"Yes, it's the oldest building in Paris. When it came up for sale, I snapped it up and had a witch place a protective spell around it. It should help protect us." Victorija led them into the building and up to the second-floor apartment. The whole building had an eerie silence, like a place frozen in time.

They arrived at the front door and Daisy said, "How are we going to get in? You don't have the keys with you, I take it?"

Victorija held her stomach and gasped, "Don't need one. The door will open for me and only me. It's part of the protection spell." Victorija grasped the handle, and with a click it was open. "Follow me."

Daisy walked in and shut the door behind her. She heard the same click, and just out of curiosity tried the door handle again, but it was locked. They were safe, for a time at least.

She followed on behind Victorija. Each room they passed along the corridor had furniture covered in white dustsheets. It had been a long time since anyone had lived in here. She watched as Victorija slowed and lingered beside one door, before moving on.

"There's a guest bedroom at the end we can stay in."

Daisy guessed that might have been Angele's room, and Victorija clearly didn't want them staying there. Too many sad memories.

Victorija let out a groan of pain and braced herself against the wall. Daisy hurried to her. "Here, lean on me." She helped Victorija along to the bedroom and opened the door. All the furniture had white sheets over it, like in every other room.

"Set me on the bed."

"Please," Daisy chastised her.

"I'm falling apart, cherie. I think I can skip getting the niceties right."

Daisy helped her over to the bed, and she slumped onto it.

"How long have you had this place?" Daisy asked.

"A few hundred years, give or take a decade."

"And Drasas doesn't know about it?" Daisy asked.

"No, I kept everything about Angele a secret. She would have thought it a weakness."

"Good. Lie back and get comfortable."

"Blood sickness is not conducive to comfort," Victorija said.

"We'll make you more comfortable. I'll get you some water." Daisy took a moment and opened herself up to the spirit of the house. She could feel the history here, the connection to her ancestors. She shivered and felt the hairs stand up on her body. This was where she was meant to be, and who she was meant to be with.

A long groan brought her attention back to the present. "I need the potion."

Daisy hurried back to the bed and sat cross-legged on the bed beside Victorija. "You can't have that any more. We dumped it, remember? It'll bring Drasas and Anka right to our door."

Victorija nodded and took a sip of water from Daisy's bottle. "I need to go cold turkey."

"You are so strong, Torija," Daisy said.

Victorija laughed, but then it turned into a racking cough. "See what happens when you make me laugh? If I was strong, I wouldn't be—we wouldn't be—in this situation." Victorija was surprised when she felt Daisy's fingers stroke through her hair. She loved the feel of it. She covered Daisy's hand and held it to her face. "Nobody's touched me like this for so long. With kindness."

Daisy slipped down the bed until she could hold Victorija. "Torija, you've done so much bad in the world, but you can do much better. Just connect to Torija inside you."

Victorija said nothing. Was it possible to be that person who Angele had loved again?

"Tell me about this person we're going to see. Are they far from here?"

"Not too far. He's called the Reaper."

"As in the Grim Reaper?" Daisy said with surprise.

"In a way. Reapers help souls stuck here on earth, both good and evil, move on to the other side and don't interfere with the living world."

"I hadn't heard of Reapers in that way. How can a Reaper help us?"

"They have a knowledge that spans time and powers that are shrouded in mystery. Gilbert went to him, after he killed my mother. He lasted a lot longer than he should have, despite the blood sickness. Maybe the Reaper knows something that can break the blood bond."

"Maybe he can tell you about this, too?" Daisy stroked her fingers along the green veins in Victorija's arm, which now reached to her elbow.

Victorija felt a stabbing pain in her stomach, worse than ever. How was she going to make it past even one more day and keep Daisy safe? She heard Daisy moan. Her yearning for blood was hurting Daisy, too.

"I want you to drink from me, Torija," Daisy said.

"No," Victorija shouted in frustration. "Stop asking me to do that. It's suicide."

"Torija, look at me."

Victorija looked up and saw Daisy, who was dangling her necklace in her hand. She had made herself completely vulnerable.

Victorija jumped away in anger and fear. "Put that back on."

"No. You said I had to feel comfortable and trust you before you would feed, and that meant taking this off."

Daisy tried not to show the trepidation she was feeling inside. This was a calculated risk. It would either bring the real Torija out even more, or Victorija would take control, kill her, or use her for blood for the rest of her life.

Every part of Daisy was urging her to take this chance. She could save Victorija's soul. Daisy walked forward slowly, holding the necklace away from her. "I believe in you, Torija. Taking this off puts me in your hands."

Victorija pushed herself right up against the wall. "Don't, I can't be that person you want. I can't be Torija."

"You can be that and so much more. Your father isn't here any more. You don't need to prove yourself—you can embrace Torija." Daisy could feel the power of Victorija's hunger. This was either the best thing she'd ever done, or the stupidest.

"Why do you believe in me? I'm a monster." Victorija snarled.

Daisy stepped closer and closer, her heart hammering in her chest. "Because Angele and Lucia did, and because monsters aren't born, they're made. If you had been brought up in the Debrek clan, you would have been a different vampire." Daisy was inches from one of the most feared vampires in the world, but no matter the cost, this was what she was meant to do. She dropped the necklace on the floor and held out her arm. "I am a Brassard, and I consent to you drinking my blood, without any coercion."

Tears were watering Victorija's eyes. "I wish I had your faith in me. I don't."

Daisy raised her wrist up to Victorija's mouth. "I know you want to be Torija again. Look in my eyes as you feed, and choose Torija, choose me." Daisy could see the tension on Victorija's face, the war going on inside her head. "I consent."

Victorija took Daisy's wrist in her hands and inhaled her scent. Daisy's body reacted to even that little bit of stimulation.

"Keep looking at me," Daisy said.

Victorija's eyes were blood red, and Daisy's body was held tight, waiting on her touch. It happened quickly. Victorija bit down on Daisy's wrist, and she gasped. Daisy didn't anticipate feeling as much as she did. Her whole body was yearning for Victorija. She wanted Victorija, needed her.

They kept their eyes locked. Daisy's breathing was building, and some moans were escaping. It almost felt like her body was building towards an orgasm. She could see colour returning to Victorija's skin. She was standing straighter and gaining strength.

But would she stop, that was the question. Was she Victorija, or was she Torija?

The answer came when she pulled her teeth from Daisy's wrist. "Thank you. I want to be Torija."

Daisy gasped when Torija licked the wound on her wrist, and it started to heal, just like Amelia's wounds did when she became Byron's blood bond. She smiled. "I knew you were in there."

"Just put your necklace on, in case Drasas finds us."

Daisy put it back on, her heart still hammering in her chest. To Victorija's surprise, Daisy led her back to the bed. They lay down, and Daisy opened her arms. "Come here."

"Why?"

"Because I want to hold you in my arms and let you sleep."

Victorija was scared, scared of having this kind of intimacy, and she didn't want to face the horrors that awaited her in sleep. "I can't. I told you, the spirits are in my sleep," Victorija said.

"But you've fed on me now. Those dreams would just have been the confusion of blood sickness."

"It takes more than one feed to get me back to full health."

Daisy patted the bed. "Just come here, Vamp."

Victorija sighed and climbed onto the bed, and Daisy pulled her into her arms. She held herself rigid, and Daisy said, "Relax, will you? It's just me. Your little old blood bond."

Victorija sighed and let go slightly, "You do realize I'm a top. I'm not used to being held in a young woman's arms."

"Oh, shut up and cuddle."

Victorija couldn't believe she was doing this, but then, who would have thought she would have turned her back on her clan for a human.

She snuggled her head into Daisy's soft breast and had the urge to cup the other breast, too. Then she felt Daisy's fingers run through her hair, slowly and soothingly. She couldn't help but completely relax and felt her body drifting off to sleep.

CHAPTER THIRTEEN

Drasas felt uneasy as she was driven back to the Dred castle. She and her vampires had no idea where Victorija and Daisy were. They found the bottles of potion disposed of in a bin. Without that tracker, Drasas was at a loss. Anka had ordered her to get the information one way or another, but no one had seen them.

The car came to stop, and Leo opened the door. When she stepped out, she saw her normal guards were not in position at the front door. These were weres—she could smell it. She looked at Leo, and he was equally surprised and worried.

"They say the werewolves in her group are from some Eastern European wolfpacks that joined her," Leo said.

Drasas felt the uneasiness turn to fear. Was she losing control?

The weres stared at her as she and Leo passed through the door. Drasas walked past some of her clan, who were looking equally worried. She arrived at the double doors that led to the throne room, and again there were werewolves guarding the door. One of them looked her up and down and opened the door for them, making Drasas feel like a visitor in her clan castle.

The first thing she noticed when walking into the throne room was Anka sitting on the Principe's throne on the dais, with Asha beside her. Arced around the steps were Anka's guard. Most of the Dred vampires were over to one side of the room, but Anka's witches and other paranormals were front and centre.

This was meant to be a partnership, she was supposed to be Anka's right hand, but it looked like *Asha* was that person. She had lost control. It was a bloodless takeover. But Anka had promised her power beyond her dreams, so losing part of her control of the Dred clan was worth the trade-off, wasn't it?

Asha whispered in Anka's ear, and Anka laughed. Anka's laugh was like honey and brought a tingling feeling all over Drasas's body. She would give anything to be near Anka and would do whatever it took to stay in her magnificent presence.

But the laughter turned to annoyance when Anka's gaze fell on Drasas. "I don't see either Victorija or Daisy MacDougall, Drasas."

Out of the corner of her eye, Drasas saw Leo slink back behind her a few paces, leaving her to face Anka's wrath alone.

"We couldn't find them after Victorija stopped taking your potion."

Anka's countenance clouded with anger. "Are you trying to shift blame for your incompetence, Drasas?"

"No, of course not, Madam Anka. But they have been so elusive. No one has seen them, not even a glimpse. It's as if Victorija has disappeared."

"I need Daisy MacDougall brought to me—she cannot be allowed to survive. Victorija has either succumbed to madness or fed from Daisy."

"Maybe she's killed Daisy MacDougall?" Drasas suggested.

"No, she is alive. I can feel it. You will find her, Drasas."

"What about Victorija?"

"Luckily I'm not reliant on you." Anka stroked the side of Asha's hip, and Asha looked at her with triumph in his eyes. A jealous surge of anger flushed through Drasas's body.

"I need a healthy born vampire, but if I can't, then I have a plan B in action. Find them, Drasas, or Asha will take the power you were offered. Don't disappoint me."

"I won't, I promise, Madam."

Drasas turned and strode off as confidently as she could. There was no way she was ever going to let that lickspittle Asha steal the power promised to her.

"Leo, let's go."

Byron got out of the car and looked up at the former industrial building. This whole area of the town was once the garment district, but most of the buildings were empty now. She looked at Alexis and said, "She might not even let me in, Duca."

"Give her a chance, Principe."

Byron nodded and together with Bhal they walked up to the buzzer. She pressed the one for the top loft apartment.

"Hello?" A broad Irish accent came over the speaker.

Byron cleared her throat. "Brogan? It's Byron Debrek, and I wondered if I could have a word with you?"

Silence was the only thing that greeted her.

"I have Alexis and Bhaltair with me."

Again there was silence, but the door clicked open.

"Well, that wasn't very warm," Alexis said.

Bhal patted Byron's shoulder. "At least she's let you in. It's a first step."

Byron nodded and led them all through the door and into an old-fashioned caged lift. She pressed the button and the lift creaked as it ascended. Byron adjusted her tie and smoothed down her coat. The lift came to a stop and opened onto a big loft area.

"This place hasn't changed a bit," Bhal said.

Their footsteps echoed on the exposed floorboards as they walked into the centre of the room. All around the walls were paintings, and some canvases were up on easels, waiting to be finished.

Alexis, who had walked further into the room, said, "Come and see this one."

Byron and Bhal went over and saw a big bearded man with trees and leaves coming out of his face.

"Who is that?" Alexis asked.

"The Green Man," Bhal said, "or the Horned God. He's called both. He's a Celtic God who marries the May Queen. She forgives him his sins, and then the new season can come."

"Well-remembered, Bhal," a lilting voice said from the side.

Byron turned and saw Brogan with two paintbrushes that she was wiping on an old painting rag.

"Hello, Brogan."

Brogan Filtiaran was every inch the dominant werewolf. Tall, strong, with a mess of honey-blond hair, today she was dressed in baggy stonewashed jeans and a sleeveless white T-shirt. But although she was a Filtiaran, she wasn't part of the pack.

"Brogan, thank you for letting us in. I need your help to find a woman."

Brogan laughed, walked away from her painting, and put her brushes down. "Byron Debrek doesn't normally need help with finding women. Have you lost your touch?"

Ah, Brogan still held a grudge.

"Alexis? Bhal? Could you give us a moment?"

"Of course, Principe," Alexis said.

Alexis and Bhal walked off to look at Brogan's other pictures.

Byron said, "Brogan, we need to get past this. We were once good friends."

"Yeah, until you slept with my girlfriend."

Byron looked up at the ceiling in exasperation. "I didn't sleep—Well, technically I did, but I didn't know she was your girlfriend. She never told me, and she pursued me."

"After all these years, you still expect me to believe that?"

"Yes, I do," Byron said earnestly. "You've known me for a long time. You know I act with honour, especially to my friends."

"She was my *mate*," Brogan said.

"She wasn't your destined mate if she slept with someone else. She was supposed to be loyal to you. Think about it."

These were all the arguments she'd wanted to make after she'd discovered that Lucy was with Brogan, but Brogan had shut down, and just left the country.

"I wanted to spend the rest of my life with Lucy."

"You wouldn't with someone who would knowingly cheat on you. I swear to you on the blood of my family that I did not know about you two, and you know what the honour of my family blood means to me."

Brogan looked at Byron attentively. "I suppose that's true."

Byron moved closer and patted Brogan on the shoulder. "You know it is, deep down. We were always good friends."

Brogan must have spotted her wedding ring because she pointed to it. "That's not a wedding ring, is it?"

Byron smiled. "Yes, I'm blood bonded. My Principessa is…well, we thought a human, but turns out she's a witch. We had a human wedding, too."

Brogan held out her hand to invite Byron to shake, and Byron was only too happy to shake hands and make up with her former friend.

"I appreciate you giving me another chance, Brogan. So, what about you? Have you been back to your pack?"

Brogan crossed her arms. "No, I can't go back."

"Your brother was at my wedding."

"How is he?" Brogan asked.

"In good health, I think." Byron never asked why Brogan didn't ever go home. It had always been a taboo subject. She changed the subject when she realized emotions were still raw between Brogan and her family. "Are you still in the private eye business?"

"Yeah, PI, tracker, bodyguard—you name it, I do it. It gives me the means to live my life as a painter."

Byron looked around. "You have some beautiful works."

"Thank you. I have a gallery that sells them for me. They make me a good living."

Byron waved Bhal and Alexis back over. "Oh, Alexis got married and blood bonded, too."

"Alexis? You're married?"

Alexis had a big smile on her face. "Yes, to Katie. She's the Debrek housekeeper."

"Good for you. I'm pleased for you, and how are you doing, Bhal?"

"Grand, Brogan. It's nice to see you again." They shook hands, each grasping the other's arm in a warrior handshake.

"What do you need my skills for?"

"We're trying to track a woman, a friend of ours called Daisy. She's with Victorija Dred."

"She's in great danger, then," Brogan said firmly.

"It's slightly more complicated than that. She's blood bonded with Victorija," Byron said.

"Victorija Dred? You must be joking."

"I wish I was. Can you help us?" Byron asked.

"My wolf is yours."

Victorija looked out of the castle window. The rain was hammering down outside while she drank a perfect goblet of blood. She felt strong and full of energy. Victorija drained her cup, then turned around and went to her bathroom to brush up for dinner downstairs with her vampires.

She could still hear the rain loudly outside the bathroom window. Victorija ran the tap and scrubbed her face in the ice-cold water. She looked up at the mirror and jumped back in shock at what she saw.

Her face was replaced by her father's, Gilbert Dred. She blinked quickly, and he was gone. It was terrifying. His very image sent fear through her body, but to see his image reflected in her own was a nightmare.

Before she got a chance to think about it any more, she heard her bedroom door slam. Victorija sped out the door into the hall and briefly caught sight of the back of a man in a dark suit. She ran and ran as fast as a born vampire could run, but she never seemed to gain on him, and even though there were no windows, the sound of heavy rain followed her as she went.

The man led her down to the dungeon, and he disappeared behind the door. There were no guards on the door, and it dawned on her that the whole castle was eerily silent, apart from the raindrops.

Victorija zoomed in the door of the dungeon and saw the nightmarish scene she used to see as a child, her mother strapped to the chair, designed so her father could drain her blood. She crouched down and clutched her head in panic, as she used to do as a child.

"No, no, you're not a child any more."

She faced her fear and went to her mother's side. Her head was bowed, her neck limp like the rest of her body, and her brown hair cascaded in front of her face.

"Mother, Mother, it's me. You don't have to be afraid any more. He's gone."

Victorija lifted her mother's head, and she fell to her knees. It wasn't her mother in the chair. It was Daisy.

"Daisy, no, you're not meant to be here."

Daisy looked drugged and barely had any life left in her. "You said you wanted to be Torija. Why are you doing this?" Daisy coughed and spluttered.

"I do, I want to be her for you."

Victorija heard heavy footsteps behind her. She turned around and saw Gilbert, dressed head to toe in black.

He smiled cruelly. "You could never be Torija. You're a strong born vampire. You will always end up here. You are the same as me, child. Your hunger for blood and your stone heart will bring you here. Accept it."

Anger, fear, and dread were building up in Victorija. She didn't want Gilbert anywhere near Daisy.

He walked over and handed her a gold goblet. "Now will you pour, or shall I?"

The anger and rage exploded, and she launched herself at Gilbert while he laughed.

Victorija woke gasping. She looked down to her side and saw Daisy sleeping safely and soundly.

"I can't do this to her. I will not be my father."

Daisy's eyes fluttered open. She felt a deep pull in her stomach and instinctively knew it was Torija. She reached to her neck and felt for her bite mark. It wasn't painful, and she couldn't feel the wound. "Torija?"

But Torija wasn't there. She looked at the clock on the wall. It was three o'clock in the morning. No wonder she still felt exhausted. She got up and went to the mirror in the en suite bathroom. "Wow, it's gone." She heard the bedroom door shut and hurried out into the room. Torija was looking solemn and pale, not as healthy as she thought she'd be after feeding on her blood. Torija was carrying a bottle of whisky. "Where were you?"

"Getting this."

"You have alcohol here?" Daisy said.

"I left a case in the kitchen. I used to come here sometimes to think."

To think of Angele, no doubt.

Torija walked over to the armchair by the window and sat down.

"Are you not coming to bed?"

"No, I don't want to sleep."

Every answer Torija gave was curt and cold. What had happened since last night? Daisy had managed to connect with Torija and finally get through all that armour she had built around herself, and now this?

"Why are you awake?" Torija asked.

"Your hunger woke me, but look—my bite mark's gone."

Torija looked at it but then said in a monotone, "Because I fed on you. Now that the bond is complete, it heals each time." This was so much different from the emotion she'd experienced last night. Torija continued, "At least you don't look like you're shackled to me."

She then took a big glug of whisky.

"What's wrong? Something's changed."

"Nothing's changed," Torija said.

Daisy walked over to the armchair and knelt down beside it. "It has. Last night we were so close emotionally, and you let go some of your past."

"I'm fine. All I care about is getting to see the Reaper tomorrow and ending this blood bond."

Daisy couldn't help but feel those words like a dagger to her guts. The goal was always to break the bond, but things had changed. Torija had come back to the surface, and she was winning at saving Torija's soul. More than that, Daisy was falling for her. She felt every pain that had been inflicted on Torija and wanted to soothe them, but now it seemed like Torija didn't want her.

"You look pale. I thought you'd feel better after last night."

"It takes more than one feed to get back to full power. Plus, this isn't helping." Torija flexed her forearm, and not only was the green in her veins still there, it had spread.

"I thought that would be gone, too, after feeding on my blood," Daisy said.

"Apparently not."

Daisy was confused. She thought she was doing the right thing and helping to save Torija, but not only did she seem to be failing at that emotionally, but physically, too. Her blood wasn't healing the green poison in Torija's veins.

"Hopefully the Reaper can explain about that tomorrow."

Daisy stood and said, "Well, at least come and feed. That's one thing that can make you stronger."

"No, not now."

"But you're hungry. That's what woke me up," Daisy said.

"Just leave it till tomorrow—now go to bed."

"Fine," Daisy shouted. "Starve yourself." She got into bed and turned away from Torija. "You don't care, so I won't care."

❖

The next day they travelled to see the Reaper in silence, and their journey was uncomfortable, to say the least. Daisy was angry at her, but she was trying to break this bond for Daisy's sake, not hers. "Why are you giving me the cold shoulder?"

Daisy stopped dead. "You must be joking. I thought we were getting so close, you know? I was actually starting to—I trusted you, I let you feed, and you stopped. You did it, made a huge breakthrough, and then nothing. You just closed that emotional door, and I was left on the other side."

Torija squinted in response. "Emotional door? What are you talking about?"

"It doesn't matter." Daisy marched on, but Torija was in front of her in half a second.

"It clearly matters."

"You wouldn't feed from me when you needed to, and you were miserable. All you cared about was breaking our bond and giving me curt replies."

"Curt replies? Oh dear gods, imagine giving you curt replies? Tie garlic around me and slice my head off."

Daisy pushed her out of the way. "I can't talk to you."

"I'm talking about breaking our bond because that's what we set out to do. To free you. Last night, I was just trying to—" Torija struggled to find the words. After her terrifying nightmare, she was just trying to pull back and keep Daisy safe because a part of her subconscious obviously thought she would end up using her, like Gilbert did her mother.

"I'm doing this for you."

"You're doing it for Angele, let's be honest."

Victorija pulled her back. "No, I'm doing this for Daisy MacDougall, the one who believed in me, believed in Torija, and is the bravest person I've ever known, someone who deserves better than being shackled to an old vampire who's committed more sins than there is forgiveness for."

Daisy looked at her silently, and Torija set off towards the river's edge. She stopped and waited for Daisy to follow.

"Why are you stopping? Where is the Reaper's house?"

"It's more of a fishing shack."

"Shack or house, there's nothing here."

"I told you the Reaper has powers. We must introduce ourselves and be invited in. That's the difficulty."

"Why is that a problem? You said you knew him," Daisy said.

Torija cleared her throat and looked a bit sheepish. "Eh…the last time we crossed paths, it wasn't under the best circumstances."

"You didn't tell me that. What if he won't see us?"

"Let me try," Torija said.

Torija held up her hands in surrender and said, "Reaper, I, Victorija Dred, wish an audience with you."

Daisy waited and nothing happened. "There's nothing here."

"Just wait."

Then Daisy saw a golden shimmer in the air, and astonishingly a wooden shack appeared by the riverside—a humble-looking shack, and a long boat tied up at the edge of the river.

"We're in. Now, just follow my lead. I know him, and he's going to be angry with me."

"Maybe I should go first, then."

"No, I'm wary of how he's going to react," Torija said.

"I'm not frightened. I faced the most bloodthirsty vampire on the planet."

"Yes, I know, you're not frightened of anything. Noted. I know him, so just let me handle it."

Daisy followed Torija up to the door. She gazed around in astonishment. This was right under the noses of the human Parisians. The paranormal world got stranger and stranger the more time she spent in it.

Just as Torija was about to knock on the door, it opened itself. Daisy peeked around Torija and saw a stocky elderly man with white hair and beard, sitting in a very worn armchair, next to a wood stove.

This was not how Daisy expected the Grim Reaper to look, but then again, she never expected to meet the Reaper.

Torija bowed extravagantly and said, "Reaper, may I enter? I seek your counsel."

Daisy rolled her eyes and said, "We aren't in the Regency period, you know."

"I was," Torija said flatly.

He said nothing and just stared at them steadily. Torija glanced back at Daisy quickly before saying, "I know our last meeting wasn't as—"

The Reaper cut her off. "That depends on who I am inviting in—Victorija Dred or Torija."

How in God's green earth did he know about Victorija's transformation, Daisy wondered. She was fed up taking a back seat, so she pushed in front of Torija and said, "She's Torija, she's changing." Daisy thought back to what Torija said outside. As mad as she was, she recognized now that Torija was probably frightened still of what she might do, and if you were a bloodthirsty vampire who hadn't cared in centuries if a human lived or died, then that was still a huge change. Even if Torija had pushed her away last night. "I mean, I'm alive, and the old Victorija would have killed me."

The Reaper laughed. "Victorija Dred with a human attorney for the defence."

Daisy could feel Torija getting frustrated. "Look, can we come in or not?"

The Reaper indicated for them to come in, and he stood up.

Now that they were inside, she could see how basic and aged his shack was. Why would a paranormal being choose to stay here?

He walked over to Daisy and said, "Daisy MacDougall. Lucia said you would come here one day, and you're as feisty as she described."

"How would the Grand Duchess know I would be here one day?"

"She was and is a very powerful woman. She supports Amelia Debrek from the spirit world, and Amelia is one of the descendants who will fight for this world against its dark forces. You are the other."

"What?" Daisy said, confused.

Torija stepped forward. "A descendant?"

Daisy had no idea what he was talking about. "What is this?"

"Sit down by the fire with me."

After Daisy sat, the Reaper said, "I don't know all the details, but your two mothers were close friends. They both found out they were pregnant at the same time."

Daisy had a sinking feeling. "Before or after my dad was killed?"

"After, Lucia told me."

"How long after?" Daisy was starting to feel her dad drifting away from her. She didn't want that. She was a MacDougall as well as a Brassard.

The Reaper cleared his throat. "I'm sorry, I don't know the answer to that question, my dear."

Daisy felt queasy. "What happened after they became pregnant?"

"They ran, together at first, then separated after dark forces came after them."

"Why did they come for them?"

"Daisy, an old prophecy said that you and Amelia will lead this world away from the darkness."

"How will I do that? I'm just a human with the ability that I know if someone is paranormal."

"You are trying to lead one vampire from the darkness now. I'd advise you to talk to a witch named Sybil."

Torija sighed and started pacing. She had a long and uncomfortable history with Sybil. "I'll take Daisy to her as soon as it's safe, but I need to ask you about our blood bond. Can it be broken?"

"Why do you ask me, Vampire?"

"My father Gilbert came to you to ask the same thing, and he survived for many years after he should have died. He lost his mind eventually, but he did live."

"I'll give you the same answer that I gave him. That requires powerful magic because a vampire blood bond is meant to be permanent. The only person willing to cast that kind of magic is a powerful witch named Anka."

"Anka?" Torija's stomach dropped.

"Wait, is it a potion? Torija, it must be that drink she was giving you. That's all she had," Daisy said.

"That's right," the Reaper agreed. "She's used it as a weapon of control before now."

Torija had pinned all her hopes on the Reaper. "Is there anything else that will give Daisy freedom?" Torija asked.

Daisy shot her a look.

"Nothing, except…"

"Except what?" Torija.

"Death, you are released by death."

Daisy and Torija exchanged a look, and then Torija said to the Reaper, "Can I speak to you privately?"

"Wait a—"

Before Daisy finished her sentence, the Reaper waved his hand, and everything froze, apart from himself and Torija. One of a Reaper's necessary gifts was the power to pause time, so that they could retrieve the souls they took to the afterlife. Torija had seen it many times.

He walked up to her and said, "Victorija Dred, feared and hated by all."

"That's why I want this bond broken. I can't trust myself to continually feed on her. She means—Let's just say she means a lot to me."

"Victorija with feelings, will wonders never cease? Come with me." The Reaper led her out of the shack and down to the edge of the pier where his boat was moored. "I've had to ferry many more vampire victims to the afterlife recently."

Torija let out a sigh. "I know. My vampires have been out of control since I have been dealing with this blood bond."

The Reaper laughed. "They weren't much better when you were in control, Torija, or will it be Victorija?"

"I'm having night terrors. All my victims haunt me. It's the first time I've had to look my victims in the face. Do you know about them?"

"Of course I do. The dead are my customers."

"What do they want?" Torija asked.

"Do you remember the last time we met?"

Torija looked down and closed her eyes. She saw the image of herself, dried blood covering her lips and chin and hands.

Just to taunt the Reaper, she brought five bodies to the door of his shack and shouted, "I thought I'd save you the trip."

The Reaper came running out the door, shouting, "Victorija Dred! One day your crimes will catch up with you, and you will lose something you love."

Victorija turned around laughing, then thumped her chest. "Impossible. I don't have a heart."

"Yes, I do. I said I don't have a heart."

"And all this time, you did. If you didn't, as your young lady said, she would be dead by now."

"Can you help me? I want to free Daisy from this bond."

"If you want to do a selfless act for the first time in your life and release Daisy from this burden, I think deep, down inside, you know what you have to do."

Death. That was the feeling in the pit of her stomach.

Torija nodded.

Death wasn't something that she had contemplated in…she couldn't remember how long. She looked back to the shack where Daisy was frozen in time. Was that the answer? She was being put in danger because of her blood bond with Torija, and her greatest fear was using her, the way she had every other human or vampire she had come across.

The Reaper continued, "But the question is, can you fight the Victorija inside who will lose herself in Daisy's blood?"

That was Torija's biggest fear. As she grew stronger from Daisy's blood, would this small window of clarity that Daisy had given her, this nudge to remember that she wasn't always this feared vampire, dissipate, until all she saw when she looked at Daisy was blood?

"I had a nightmare about that last night. I saw myself as my father, using Daisy like he did my mother. What should I do?" Torija said.

"If you truly don't want that to happen, then take her back to her grandmother's house in Scotland and think about what comes next."

Torija nodded, then pulled up her sleeve. "Do you know what the green in my veins is? Is it poison?"

The Reaper looked at it closely. "Ask Sybil. She will tell you everything."

"Thank you, Reaper. I'm—"

He grasped her arm, and Torija noticed the green was creeping further up her arm. "I don't need empty apologies, Vampire, none of your victims do. They need to see action. Now go and try to think only of Daisy MacDougall."

❖

"Yes, we are all fine," Amelia said. "I'm just worried about Daisy and you." Amelia paced up and down her bedroom. She'd been not so patiently waiting for Byron to call for hours.

"I'm sorry for not calling sooner, mia cara. We have tried all the places Victorija might have taken her, but nothing yet. I don't know why, but I have a gut feeling Victorija won't harm her, or at least not yet."

"Why do you think that?"

"She's not at the Dred castle, and our information says that Drasas and Anka are looking for her, too. In any event, we've met up with an old friend called Brogan who can help us track her."

"Brogan? Doesn't sound very French."

Byron laughed softly. "She's not, she's one hundred percent Irish werewolf, but she's an excellent artist, so Paris suits her well."

"So what is Brogan going to do?" Amelia asked.

"She works as a private investigator, tracker, fixer of sorts."

"Brogan doesn't work on the right side of the law, then?"

"Hmm…treads a fine line, I'd say. Anyway, her wolf is the best tracker I know. I'm sure we'll find Daisy. I better go—tell Sera to keep on her toes."

"I will. Bye, sweetheart, I love you."

"I love you too, mia cara."

When she hung up the phone, there was a knock at her door.

"Knock, knock, can we come in?"

It was Sera and, she presumed, Katie. "Yes."

They came through the door with big smiles. "We've come to distract you from worrying," Sera said. "Well, we need to distract Katie, too, because she's pining for Alex."

Katie gave her a mock glare. "I am not. It's just the first time Alex has been away on a mission like this."

"I'll keep both of you occupied. We brought Monopoly." Sera held up the box.

"Come on then. Byron's just called."

"What did she say?" Katie said as she sat on the bed.

"They're all fine, and Byron says you're to keep on your toes, Sera."

Sera rolled her eyes, sat on the bed, and set the Monopoly box down. "She never trusts me. So, what did she say?"

"Victorija and Daisy are not at the castle, so they tried all the usual places Victorija might be, and nothing, but they've met up with an old friend who Byron thinks could help them track Daisy. A werewolf called Brogan."

"Brogan?" Sera said with surprise. "But they haven't spoken in years."

"Oh? Why?" Amelia asked.

Sera rushed into her answer without thinking. "Oh, it was this girl that turned out to be Brogan's girlfriend and—" Sera stopped abruptly.

Amelia narrowed her eyes. "What about Brogan's girlfriend?"

Sera looked at Katie, then back to Amelia. "Um, this girl pursued Byron, and Byron didn't know she was Brogan's girlfriend. Brogan said she must have known, and they had a big fallout."

Amelia felt the twist of jealously in her stomach. "In other words, she had sex with Brogan's girlfriend."

Sera let her head fall back and said in a low voice, "Byron's going to kill me."

"You don't have to feel weird about it. I know Byron has a past centuries old." Amelia tried to be as adult and mature as she could possibly be.

"She didn't know the woman was Brogan's girlfriend, honestly, Amelia, and they seem to have patched things up."

Amelia put on her best smile. "Don't worry about my feelings. I'm fine. Really."

But there was clearly a tense feeling in the air. Katie tried to change the subject by saying, "Let's get playing. Monopoly is a long game."

Amelia watched as Sera and Katie set up the board. It shouldn't matter, and if she was immature for being jealous, then so be it. She wasn't perfect by any means, but one thing she was sure of—she was married, blood bonded to Byron, and carrying her baby. She might feel the odd twinge of jealousy about Byron's past, but the right now was the most important.

DYING FOR YOU

CHAPTER FOURTEEN

Daisy was woken up by an even worse ache than the night before, growing inside her. The ache pulled her to feed Torija, but she wasn't in the bed or the bedroom. She got up and put her feet on the cold, wooden flooring.

All she had on was an oversized T-shirt they found in one of the wardrobes. It barely went over her thighs. She got up and shivered from the cold inside the room, then walked out of the bedroom and along the corridor.

She tried to concentrate on the pull she felt towards Torija, the natural desire to feed Torija that the blood bond had given her. Daisy followed it to a door that was half open and peeked inside. Daisy saw Torija sitting on the bed in the room with a drink in her hand.

"May I come in?"

Torija nodded.

"Is this Angele's room?" Daisy asked.

"Yes."

Daisy went in and sat beside Torija. "Did you used to visit Angele here?"

"Yes, I used to come in that window. Her father would have put a stake through my heart if he'd found out."

"You still miss her a lot?"

Torija took a sip of her drink and stood. "Yes, but until my grandmother unpacked some of my memories, I managed to block out the pain."

Strangely, Daisy felt slightly jealous. The love Victorija—the most feared vampire, who'd chosen the dark path—carried for her, the love that stopped her from giving in and draining Daisy of her life-giving blood, was incredible. The love for Angele.

"I bet you wish you could get Angele back here in my place." There was jealousy in that question.

But to her surprise, Torija shook her head. "I was seventeen years old. I hadn't transformed into a born vampire. It was easier for Angele to keep me on the straight and narrow path, but the Victorija you first met? I don't think she could've gotten through to me."

"And I could?"

Torija stood and walked over to the window. She put her glass of whisky on the sill and braced one arm against the wall.

"Torija?" Daisy said. She could feel Torija's need for blood rising by the second, but also a confusion over what she was feeling. Daisy was pulled to her like a magnet. She walked up behind Torija. "Torija? Could I?"

Torija balled her fist and softly smacked the wall. "You're stubborn, obstinate"—she turned to face Daisy—"kind, and the bravest person I've ever met. Why you took the chance to come and find me, I'll never know."

Daisy took a step forward and put her hand on Torija's chest. "Because I knew there was a better person there. Every time I went into Angele's memories, you called to me for help. The hurt, the pain, the trauma you went through, it was too much for anyone. I believed that you could be redeemed."

Torija could literally feel the warmth from Daisy's palm on her chest. It was seeping into her chest and spreading around her upper chest and arms. This was more than blood hunger or because Daisy was her accidental blood bond. Her heart was cracking open from the warmth and care Daisy was giving her.

Torija was frightened to put a name to the feeling that was growing for Daisy, but one thing she did know—the answer to Daisy's question. "You could, you have."

Daisy looked slightly confused. "What?"

"You asked if you could get through to this Victorija, and the answer is, you have."

Daisy smiled softly and, with her free arm, took Torija's hand.

Before Daisy could say anything she said, "I can't ever change what I am, and what I've done. I've killed, I've hurt, I've destroyed—"

"But you can do better. *We* can do better together. You heard what the Reaper said—this descendant thing I'm meant to be, you, me, Amelia, and Byron can draw all corners of the community together against Anka."

Little did Daisy know that Byron would take her head if she went anywhere near her home. But the warmth from Daisy's hand had now spread all over Torija's body. She felt lighter, energetic, and aching to touch Daisy.

She cupped Daisy's cheek and said, "Why would someone like me, having done the things I've done, help bring the community together?" She felt Daisy shiver at her touch, and every sense was on fire.

"Because you recognize the darkness. You've been in it, you've drunk it in, then found that there was still light there to grasp hold of and hold on to."

"I want you so much it hurts me here." Torija thumped her fist against her heart.

Daisy responded by moving in and giving her the sweetest kiss. It totally disarmed Torija. She was not used to kisses like that. Soft, loving lips that were a balm to her soul. Daisy took her hand and started to lead her from Angele's bedroom.

Once they were in the guest room, Torija stopped. She was at a loss as to what to do, how to handle this. She had never felt like this, not even with Angele. They'd never got this far. *Victorija* was used to taking pleasure. This was different. Her heart wanted simply to touch Daisy and show her what was in her soul.

Daisy turned around and stepped closer. She stroked Torija's blond locks from her eyes. "Torija, I want you to feed. I need it as much as you do."

Torija leaned her forehead against Daisy's. "How do you know that's not the blood bond talking?"

Daisy placed small, tender kisses on her cheeks and lips. Torija felt hunger in her heart for the first time. She knew it didn't come from the same place as blood hunger—that, she was certain of. She watched as Daisy pulled off her shirt and unclasped her bra, letting her full breasts tumble out. They were simply beautiful, and her hands ached to touch them. Then Daisy encouraged her to take off her T-shirt.

Her body was athletic and breasts small, so she rarely wore a bra. Daisy dragged her nails between Torija's breasts, and she shivered as her nipples hardened. Torija was never this passive when having sex. Never had been, but this was different. This wasn't purely a physical need for release. This was one heart, one soul, bringing light and love to an old, dark heart. Daisy stepped into her arms, and their two naked torsos came together.

Torija pulled them closer and rested her face in the crook of Daisy's neck. Daisy was so soft and so warm. She ran her hands up and down Daisy's back while breathing her into her soul. She simply wanted to melt into Daisy.

It was only then that she noticed her fangs had already erupted. That had never happened before, because normally her sexual feelings were separate from her hunger for blood. She was hunger driven and so becoming ready to drink was at the forefront of her mind. But now, instead, the feel of Daisy's breasts pressing against her was what was occupying her mind and body.

Torija ran her hand up to the side of Daisy's breast, and she felt her shiver.

"Take my blood," Daisy moaned.

"Not yet." Torija experienced a rush of confidence after initially struggling to cope with the emotions she was experiencing. She took Daisy's hand, led her over to the bed, and took a step back to stroke her hair away from her face. "You're beautiful, Daisy MacDougall, but you have an even more beautiful soul. You're the only one who could have saved me."

"You've always had the light inside you. You just needed someone to help you look for it."

"I want you," Torija said. She picked Daisy up easily, and Daisy wrapped her legs around Torija's waist. Then Torija got on the bed and moved them both to the middle of the bed. She sat down, and Daisy sat on Torija's lap, on her knees.

They kissed softly at first, slipping her tongue into Daisy's mouth, taking the time to taste, feel, and discover everything that made Daisy the woman she was falling in love with.

Torija's heart pounded to the same beat she was experiencing deep inside her sex when she felt Daisy's hot, wet heat on her abdomen. For the first time since she turned into a born vampire, Torija perceived what it was like to be flesh and bone again, and for once, simply human.

❖

Daisy was getting lost in her need for Torija. The slow, loving pace was everything she hoped it would be, but she wanted more. Daisy took Torija's hand and placed it on her breast. Torija moaned into her mouth, and Daisy felt an electrical pull down to her clit. She started to move her hips, aching for some sort of stimulation. "Tor, please touch me."

Torija nodded, and Daisy gasped when she felt Torija's fingers slip between her legs and start to softly, gently stroke her clit. Daisy wrapped her arms around Torija's neck, holding her closer as she thrust her hips along with her lover's strokes.

"That feels so good, Tor. Drink my blood."

"Not yet, cherie," Torija whispered in her ear.

Daisy then groaned when Torija teased her opening and pressed two fingers inside her.

"Oh God, yes." Daisy loved the position of kneeling astride Torija's lap. It allowed her to control long, deep thrusts inside her. She was soon speeding up her hips and breathing as her orgasm built. As her orgasm got closer, she dug her fingers into Torija's hair.

"I'm going to come, Tor."

"Do you consent to me taking your blood?" Torija asked.

"Yes, yes, I consent. I just want your teeth in me when I come."

Daisy was nearing the precipice of her orgasm when she felt two sharp fangs pierce her neck. It nipped at first, and then it felt so good, as a rush of feel-good endorphins rushed over her body.

"Yes. Yes," Daisy shouted.

Then, all at once, she crashed into a white-hot blast of pure joy and ecstasy. She thrust her hips fast, then went rigid and held on to Torija's neck.

Torija pulled her teeth out and allowed Daisy to fall backward onto the bed. She looked up at Torija, who was breathing hard, Daisy's blood painted on her mouth and chin, but the sight didn't frighten her. To know that she and only she could feed Torija made her heart swell.

"I love you, Tor." She could see the confusion in Torija's eyes. All these new feelings were clearly overwhelming to her. "It's okay. You don't have to say anything."

Torija simply said, "More, I need you more."

❖

Torija lay on top of Daisy, with Daisy's thigh between her own, so she could thrust her sex whilst drinking from Daisy's neck. She hadn't felt this ready for sex in a long time. Her body was finally working again. As Torija thrust against Daisy's thigh, Daisy pulled her head down for a kiss. Then Torija said, "Can I drink from you again? I need to come so badly."

Daisy stroked her face. "You never have to ask."

"Yes, I do. I always do." That answer came from deep inside her soul.

"Then, yes. Drink from me and come on me," Daisy said.

That sentence shook Torija and sent her back to Daisy's neck. There was not a better feeling than drinking from a lover who had opened up her heart and her body. Torija could never have imagined how good her bonded's blood would taste and feel. It was overwhelming, and on top of that, her body was gaining strength with every mouthful.

Soon her orgasm was soaring out of control. Her body needed to come so badly. It had been so long. She thrust harder and faster on Daisy's thigh, and Daisy rubbed her back soothingly.

It was almost as if Daisy's love carried her into her orgasm. A couple more thrusts and her hips jerked erratically, and she fell tumbling into a bliss she'd never felt before.

❖

Despite vowing not to fall asleep, Torija slept as she lay in Daisy's arms, her cheek resting on Daisy's breast, while Daisy stroked Torija's back. What she had shared with Torija was like no sexual experience she had ever had, not that she'd had loads of experience. She'd had three girlfriends in her life, and it had been nice, but nothing so all-encompassing, all-consuming as making love with Victorija.

She had been jealous of Amelia's deep connection to Byron and the passion they shared, but she could understand it now. Sharing life-giving blood with the one you love and them being dependent on your survival was unlike any other passion in the world.

Torija started to murmur in her sleep. "Rain, rain, no, can't."

It must be one of the nightmares. The reason she didn't want to sleep. Daisy stroked her hair and kissed her brow. "Shh, shh. It's okay, Tor."

Torija woke up with a gasp and then realized where she was. "Fuck."

"It's okay, you're safe."

Daisy was surprised when Torija pulled her to her, wrapped her arms tightly around her, and murmured into her neck, "You're safe, it was just a dream."

"Of course I'm safe. I'm with you," Daisy said.

Torija kissed the side of Daisy's head, closed her eyes, and saw the movie in her mind that had terrified her in her dream.

She was back in the castle in her grand four-poster bed, waking up in the morning with Daisy by her side.

She put her arm around Daisy's middle, spooning and anticipating going back to sleep, but she felt Daisy shiver and shake.

"Daisy? Are you—" Torija pulled Daisy around but felt sick at what she saw. She was pale, the flesh of her throat just about ripped out, and tears were streaming from her eyes. Torija was in shock. She jumped up in panic.

"No, no. What have I done?"

She held Daisy's head and placed kisses on her forehead. She heard Daisy struggle to say something, and she placed her ear near Daisy's mouth and heard a low whisper, "Kill me or let me go, please?"

Torija felt like she had been stabbed with a stake through the heart. She jumped up and out of the bed. She felt true terror and disgust at what she had done. Torija grasped her hair and bent over in pain and despair.

Just as she thought she was going to vomit, one of her vampires came into the bedroom and said, "Shall I take her back down to the dungeon to heal?"

Of course. Now that Daisy was her blood bond, she would heal and live for as long as Torija was alive. Daisy didn't even have the escape of death from her torment.

Then she heard rain battering down, but it almost sounded like it was inside the room.

Another voice said, "I told you, didn't I?"

Torija turned around and saw her father, sitting on the windowsill of her castle bedroom in a black suit.

He was smiling. Then he repeated, "I told you that you couldn't keep up this *Torija* facade." Gilbert pushed off the windowsill and walked over to her. "You're a Dred, Victorija, and you always will be. Blood and hunger are not things we Dreds can control."

Torija couldn't speak. She looked over at the bed and felt tears fall down her face.

Gilbert stuffed his hands in his pockets and sauntered over towards Daisy.

"And why should we control it? Humans are weak, they are food and there to serve us. That's the natural order of things."

Torija was shaking with fear and disgust. Gilbert leaned over Daisy and said, "Beautiful human, looks like she'd have delicious blood. Maybe I'll have a taste of Daisy MacDougall too."

Torija didn't need any time to think. She ran at her father and pushed him to the floor—

"Tor? Tor?"

Torija came out of the replay of her nightmare to the sight of Daisy looking down on her. "Are you okay? Where did you go? What happened?"

"My nightmares, that's all. Come here."

"Wait," Daisy said. Daisy pointed to the green vein that was now well up her bicep. "We need to go and see this witch, Sybil. I think that has to be our top priority."

Sybil was not on Torija's agenda now. As the Reaper said, the only way to release Daisy was Torija's death. That became even more acutely clear after her dream. Sure, she might be doing well now, but as time passed, and she came back into the paranormal world, her selfish impulses and hunger for blood and violence might return, just as Gilbert had suggested in her dream. She was a Dred, after all.

Her mind was made up. "We will, but I think first we should contact your grandmother and tell her you're—we're coming to stay."

"Why? I mean, I need to call her, and Amelia and Byron. God, they are going to kill me. We need a phone."

"We can't call anyone. We might be tracked, and you don't want vampires heading to your grandmother's home," Torija said.

"But why don't you want to go straight to Sybil? You need help with whatever this green poison is. It should have gotten better when you fed from me."

Torija had to think on her feet. "When I was talking to the Reaper—"

"You mean when he stopped time just so you and he could have a private conversation and leave me out of things?"

Torija sighed. "I told you, the Reaper and I had a lot of history to work out. Anyway, he said that he knew of your grandmother's work within the paranormal community and that she could help us with information and planning for what comes next. The descendant issue and other things."

"Okay, but how do we get back to Scotland? I was abducted here. I don't have a passport or any official papers. You jumped out of the Dred castle window, so I don't expect you have anything we could use, like money?"

"A vampire doesn't need money. You've been eating, haven't you?" Torija said firmly.

"Yes, and I feel terrible about it. You're using your powers to steal."

"I know you're here to redeem me, Daisy, but it's only a sandwich or two. Needs must."

"Don't forget the whisky." Daisy gave her a half smile.

"Fine, once we have cured me of this poison, transported you back to Amelia, so you can do your descendant thing, destroyed Anka and her dark forces, then I will come back here to Paris and pay for every sandwich, every bottle of water—"

"And whisky," Daisy reminded her with a smile.

"And whisky, and all will be right with the world."

Daisy leaned over Torija's lips and said, "Have I ever told you how sexy your accent is? Even though you were being sarcastic."

Torija couldn't help but smile at the comment. She didn't think she had smiled and laughed so much in her life as since she met Daisy.

"Did I ever tell you how sexy your Scottish brogue is?"

"I don't have a brogue. That's the Highlanders—I'm a strict lowlander. Haven't you ever been to Scotland?" Daisy realized in a second what she had just said, and Torija's smile faltered.

Of course she had been to Scotland. Very recently Victorija, as she was then, chased the Debreks to their castle on the very far end of Scotland and killed her grandmother.

"I'm sorry, I didn't mean—It was just a joke. I'm sorry if I upset you."

What a beautiful human being Daisy was. She never thought of herself, only others, and had taken the chance on redeeming an old vampire who could have killed her.

Torija stroked Daisy's hair. "Don't worry about it. I know what you meant. I have been to Scotland many times, but maybe it's best not to dwell on it just now."

"So, how are we getting to Scotland?"

"I know someone who has a private plane. We can fly into a small private airfield at night, and hopefully we won't be spotted by any authorities."

"Hopefully?" Daisy said.

"Well, let's just say he is an expert at getting things into the country without anyone noticing."

"And how do you pay this someone?"

"Just let me worry about that," Torija said.

"Nuh-uh. That's not how this blood bond thing between us is going to be. I want to know what's happening in that brain of yours."

Daisy's incessant questions were going to make it difficult to leave her at her grandmother's, but that was exactly what had to be done.

Torija flipped Daisy onto her back. "Let's just say I have some information about someone that he would pay a lot more than a plane ride for."

Now to distract her. Just as Daisy was about to speak and no doubt ask more questions, Torija kissed her deeply on the lips until Daisy moaned. To Torija's delight, Daisy took her hand and placed it on her breast and encouraged her to squeeze.

Torija loved Daisy's breasts and hungered to put her mouth on them. She pulled back from the kiss and said, "Do you want me to make you come?"

"Yes, while you feed on my neck."

Torija again got a flashback to her dream, where Daisy's neck was ripped to shreds. She couldn't feed from her there, not now.

"No, I want something better. You know, a vampire can feed from more than your neck and wrist…"

"No. Where?" Daisy said breathily.

Torija smiled, disappeared under the covers, and Daisy gasped in surprise.

Chapter Fifteen

Drasas took her seat beside Anka in the back of her limousine. Asha leaned in and said, "I'll report in when I locate the target."

"Thank you, Asha."

"Where is Asha going, Madam?"

Anka twisted the ever present gold ring with the purple stone in it on her finger. "Just a little side mission. Nothing for you to worry about at the moment."

"And where are we going?" Drasas didn't have much power over the way things were going now, but she would. Anka promised, and she'd follow her anywhere.

"One of my people on the ground has discovered the location of an old adversary of mine. A man I have been seeking for quite a long while. Your former Principe led one of my witches there."

Drasas turned around in her seat. "Victorija?"

"Yes, she took her little woman to visit the Reaper. Have you heard of the Reapers?"

"Yes, they come to take the dead to the other side, like the Valkyries of old. Victorija met the one for our region, I think, a few times. I never did."

"I've been looking for this Reaper for a long time. He helped trap me some years ago, and it was a long time till I got out again," Anka said.

"How did Victorija know where to find him?"

"Gilbert Dred, I believe, went to him once, about his own blood bond with his wife."

"That was before my time, and Victorija didn't share that information with me, I can assure you," Drasas said.

Anka put her hand on Drasas's knee and squeezed. "I know, my little vampire. You are so important to my plans, and I trust you would do anything you could to help me."

Drasas was hungry for every touch Anka gave her. Around Anka she felt like she was constantly on the edge of orgasm, but never quite got there. Drasas would crawl for Anka, as she had before, to get any attention from her.

"I would do anything for you, Madam."

Anka smiled and rubbed her hand up and down Drasas's thigh. "That's good, because I have a job for you today, and after losing Victorija and Daisy, I know you will do this to perfection."

Drasas's body was on fire. She could hardly think straight. "I won't fail you."

"Good, because this is the first test to see if you can handle great power."

That thought doubled the fire scorching over her body, and she started breathing heavier and heavier.

Anka took off her gold ring and handed it to Drasas. "Put this on."

When Drasas did, she felt a surge of power run through her. It made her feel confident and full of boundless energy. "Wow, what is this?"

"This ring is powered by some of the greatest paranormals the world over. I have collected that power diligently for many, many years. I had hoped that Victorija would be the last one to have her power taken and given to the one I deem fit enough to hold this power."

"I can still get Victorija for you if you give me another chance," Drasas said, as the ring fuelled her confidence.

"We will get a born vampire, one way or another, but the Reaper is an unintended bonus. He has great power"—Anka turned and stroked Drasas's face—"and it will make you so much more powerful than I imagined you could be."

Drasas was nearly shaking apart. "Yes, Madam. I need you to touch me."

Anka sat back abruptly. "Later, if you accomplish what I want you to."

The car finally stopped, and when Drasas got out, she found she was at an area of desolate ground, by the banks of the river Seine. Anka walked around the car to join her. "Where are we?" Drasas asked.

"We are at the current location of our man of the moment, the Reaper."

"But there's nothing here," Drasas said.

"Just trust me, Vampire." Anka led them slowly down to the river's edge.

"Are there many Reapers in the world?" Drasas asked.

"Ten. There is a large world out there to cover, and ten is a perfect number in many ancient cultures. Come with me."

Drasas followed Anka, but all she could see was wasteland.

Anka held her hands up and then, as if undoing a zip in a tent, brought her hands down, and an old fishing shack appeared out of nowhere.

"This has been here all this time?" Drasas said.

"His base moves around. That's why he's so difficult to find. Come."

Drasas followed Anka towards the shack. She noticed a long boat tied to a small pier beside the shack. "That's an unusual boat."

"It ferries the dead to the other side," Anka said. She stopped a few feet away from the door and turned to Drasas. "The Reaper is extremely powerful. He can freeze time, amongst many other things, but I want you to follow me in and destroy him and take his power."

Drasas was not expecting that. "I can't do that. I'm not even a born vampire. I'm turned and can't go up against someone as strong as that."

"With this ring on, you can. For every power and blow he casts upon you, the ring will steal that energy and give it to you. You can handle this, can't you, Drasas?"

Drasas was scared, if she was honest, but she would never let Anka know. "Of course, Madam."

Anka smiled. "Then follow me, Vampire."

They walked up to the door, and with a bolt of red light from Anka's hand, the door blew open. Drasas saw an elderly-looking man sitting in his armchair. This was not how she imagined the Reaper would look. She felt more confident now.

He looked up and calmly said, "You could have just have knocked, Anka. That was a perfectly good door."

Drasas was surprised at his calm in the presence of Anka.

"I like to be surprising, Reaper."

"So it seems. It's been a long time," the Reaper said.

Anka walked further into the room. "Yes, well, it took me some time to get out of the trap you and your little helpers caught me in, but nothing keeps Anka trapped forever, Reaper."

"Who is your friend?" he asked.

"The new Principe of the Dred clan, and she's here to take your power."

The Reaper chuckled. "Well, I better get out of my armchair for this one. Do your worst, Principe of the Dred clan."

This was Drasas's chance for greatness and for Anka. She wanted her more than anything she'd ever wanted in her life, but would she be able to do this?

Anka surprised both her and the Reaper by shooting a bolt of red light at him. He held his hands up to catch it.

"Now, Drasas!" Anka shouted.

Drasas ran at him, and he deflected the light at her. She had the most incredible sensation, starting from her ring finger, traveling up her arm, and then spreading all over her body.

She felt stronger than she ever had in her life. Her fangs sprang from her gums, and she struck the Reaper. He responded by throwing a large glowing white ball of light, which the ring on Drasas's finger drank up greedily.

The Reaper's knees started to buckle as his energy was drained from him.

Drasas smashed the Reaper to the floor, and instinct made her rip at his throat. She drank from him, strong blood like she hadn't experienced before.

"No, you can't—" He gurgled as blood flowed from his neck.

"Drasas, enough."

But Drasas could hardly hear her. She was high on the energy she felt and the rich blood. She was then pulled back by a force at her back. Drasas landed on her backside, and Anka stood over her.

"Stop when I tell you to, Vampire. Stand up."

Drasas jumped up. She had never felt this good in her life. Wearing this ring and drinking from such a powerful paranormal bathed her in a sensation of ecstasy. She wiped the dripping blood from her mouth and saw that it was black, not red.

Anka must have noticed her surprise, because she said, "Reaper's blood always runs black, the colour of death. It's much richer than human blood."

Drasas licked it from her fingers. Her breathing was heavy, and all she wanted to do was to have Anka touch her.

Anka beckoned her with a crooked finger.

"Did I do well, Madam?" Drasas asked.

Anka grinned. "You did very well, Drasas."

Drasas felt the ring fly off her finger and rest back on its owner's. She felt its loss but was still on a high, and a sexual high at that.

Anka turned her around, and with her palm pushed her back against the wall of the shack. She scratched her nails down Drasas's T-shirt and put her lips close to Drasas's. "How did that feel, Vampire?"

"Like nothing I've experienced, Madam." Drasas moaned, and the heavy beat inside her increased tenfold when Anka teased her belt. "Please, Madam?"

Anka grinned and palmed Drasas's crotch. "Please what, Vampire?"

Drasas felt a white-hot heat radiate through her trousers and surge into and around her sex. She pushed back against the wall, as all of her sex was stimulated. Under her clit, she felt incredibly full, and Anka wasn't even touching her directly. "Fuck," Drasas said as she began to thrust her hips in time with the stimulation.

Anka whispered in her ear, "The power you felt there, as you drained and killed the Reaper, is nothing to what is coming, so keep following my orders, and I will give you exactly what you need."

Drasas was starting to lose control at the exquisite pleasure built with Anka's stimulation and words. "Yes, I want it," Drasas groaned. She tried to touch and kiss Anka, but Anka's hand went gently around Drasas's throat to push her back.

"Uh-uh, Vampire. You can't touch me yet. You have still a lot of service to do for me."

Drasas felt the gentle pressure on her throat increase and increase the closer she got to the edge of her orgasm. Instead of panicking her, it made all her sensations increase wildly. Finally she fell off the edge and into an incredible orgasm.

"Anka," Drasas croaked when she found taking a breath difficult. But she almost didn't want it to stop, as her orgasm submerged her in pleasure.

Anka released her hold on Drasas's throat, and Drasas fell to the ground, shaking and gasping for breath. After a few big breaths, Drasas started to regain control. Anka grasped her hair and pulled her head up.

"Did you enjoy that, Vampire?"

"Yes, yes, Madam," Drasas managed to say.

"That is only the beginning of the pleasure I can give you. Do you pledge your life and soul to me, Vampire?"

Drasas would have given her anything at that moment. She grasped Anka's hand with her own shaky one and reverently kissed the back. "I pledge everything to you, Madam. Mind, body, soul."

"Very good."

Anka abruptly let go of her hair and started walking out of the shack. "Let's go, Vampire."

❖

Amelia laughed reluctantly as she lay on her bed with Sera and Katie. Determined to distract Amelia from her worry about Daisy, they played Monopoly, and then Sera found some old photo albums that were in a locked chest in the attic and was talking them through each picture.

"These are just wonderful, Sera."

A large box of chocolates sat within all their reaches. Sera and Katie had cocktails, and Amelia had a virgin Mary. "This was a great idea, girls. I just needed distraction. I'm so worried about Daisy."

Sera clasped her hand. "Byron, Alexis, and Bhal will find her."

Katie said, "Victorija better hope Alexis doesn't find her first. After she turned her, without her consent, she's despised her ever since, not to mention the Dreds killed her first girlfriend."

There was a knock at the door, and one of the guards said to Sera, "Ms. Debrek, there's a phone call for you."

"Okay, I'll just be five minutes, girls."

"Bring some more snacks from the kitchen, will you? I'm really hungry," Amelia said.

"I think baby Debrek is going to be a big baby at this rate," Sera joked.

Sera zoomed downstairs and lifted the phone that sat on a table in the entrance hall.

"Hello?" Sera said.

A shaky voice said, "Hi, Is this Serenity Debrek?"

"The very one. How can I help?"

"My name's Zane. I'm part of Daisy's Monster Hunters group."

Zane? Oh yeah. Zane was the one who was a bit handsy with Daisy, she remembered. "Of course, Zane. How can I help?"

"I've got Daisy here. She needs help—can you come over?"

"Why did she go to you?" Sera asked.

"I was the closest. Um…she's really scared. Could you come over?"

This was Sera's chance to prove her worth to Byron. Her time to shine and show her that she was worthy of the name Debrek.

"I'll be right with you. What's the address?"

She called Henri, her bodyguard, and asked him to gather together a team of five vampires and warriors, while she made sure the guards left in the house were on alert. Sera put the address in her phone's map and raced out of the house with her team of vampires and warriors.

Sera's time was now, and she was going to make Byron proud.

Zane hung up his phone with shaking hands.

Behind him Asha said, "Good choice, Zane. Maybe I won't have to break your neck like your flatmate's there, if you do what I say."

Zane looked down and saw the result of his flatmate Mikey's attempt to help Zane. Asha had killed him, broken his neck with the flick of the wrist.

Asha had his hand at the base of his skull, and Zane believed he would snap his neck just as quickly. When the man had asked him to make a phone call to Serenity Debrek about Daisy, he'd panicked and refused. From what he knew about Byron Debrek, she would hunt him down if anything happened to her sister.

But what choice did he have?

"I will do whatever you want."

Asha took his hand off Zane's neck and walked over to a noticeboard on Zane's bedroom wall. It was covered by photographs of Daisy. Some taken from the Monster Hunter's expeditions, and some taken when Daisy didn't know he was there.

"It's no wonder Daisy can't stand you. You're a coward. A coward who takes secret photos of women?"

Zane felt deep shame. He knew it wasn't right, but he just loved Daisy so much. If she would just give him one date, he could show her how right they could be.

Asha leaned over Zane and said, "You do as I say, you stay alive. Got it?"

Zane nodded.

"And who knows? When this is over, I might give you a chance to see Daisy again."

❖

Byron paced as she, Alexis, and Bhal waited for Brogan to come back. Alexis had offered to go as well, but Brogan said she could work more quickly solo, following the scent alone.

She'd shifted to pelt and her wolf had set out about two hours ago, after she inhaled Daisy's scent from her phone. Alexis got up and started pacing herself. "That's two hours she's been away. Surely she'll be back soon?"

Bhal, who was at the kitchen table, sharpening the sword she kept on her back, said, "Have patience, Duca. Tracking is a tricky business. Even for a wolf."

Just then, they heard a bang from the balcony at the back window. Byron turned around and saw Brogan's wolf nose through the window, which had been left on the latch, and jump onto the floor. Brogan's wolf was impressive by any dominant's standards—big, grey pelt, with a streak of red and brown down her back.

She started to shift back to skin, and Alexis grabbed the jeans and T-shirt Brogan had left on the table. Brogan panted as she stood from all fours, and her skin was covered in a fine sheen of sweat.

"Anything, Brogan?" Byron said.

Brogan pulled on her jeans and T-shirt, and then went to the fridge for a bottle of water. "Yeah, just give me a second." Brogan gulped down the water greedily, and ran her hands through her hair. "Oof, that was a longer hunt than I thought it would be," Brogan said.

"What did you find?" Alexis asked.

Brogan rested her hands on her hips. "I didn't find your friend Daisy, or Victorija, but I did track them to a boating shack down by the river. I've never seen it before. When I arrived, I saw a woman and the vampire Drasas was with her."

"Drasas?" Byron said.

Bhal walked over to them. "Maybe the woman was Anka, Principe?"

"Was she elaborately dressed? Light brown skin with black hair tinged with blond highlights?"

Brogan snapped her fingers. "That's her. Your friend Daisy was there earlier. I came right back to take you over there."

"Let's go," Alexis said.

Byron got in the back seat of the car with Brogan. She leaned forward and said to Bhal, "Go straight ahead for about two miles."

"Aye, will do."

When she sat back, Byron said, "Thank you for doing this for me, Brogan."

"I'm sorry it took so long for me to come to my senses. I missed our friendship."

"As did I, but don't worry about it. Love makes us do funny things," Byron said.

"Well, it won't get me again. I'm not looking for love or a mate."

Byron chuckled. "Sometimes it doesn't take no for an answer." A thought flashed across Byron's mind. "Wait a minute. Alexis? Bhal? A shack by the river—could it be the Reaper?"

"Could well be, Principe," Bhal said.

Alexis turned around in the front passenger seat and asked, "Why would Victorija take Daisy there?"

"No idea, but hopefully we'll find out."

Brogan said, "I never knew there was a Reaper in Paris."

Byron nodded. "Yes, for many years. Our paths have crossed a few times."

The car pulled up by the river, and they all got out of the car.

Byron immediately knew something was wrong. The Reaper's base was in full view. Reapers' homes were always disguised.

"Blood, Principe," Alexis said.

"I smell it, Duca," Byron said.

"Let us go ahead, Principe," Bhal said.

Alexis and Bhal led the way down to the door of the shack. The door was in bits, blown apart by the looks of it.

Bhal took a tentative step inside, followed by Alexis. The smell of blood was getting stronger, and Byron feared the worst. She took a step inside and saw the Reaper, or what was left of him, lying on the floor, black blood seeping from his body.

Around his body, a circle was marked with some symbols. Bhal walked forward and knelt down. "This is Anka's work, Principe, dark magic. It's a message. Anka is back, and she is powerful."

Byron, Brogan, and Alexis joined her at the circle, and Byron said, "Can you imagine the power needed to destroy a Reaper?"

"She's gaining power, Byron," Bhal said.

Alexis knelt beside Bhal. "What do we do?"

"We get back to London quickly," Byron said grimly. "Our clan may be next."

CHAPTER SIXTEEN

Torija organized the plane trip to Scotland with her acquaintance, who was only too pleased to help in exchange for a dark witch that he was looking for. By nighttime, they'd landed in Scotland on a private airfield and were met by a car to be driven to the nearest town.

From there they took a taxi to Daisy's family home on the outskirts of Edinburgh. As the taxi pulled up at Daisy's granny's, Daisy said to Torija, "We'll need to phone Amelia and let her know I'm okay."

Torija did not want that. She wouldn't risk Byron sending her vampires up to Scotland to bring Daisy back to London. Torija needed Daisy to stay here with her grandmother, while she went to London and handed herself over to Byron, where she would meet her death, thus bringing her blood bond with Daisy to an end, and freeing her.

If Daisy came with her to London, it would cause her hurt and pain to see what had to be done, and she didn't want Daisy to lose her bond with the Debreks. They would be her security after Torija was gone.

"Let's just wait till we see how the land lies. We don't want Anka's people being attracted to your grandmother's home."

"Fine, but let me do the talking, okay?"

"Fine by me." Torija paid the driver and got out of the car. She winced in pain and held her arm gingerly. The green poison was now at her shoulder and making its way to her heart. She had tried not to show Daisy how painful it was, and how tired she was. Now that Daisy was sharing her blood, Torija shouldn't be feeling tiredness, whether she was sleeping or not sleeping. It must be the poison. It was weakening her by the second.

Torija heard the front door of the house open, and an older woman called out, "Daisy, thank God."

Daisy ran into her arms, and the woman—her granny—held her tightly, while she stared over her shoulder with anger and distrust at Torija. Torija hung back at the garden gate.

"I was so worried about you. Amelia Debrek called me and told me you were missing. I thought I'd lost you."

Daisy kissed her granny on the cheek. "I'm fine. I had a protector."

"Victorija Dred. One of the worst vampires in the world?" Granny said with anger.

"She *was* Victorija, but she's changing," Daisy said.

Daisy had such faith in her. It was unshakable and made her feel even more for her.

"A vampire changing? I don't think so," Granny said.

"Please, Granny. Let her come in."

"All right, we have some extra protection anyway."

"Who?" Daisy asked.

"Sybil. A powerful witch from the cunning folk coven."

Torija let out a sigh. Sybil had been a thorn in her side more than once. This was going to be difficult.

Daisy took Torija's hand and said, "Come inside."

"I don't know if it's a good idea."

"Please, for me?"

She had to say it, didn't she?

Daisy's granny led the way inside, and Daisy and Torija followed into the kitchen, where Sybil was sitting at the table.

"This is my granddaughter, Daisy," Granny said, "and I think you know this vampire."

"We have crossed swords. Could we have five minutes alone, please?" Sybil said.

"No, we've seen what magic can do, even to a paranormal," Daisy said fiercely.

"You have my word, she will be unharmed."

"It's okay," Torija said. "Sybil and I go a long way back."

Reluctantly Daisy was taken out of the kitchen by her granny.

"Tea?" Sybil said.

"Yes, why not," Torija said.

Sybil lifted the teapot and poured it out into a china cup. "Sit down." She passed the cup and Torija added milk and sugar. Torija took a sip, stalling for time, really.

Torija gulped. "I'm sorry about sending my vampires to try to kill you and what's left of the coven."

Sybil smiled. "Water under the bridge. I was never in danger anyway." The old witch was surely confident in herself. "What made you turn your back on your clan, Vampire? Tell me the truth."

Torija thought carefully before saying, "Three women who believed in me—the Grand Duchess, Angele Brassard, and Daisy MacDougall."

"Lucia never gave up on you. She gave up her life, walked into death, to prove it to you," Sybil said.

"I know, and I don't deserve it."

"Don't be self-pitying—just make best use of this situation. You and Daisy are going to be needed in the forthcoming endeavour against Anka."

"What does Anka truly want?" Torija asked.

"She wants to bring darkness to the world. An ancient dark power gives Anka her magic, and to bring that darkness, she needs the strength of many powerful paranormals. She's travelled all over the world, gaining power from werewolves, witches, fae, shapeshifters, and the last thing she needed was a born vampire. You were it, but she didn't count on you finding your light."

"Daisy is my light," Torija said, "so I have to find a way to break our blood bond. I can't have her saddled with me."

"Why?" Sybil asked. "Her defence of you shows she has feelings for you."

"Feelings for the most evil vampire ever," Torija replied.

Sybil laughed. "Not by a long chalk. You might have thought that in your arrogance, but there have been a lot out there, including your father."

That was true. Gilbert was worse, and sadistic with it. He could strike fear in Torija daily, even after she became a born vampire.

"Why do you really want it broken?" Sybil asked.

Torija rubbed her face with her hands and pulled the answer from the depths of her soul. "I don't know if I can continue to be this vampire, or if I'll become the Victorija from before when I get used to Daisy's blood. I could make her life a living hell like Gilbert did to my mother. I went to ask the Reaper's advice, and he said only death could break a bond."

Sybil took a sip of tea. "He's right. Like your grandmother, you would need to walk willingly to your death. Angele was your beginning, and Daisy will be your end."

Just as Angele had said. Torija's destiny was clear.

❖

"I knew this would happen if you knew the truth about our family," Granny said as she paced around the living room.

"I'm a Brassard, a vampire hunter—you have to let me be who I was meant to be," Daisy said.

Granny covered her mouth with her hand. "I can't believe you just let the Dred vampires take you. You could be dead or living in misery as a Victorija Dred blood donor the rest of your life."

Daisy walked over to her granny and said, "But I'm not. I'm not because I believed in Angele Brassard, our ancestor. She showed me Victorija's life, what shaped her into what she was today, but also that there was still light in her soul. Sybil must have told you that Lucia Debrek agreed."

"She did, but remember—Victorija ripped her grandmother's heart from her body, so forgive me if I'm worried about you having faith in a Dred vampire." Granny stayed quiet for a minute, then said, "Why did it have to be you?"

"It couldn't be anyone else, Granny. I'm a Brassard, and Angele chose to tell her story to me."

"I can't bear to lose you to a vampire, too, Daisy," Granny pleaded.

"Torija saved me. The Dred vampires were after me, as well as Anka's people, but Torija saved me. She kept a long-held vow to a young Brassard she loved when she was seventeen. Can you imagine how hard that must have been for her?"

"Nothing can truly replace a vampire's lust for blood."

"I'm giving it with consent. Torija is behaving with consent."

"How do I know this isn't just your blood bond talking?" Granny asked.

"I suppose you'll need to trust me, Granny. I need to get back to Torija, but I promise she won't hurt me."

❖

Daisy came marching into the kitchen. "What's going on? Don't do anything to her, Sybil. She's changed."

"I see that." Sybil smiled and leaned back in her seat. "I can see why Angele Brassard chose you to take on the formidable Victorija Dred. No one else would have the courage to stand up to her."

"It's okay, Daisy. We were just having a chat."

"Did you ask her about the poison?" Daisy asked.

"I was just going to when you came in, guns blazing," Torija said.

"Go on then."

Daisy and her granny sat down, while Torija stripped off her jacket and shirt. She held out her arm.

"Come closer," Sybil said.

Torija stepped right up to her and pulled her sports bra to the side, so Sybil could see the green, now just above her breast.

"Indeed, that's poison. If it reaches your heart, it will be poisoned, born vampire or not."

"How did she get it?" Daisy asked.

"From you, when she bit you."

"What? How?"

"To answer that I'll have to tell you a story."

Torija put her shirt back on and took a seat.

"Daisy, I understand you and your Monster Hunters were at the Beltane festival," Sybil said.

"Yeah, in Edinburgh. Why?"

"It's a modern retelling of an ancient Celtic festival, whose two main characters are the May Queen and the Green Man."

Daisy butted in enthusiastically, "The Horned God, or the winter aspect of the Green Man sees the May Queen." She slowed her storytelling, took Torija's hand, and said more softly, "When he sees the May Queen in her maiden form, he realizes that to be with the woman he loves, he must undergo a complete change."

"I'm the Green Man?" Torija said to Sybil.

"Indeed, and that's why you were destined to meet. Daisy is your poison, but she also leads you to your cure."

"What is the cure?" Daisy asked.

"Victorija must face her misdeeds, must face the untold pain and destruction she caused," Sybil said.

"How does she do that?"

"That's for Victorija to find out."

While Daisy tried to find information on the net about the myth of the great witch Anka, Torija went downstairs to find a drink. There was only a bottle of vodka in the cupboard, so she poured out a generous glass and sat down at the kitchen table.

Not long later, Daisy's granny came into the kitchen.

"Sorry, I just came for a drink." Torija held up her glass. "I hope you don't mind."

"I don't care about the drink. I want to know what you are up to and what you're going to do next."

"I'm not up to anything. I'm simply bringing Daisy back to safety," Torija said.

Margaret Brassard got a glass and poured out a drink for herself. "We both know Victorija Dred will eventually be pulled towards the darkness."

"I suppose so."

"So what are you going to do about it?"

Torija emptied her glass and stood. "I'll leave her here for safety, and then I will deal with it."

"There's only one way, you know."

"I do," Torija said solemnly, "I'll take care of it."

Torija left the room and walked upstairs. She walked into Daisy's bedroom and found her tapping away on her iPad. Her brown hair cascaded over her bare shoulders. She was beautiful.

Torija hadn't seen the beauty in things or people in a long time, but she was now, as Daisy had awakened her from her darkness.

Daisy looked up from her screen. "Where did you get to?"

"I just wanted a drink."

"Well, come here, I've got lots to show you. I found some information on the myth of the witch Anka."

Torija felt claustrophobic. The room's walls were closing in on her just as Daisy's expectations were. She walked over to the window and opened it, hoping the fresh, cold Scottish air would help.

Daisy carried on, regardless. "If I'm one of these descendant people with Amelia, I'm to help bring together the paranormals who are on the edge, so they choose the path of light, like you."

The pressure in Torija's head was increasing by the second, aided and abetted by the stinging pain travelling around her veins, and heading for her heart.

"Tor? Come to bed. We've got a lot of work to do."

Torija shook her head and muttered, "It's all so easy, isn't it?"

"What? What's wrong, Tor?" She didn't answer, but she heard Daisy get out of bed and walk up behind her. "Torija? What's wrong? Tell me."

Torija didn't turn around but kept staring out of the window. "You think it's easy."

"What's so easy?" Daisy asked.

"Attracting people like me to the cause of good, reaching out to them." Torija felt like she had a tight band around her head and chest, squeezing the breath out of her.

"Not easy, but doable. Nobody would have given you a hope, and yet here we are."

Torija spun around to face Daisy. "Worked for me? In case you haven't noticed, I have poison taking over my body because of my misdeeds, and it will kill me."

"You just have to face your past."

"Just? Just? I don't think you have the first idea who I am and what I've done. I've killed countless, I've maimed, I've hurt, and you think I'm redeemed just because you say so? I'm Victorija Dred, and I can never make up for what I've done."

Torija ran out the door and fled the house.

Daisy pulled on some shoes and her leather biker jacket, then hurried downstairs after Torija. She was in a panic. She had pushed Torija too far, too fast.

What if she hurt someone?

By the time Daisy got outside into the black of the night, she thought maybe the nightie and leather jacket left her a bit underdressed. Her granny's house was in a relatively rural area without many street lamps. The road was lit up, but the fields and trees on either side of the road were shrouded in darkness.

Daisy hugged herself and shivered. She was more than slightly vulnerable, and to top it off her spidey sense was tingling. Daisy had noticed they were getting stronger since her bond with Torija.

Someone out there in the dark was watching, and she prayed it was Torija. Everything was telling her to go back inside the house, but Daisy couldn't risk Torija running. Maybe she was already gone.

This was her one task, set to her by the Grand Duchess, Angele, and destiny, and it seemed she was on the verge of failing. She took a deep breath and walked around the perimeter of the house. Daisy's heart was pounding. When she reached the back of the house, the security light came on just as a male with vampire teeth and red eyes launched at her.

Out of nowhere, Torija was with her and held the male by the neck and stared into his eyes. "Who sent you?"

"Anka."

"When you recover from the broken neck I'm going to give you, you'll disappear, forget who and what you found here, and tell Anka that you'd heard Victorija Dred and Daisy were still in France."

Daisy watched with bated breath as Torija easily dealt with the intruder. She could see how much stronger and faster Torija was than the normal turned vampire. She squeezed her eyes shut when she heard the vampire's neck snap. Even though she knew the vampire would heal, it was still horrible to watch.

When she opened her eyes, Torija was in front of her, breathing heavily, teeth elongated, and wild looking.

"Why are you out here on your own? It's dark."

"I was looking for you, I wanted to talk—I didn't mean to upset you in the bedroom."

"Look at you. You're in a nightdress and not much else."

"I didn't want to risk losing you."

"For your noble cause as a descendant?" Torija asked.

Daisy reached for Torija's cheek. "No, for you, for my heart."

Torija closed her eyes and shook her head.

Daisy cupped both of Torija's cheeks and said, "You were right upstairs. I don't know all you've done, but I know who you were because of Angele and your grandmother, and I know who you are becoming because I see it in your actions, in your eyes, and in your heart. Maybe you're right—maybe you have done unforgivable things, but you can spend the rest of your immortal life doing good, and that's the vampire I'm falling in love with."

Torija looked stunned and opened her mouth, but no words came out at first. Then she moved her lips close to Daisy's and whispered, "How do you love a monster?"

Daisy's fingers caressed Torija's cheeks. "By taking their mask off." She then kissed Torija gently, and Torija's lips were so soft, Daisy melted into them.

Torija's kisses became more intense. "I want you," Torija said.

Daisy wanted Torija, too. She was aching to be touched by her. Daisy took her hand and said, "Follow me." When they got up to Daisy's bedroom, Daisy locked the door. "My granny's room is on the other side of the house, but we still need to be quiet."

Torija pulled off her clothes quickly. She was going to be leaving when Daisy fell asleep and wanted to love every part of her before she left. Daisy took off her nightie, and Torija lifted and carried her over to the bed.

Daisy pulled Torija's head down into a kiss. Torija feverishly kissed her way down to Daisy's breasts. She sucked in Daisy's nipple and grazed it with her fang. Daisy showed her she liked that by pushing the back of Torija's head down onto her breast and grasping her hand and putting it onto her sex.

Daisy was already so wet for her. Torija split her fingers and stroked the outside of her clit.

"Don't tease me, Tor. I need to feel you inside," Daisy said.

Torija left Daisy's breasts and went back up to her lips. Daisy's hips were jerking, trying to encourage her to slip her fingers inside.

"Is that what you want?" Torija asked.

Daisy moaned and said, "God, yeah. I want it so deep. I wish we were in my flat in London."

"Why?"

"I have a new strap-on in my bedside drawer. I've always wanted someone I cared about to use it on me. I want you so deep inside me."

"Then I'll give you deep."

Torija shuffled back on her knees, then lifted Daisy's legs over her shoulders.

"What are you doing?"

"Just relax. I'm giving you what you want."

Torija pulled Daisy back further so that her buttocks were virtually resting on Torija's thighs.

Daisy was watching her carefully and breathing hard. "Tor?"

Torija kissed Daisy's ankle tenderly while giving her clit a few more strokes before she slowly pressed two fingers inside her.

"Shit." Daisy's hips jerked.

"Relax, slowly." Torija started a gentle thrust and inched deeper every time. The sensation must have been intense, going by Daisy's reactions. She was grasping and squeezing her own breasts and thrusting her hips along with Torija's.

Torija was going to remember every detail of this moment. The pleasure on Daisy's face, and her beauty. Her willingness to trust and give herself to a truly frightening vampire, as everyone else saw her.

Her fingers were now fully in, and she quickened the pace.

"It's too much," Daisy moaned.

"It's never too much. Just let go, cherie."

Daisy threw her hand over her face, and her legs started to shake on Torija's shoulders.

"That's it, let it go, my love," Torija said as she felt Daisy's walls flutter around her fingers.

What a beautiful sight this was, Daisy overcome with her impending orgasm, breasts bouncing with every thrust of her hips, and then her head thrown back as the rest of her body went rigid.

Torija smiled when she saw Daisy put her hand on her mouth to stop the loud noise she naturally wanted to make, with her grandmother not too far away. She slowed her fingers, eased them out, and gently put Daisy's legs down.

Daisy's body was shaking. Torija got up to her quickly and pulled her into her arms.

"Oh God," Daisy said breathily. "That was intense."

"Being with a vampire is intense." Torija said, kissing Daisy's brow.

When Daisy calmed a little, she said, "Did I hear you say *my love* when we were making love?"

It would be easier to brush it off, since she was leaving, but Torija didn't want Daisy to doubt how Torija felt.

"Yes, I did. Je t'adore."

Chapter Seventeen

One of Anka's were guards opened the door to an old disused garage. Anka's high heels clattered on the dirty floor. She looked down at it with disgust and walked on until she reached a pacing Serenity Debrek. Serenity's bodyguard and the rest of her people were unconscious and being held in a casting circle over in the corner.

"What is this about, Anka?"

Asha was standing a few paces away. Anka nodded to him and sat down on a seat that was prepared for her.

"You know my name then, Serenity? Won't you take a seat."

"No, thank you." Sera kept looking at a TV screen Anka had put up.

Anka took off her leather gloves slowly. "If you insist, but you'd be more comfortable."

Sera, instead of sitting, leaned on the back of the chair. "So, what do you want?"

"Want from you?" Anka chuckled. "Nothing from you. You are simply the bait. I need a powerful born vampire."

"I'm a born vampire, if you hadn't noticed. Now let *them* go." Sera pointed up at the TV screen. On it were five men and women who looked terrified. Each was holding a knife to their throat.

"Ingenious, isn't it? That was the one problem I had. How to trap a born vampire—stronger, faster, than any other vampire—and keep them compliant and under control? The answer for a Debrek born vampire, who believes in the value of humans and consent and other such disgustingly pious ideas, was simple: test those pious ideas."

Sera sat down in frustration and crossed her legs and arms, thoroughly pissed off. "Can we get to the point?"

"I understand that Asha explained to you that these humans are locked in a room somewhere in this building."

"Yes, yes," Sera said.

"And that they have been compelled to cut their own throats, at one press of a button by Asha, or me, or any one of my people around this place. When those people see a flashing red light, they will go through with it. You couldn't possibly get there on time."

Sera gave Anka a sarcastic handclap. "Good for you. I'm obviously not going to risk that, so you've caught me. Well done."

Anka laughed at her attitude. "Poor Sera. The ditzy blond airhead born vampire, who loves partying more than serious work."

"You don't know anything about me," Sera spat back.

Anka leaned forward. "I know more about you than you think. You were a spoiled child before you became a born vampire at eighteen, and still are spoiled. Everyone indulges you." She was getting to Sera, Anka could tell. She stood up and started to casually walk around Sera's chair. "You were the pretty girl, the second child that had no role in the Debrek banking business and could never live up to the magnificent and shining Byron Debrek."

"I love my sister. She is the perfect leader."

Anka moved around to Sera's front, leaned over, and whispered, "The charismatic leader, who will always outshine you, but I understand that. I had an older brother who outshone me until I found a way to outshine him. But you? I doubt it."

"Are you going to just run down my character or tell me what this is about?"

Anka walked back to her chair, picked up her leather gloves, and slowly pulled them back on, one by one. "You wanted to know why you weren't the born vampire I wanted, why you were just the bait, and I'm telling you why. Your great-aunt Victorija and your sister Byron will always be better than you, because they have a darkness in their souls that makes them ruthless, but you? You're more concerned with drinking cocktails with your friends in Monaco, or skiing in St. Moritz, or saving puppies or whales or kittens."

Sera said nothing but glared angrily.

"Your great-aunt Victorija I thought would be the easiest target, since your sister is the most powerful vampire on earth, but I didn't expect her to feel compelled to save her blood bond, Daisy MacDougall."

Sera was shocked. "What? Victorija saved Daisy?"

"Hmm…quite annoyingly, yes. I don't know what came over her. They are on the run together as we speak."

Sera laughed with surprise. "Wow, I'd never have thought Victorija had it in her."

"My only option was to go for Byron, which was always going to be trickier. Hence why I needed you as bait."

"Why do you need a born vampire anyway?" Sera asked.

Anka smiled. "To bring on the darkness, of course."

"Byron will kill you, you know."

"People have been trying that for centuries, but I always come back." Anka started to walk away. "Sit tight, Serenity. Your time will come."

Daisy's eyes flickered open, and she heard shuffling around the room. She saw Torija packing a bag and trying to be as quiet as possible. Daisy got a sinking feeling.

She sat up quickly and said, "What the hell are you doing?"

Torija sighed and swore under her breath. "Go back to sleep."

Daisy jumped up and crossed the room to Torija. "I bloody will not. What are you doing?"

"I'm going to find someone who can give me death."

"But our plan was to go to Byron's tomorrow," Daisy said.

"It wasn't *my* plan. I always had the intention of leaving you with your grandmother."

"What?" Daisy was shocked and angry. "Why?"

Torija zipped up her bag and then turned to cup Daisy's cheek. "Because I don't want you shackled to me for all time. I want you to have a normal happy life, and I don't trust that I won't let the darkness take me over again."

"I won't let you do this," Daisy said firmly.

"You don't have a choice. I move too fast. I'll be out of here before you know it."

"I'll come after you, or I'll let Anka capture me," Daisy said.

Torija turned back to her bag and put it over her shoulder.

"Is that what last night was about? Was it a goodbye?" Torija kept silent, which made Daisy panic more. "You know I'll be in much more danger when I follow you."

"You won't follow me," Torija said.

"Won't? Why?" Daisy had a sinking feeling. She went to grasp for her necklace that protected her from compulsion, and it wasn't there. "No, no—tell me you haven't."

Torija turned back to her, holding her necklace.

"You took it while I was sleeping?" The shock and hurt made tears come to Daisy's eyes.

"I had to. I'm doing this to protect you."

"You're insane," Daisy shouted. "If you ever cared about me, you'll take me with you."

Torija put the necklace down and tried to take hold of Daisy. Daisy pulled away, but Torija was too quick and got hold of Daisy and compelled her to stay still. She cupped Daisy's cheeks and stared into her eyes that were flowing with tears.

Daisy didn't move but she could talk. "Please don't do this, Tor. I love you. Don't make me forget what we are to each other."

Torija was in torment. This was the hardest thing she'd ever had to do, and it was tearing her apart inside. She also had tears come to her eyes. "I'm sorry. This is the hardest thing I've ever had to do, and I'm doing it because I love you with all my heart."

Daisy was distraught. "We were supposed to fight the darkness together. Please don't do this."

Torija's eyes bored into Daisy, and she said the words silently to herself. *You'll forget that you loved me. You'll stay here with your grandmother and have a happy life.*

Now she just had to say them out loud, but the words were caught in her throat.

"Please, Tor. If you love me, don't do this," Daisy said again.

Torija's hands shook, and then she released Daisy, suddenly.

Daisy leaned over, touching her knees, trying to her get her breath back. "Don't you ever try anything like that, ever again."

"I'm sorry." Torija handed her back her necklace, and Daisy put it on straight away. "I won't."

"Swear on my life that you won't do it again," Daisy said, fighting back the tears.

"I swear on your life that I won't try to compel you again. Forgive me? I'm just frightened I'll go back to the darkness, or that the enemies who follow me will try to hurt you," Torija said.

Daisy threw her arms around Torija's neck. "I love you, and we'll face anything together."

"I love you," Torija said.

"So we'll use one of Granny's cars and drive to the Debreks' home, in the morning."

"Yes, I promise."

Byron paced as Amelia spoke to Daisy's friend Skye on the phone. She had discovered on returning from France that Sera had left the house with her guards and gone in search of Daisy. Amelia had said Sera had been contacted by Daisy's friend Zane, who'd said that Daisy was with him.

Byron knew how eager Sera was to prove herself, but she couldn't help but worry about her. Sera would always be her baby sister.

Amelia finished her call and said, "Skye hasn't heard anything from Zane and can't get him to answer his phone. One thing she did know was that Zane thought he was in love with Daisy, obsessed with her."

"But if it's this boy Zane," Byron said, "then he is no match for Sera and our vampires. Why isn't she back home with Daisy, and why can't we get hold of her on her phone?"

Amelia shook her head despondently. "I don't know."

Bhal came striding into the drawing room. "Sera's idiot bodyguard is clearly not doing his job."

Byron could tell how worried and angry she was. Bhal always made it her personal responsibility to keep Sera safe and train her to be the best Debrek she could be, but Sera butted heads with her because of this. But Bhal did care for her, and Byron suspected that's why she was hard on Sera.

"It's not Henri's fault, Bhal. She wanted the responsibility to lead and protect our home, and I'm sure there's a reason why they aren't back as yet." Byron tried to sound as calm as possible, but inside she felt such a deep fear for Sera. If only she had been here.

"She should have waited until we returned," Bhal said with frustration.

Amelia squeezed Bhal's arm. "She was trying to do the right thing. She was being a Debrek, Bhal."

"My sister doesn't think, she just responds. Mother and Father are going to be beside themselves with worry. We need to find her."

Bhal walked up to Byron and said fiercely, "That is why Henri is at fault. I would never have let her get into this position."

Byron frowned. This wasn't like Bhal.

Bhal seemed to realize her mistake and said, "I'm sorry, Principe. I'm just so—"

"It's all right, old friend. I know."

Just at that, Byron's phone beeped with a text message. "It's Anka. Anka has Sera," Byron growled. "If she so much as puts a finger on my sister, I will hunt her down for the rest of my life."

Bhal added, "I will be at your side, Principe, and I will take Anka's head from her shoulders."

"What does the text say, Byron?" Amelia asked.

"If you play along, Serenity won't be harmed. I want a strong born vampire, and since I can't get my hands on Victorija Dred, you will have to do. I'll be back in touch soon about the exchange."

"I can't lose you, too, Byron," Amelia said with worry in her voice.

Byron pulled Amelia into her arms. "You are not going to lose me. I'm Byron Debrek, and no dark witch is going to hurt my family."

"I will die before Byron or Sera is harmed, Principessa," Bhal said passionately.

Alexis came striding into the room. "All our people are on alert. If someone comes for us, they won't last long."

"Thank you, Duca."

"Everything's so confusing," Amelia said. "Daisy and Sera going missing, and Victorija—who knows what's going on with her."

Byron kissed Amelia's brow. "We'll get to the bottom of it, I promise, and all will be well."

CHAPTER EIGHTEEN

"Put your foot down, for God's sake. You're driving like an old woman," Torija said.

Daisy looked to the passenger seat of her granny's car and gripped the steering wheel tightly. They had left her granny's house at the crack of dawn this morning, to drive down to London. Although Daisy and Torija had sorted out the near-ending of their relationship last night, things were tense between them. They were five hours into their journey, and Torija had been getting worse, mentally and physically.

"I'm not going to reply to that comment because you're in pain."

"Oh, how good of you. I don't know why you wouldn't let me drive." Just at that moment she clutched her shoulder and grimaced in pain.

"Well, for one, you're ill and in pain. Two, you don't have a driving licence."

"Vampires can't exactly apply for a licence. *When were you born?* Hmm, quite a number of centuries ago."

Daisy just replied with, "And three, you were born in a time when the fastest vehicle was a horse and cart. So just calm your jets, as we say in Scotland, and we'll be there in no time."

Torija shifted uncomfortably in her seat. "You know I'm not an expert on love, but aren't you supposed to be nicer?"

"Look, it'll just be a little while longer."

Five hours later, they arrived in London, and things were even more tense. Torija was in pain and, having been stuck in the car for all that time, was deeply uncomfortable. Her mood was also dark because she knew what she was walking into. They found a place to leave the car and walked the final mile to the Debrek house.

"Don't be nervous, okay? I'll explain everything," Daisy said.

"Born vampires don't get nervous."

As Daisy and Torija walked down the early morning London streets to the Debrek mansion, nerves weren't what Torija was feeling, but resignation and sadness that she was leaving Daisy, the Brassard that saved her.

The Reaper and Sybil both told her that she had to walk willingly into death to be redeemed, and that's what she was doing. After all she had done, Byron would take her head and her heart. She would then face those she had harmed in the next world, till the end of time, no doubt.

They approached the steps to the house, and Daisy said, "Stay out of sight for a second. There's cameras on the front door, and I need time to explain before they go crazy." Daisy went up the steps and pressed a buzzer on the door, then waved at the camera above the door. "Hi, it's Daisy." The door lock clicked, and Daisy turned to her and said, "Give me five minutes."

Daisy disappeared through the door. This was Torija's moment. Walk willingly into death? She ran in so fast, she arrived in the middle of the entrance hall before Daisy.

"I told you to stay outside," Daisy said with annoyance.

"Born vampires don't follow orders."

Daisy rolled her eyes. "It's really quiet. Normally there's vamps all around."

The front hall area was empty, but not for long, Torija knew. "Give it a minute, and there'll be vampires everywhere." Time to do the right thing. Torija dropped to her knees and put her hands behind her back in a sign of surrender.

"What are you doing?" Daisy asked.

"Trust me." Ten seconds later there were guns pointed around her head. "You do know I'm immortal—"

Before she could finish her sentence, Torija found herself flying through the air and smashing into the wall. Plaster and brick crumbled around her as she slid to the floor. Immortal or not, being smashed against a wall by another vampire still hurt.

Torija tasted blood in her mouth and spat it onto the floor. She heard Daisy's voice saying, "No, please wait. She saved me—"

But the vampire who had thrown her so hard wasn't listening. Alexis was bearing down on her, with pure red fury shining from her eyes. She lifted her again and smashed her repeatedly into the wall. "Fight back, what's wrong with you?"

"I won't fight you, Alexis." Torija coughed up blood on the floor.

Daisy ran over and used herself as a human shield. "Stop, Alexis."

"Get out of the way, Daisy. She turned me and killed my girlfriend."

"Please give us a chance to explain," Daisy said.

"Duca?" Byron's booming voice cut across the chaos of the scene. "Stop."

Alexis was breathing heavily. Torija didn't blame Alexis. She had years of resentment piling on top of her.

Then Bhal was on her with her sword at her throat. "Where is Sera?"

"Sera? What?"

She had never seen Bhal like this, pure rage radiating from her. Normally she was a calm, cool warrior.

"Bhal, please, let me explain," Daisy tried again.

Byron touched Bhal's shoulder. "Step back, Bhal. She is clearly not with her clan any more."

"Alex!" One of Byron's staff came downstairs with Amelia and ran over to Alexis. "Calm down. Let Byron deal with this."

"You know what she did," Alexis spat.

The way this woman was touching Alexis suggested she had found a new love at last.

Byron stepped in front of them all and gazed down at Torija. "Katie, take Amelia and Daisy upstairs."

"Not bloody likely," Amelia said.

"I'm not letting you hurt her, Byron," Daisy added.

It was such a strange experience to have someone care enough to try to protect her. Torija liked it. Daisy was worth the sacrifice of her immortal life. She deserved so much more than Torija could give her. She spat more blood from her mouth onto the hall floor, then smiled up at Byron. "Hello, niece."

She was met with stony silence, then, "No one will harm her for the moment." Byron pointed to two of her nearest vampires and said, "Take her down to the holding room."

"Yes, Principe."

They helped Torija to her feet, and Daisy held onto her arm. "Don't take her away. She's not who she was—she's changed."

"Victorija Dred will never change," Alexis shouted.

Byron held her hand up, bringing the argument to an end. "She will be safe. We just need to find out what's been happening with Daisy."

"I will be okay, mon cherie. Let me go."

Daisy's great courage was displayed to Torija again when she pointed at Byron, the most powerful vampire in the world, and said, "If anything happens to her, I'm holding you responsible."

Byron raised an eyebrow, then nodded. "Very well."

"You have to believe me. She's not Victorija Dred any more."

Daisy paced up and down in front of the dining table as the group tried to understand what was going on. Alexis was not seated, but leaning against the wall, with her arms folded, steam nearly coming out her ears, while Byron, Amelia, Bhal, and Katie sat around the table.

"It's just your blood bond talking. She's manipulating you," Alexis said angrily.

Daisy was so frustrated. How could she explain what she and Torija had been through? "Nobody can manipulate me, Vamp," Daisy replied, equally as angrily.

Katie jumped up and said to Alexis, "Alex, let Daisy explain."

Daisy came back to the table and leaned on the top. "I don't know how else to explain." She let out a big sigh. "Byron, you said you'd heard of the Brassard family of vampire hunters."

"Yes, the Brassards and the Debreks have crossed paths at one time or another, but once my family enshrined the value of consent into our beliefs, we came to a truce. I never connected you to the Brassards because of your MacDougall family name."

"Yeah, my mum was a Brassard. I didn't know until recently that they were both killed by a vampire. My granny always told me they died in car accidents. She lied to me, but somehow I was always drawn to this other world."

Amelia sat forward in her seat. "I'm sure she thought she was doing the right thing to protect you. I was in the same boat. Sybil and my parents—adopted parents—thought it was safer for me not to know I was born a witch."

"I know, but I just wish I would have known sooner. People always made fun of me because I believed in this world. Now look at me, surrounded by vampires."

"Tell us what you found out about Victorija," Amelia said.

Amelia felt she had to be the voice of reason here. Since Sera had been taken by Anka, Byron, Alexis, and Bhal had been so emotionally charged.

"Granny gave me a chest with lots of family heirlooms. One of them was a locked notebook. Granny said every Brassard has tried to open it but couldn't. I opened it easily."

"Do you think you were meant to open it, then?" Byron asked.

"I must have. That's when the enchantment kicked in." Daisy began to explain that she was pulled into Angele's memories.

"It's strange. I can't picture my great-aunt as a young, vulnerable seventeen-year-old," Byron said.

"She had a terrible start to life. Angele helped her, gave her hope, taught her to love," Daisy said.

Bhal then piped up. "We all have bad times in our lives. How can she possibly redeem herself from what she has done?"

Amelia was impressed when Daisy replied quickly, "That's my job. She has to face what's she's done."

"Principe? The blood bond," Alexis said. "It must be having an effect on Daisy."

"I suspect the same. Daisy, I have to question your blood bond. You left safety here and allowed yourself to be picked up by Victorija's vampires," Byron said.

Daisy sighed and sat down. "I'm sorry I took off without telling you, but I trusted what Angele and the Grand Duchess were telling me. I had to take a chance, and it was worth it. Torija chose me over her clan. She tricked them just to get me to safety, and now the Dreds and Anka are looking for her as well as me."

Byron got up and started to pace at the head of the table. "The Grand Duchess did leave a letter for me after her death. She implored me to give Victorija a chance, to pull her back from the darkness."

"That's what I tried to do," Daisy said.

"Of course, she did rip the heart out of her grandmother, the Grand Duchess," Byron said.

"I know. It haunts her, but Lucia said it was her destiny. She had to walk willingly into death, because she should have tried to get Torija and her mother away from Gilbert's cruelty. Please, at least talk to her."

Amelia saw Alexis shaking her head, and Bhal was staring at the table, lost in her thoughts and worries. Bhal was taking Sera's disappearance badly. She had spent most of her long, long life protecting and teaching Byron and Sera and was bound to feel deeply for them both.

"I will speak to her," Byron said. "Bhal, Alexis? You're with me."

As they left, Amelia said to Katie, "Could you give us a few minutes, Katie?"

"Yeah, of course," Katie said.

When she and Daisy were left alone, Amelia said, "You know how worried I was about you? You're like the little sister I've never had."

"I'm sorry. I didn't mean to worry everyone. I just knew no one would let me go, but I had to—I had to see if what Angele and Lucia said was true."

Amelia rubbed her baby bump in a soothing fashion. "It's just so hard to accept this Victorija. Although…"

"What?" Daisy asked.

"Remember she took me out to dinner when Byron and I were broken up?"

"Yeah?"

"Victorija told me she had felt every kind of pain there was, and on that one thing, I could see truthfulness in her eyes."

"She has. What she went through as a teenager…I watched her howl in pain when her dad, Gilbert, made Angele take her own life in front of her. After years of watching her mum be abused and the mental and physical abuse Torija endured, that day just broke her soul and nearly snuffed out all the light in it."

"You really care about her? And you're sure it's not the blood bond?" Amelia asked.

"I fell for who she was, the woman I saw in the notebook vision, but then I met the real Torija, who was still there under that monster mask she wore. She's the vampire that honoured an oath made centuries ago, the vampire who turned against her own clan because of me and was willing to suffer pain, illness, and death, rather than take my blood—and I'm falling even harder. Please trust me, Amelia?"

"I do, and if we are the descendants who were foretold to bring the paranormal world together, against Anka and whoever she serves, then it makes sense. I bring the witch and vampire community together, and you bring those vampire clans, paranormals whose sympathies normally lie with Victorija's way of thinking, and the vampire hunters."

"I don't even know who the families of vampire hunters are. My family history is so new to me. There's so much we have to do if we're going to be ready for what's ahead."

"I'm pregnant. Not exactly ideal for fighting an ancient evil."

Daisy took her hand. "You're a powerful witch, and we will all be beside you."

"Together?" Amelia said seriously.

Daisy repeated the pledge. "Together."

Byron's stride was fast as she made her way downstairs to the holding room. Bhal and Alexis were keeping pace behind her. Her mind was whizzing with worry, fear, and dread. The fear she'd felt on receiving word that Sera was with Anka was overwhelming.

It was bad enough when Victorija took Amelia. At the very least Byron knew what she was dealing with, with Victorija and the Dreds. But now that Anka had the Dreds under her control, along with her own people, she was a much more dangerous enemy.

Behind her, Bhal and Alexis were talking back and forth in panicked tones. It wasn't like them, especially Bhal, but Sera's kidnapping had been a shock to everyone. They arrived at the holding cell.

Byron turned around and said, "I'll go in myself."

"But—" Alexis started to say, but Byron silenced her with a wave of her hand.

"I'll go in myself. You'll be outside if I need you."

They both nodded, and one of the vampires by the door unlocked it for Byron.

"Thank you," Byron said. She walked into the cell to find Victorija lying back on the bed, with her arm shielding her eyes.

Without moving a muscle, Victorija said, "You really must redecorate in here. It's quite dull and dreary."

"I'll file that on my to-do list," Byron said, "but for now I want you to tell me why you're here."

Victorija sat up. "Is that any way to greet your great-aunt?"

Byron walked to the other side of the room and brought a chair over to the bed.

"It is when that great-aunt has maimed and killed many of my clan. In fact, you should be lucky you're just sitting in a cell. Every member of my clan would gladly destroy you." Byron sat on the chair, crossed her legs, and looked at Victorija with a steady gaze. "Why are you here, and why did you save Daisy?"

Torija clasped her hands and gazed down at her shoes. "I saved her and turned my back on my clan because I made an oath to someone I loved, a long time ago."

"Forgive me for sounding sceptical, but love has never been an emotion that I associate with Victorija Dred."

"I didn't believe it either, but apparently three women, much more in touch with their emotions, have told me that. My first love Angele, Lucia, and now Daisy."

"You killed the Grand Duchess, your own grandmother—how can you move on or be forgiven for that?"

Victorija looked up at Byron and said, "I don't think I can be, but those three women seem to think I can do the right thing, and I'm trying."

"Daisy is upstairs trying to convince everyone of that fact."

"She is exceptionally stubborn and determined," Victorija said.

"Are you sure this isn't the blood bond talking?"

"Yes, but the bond is why I'm here. Daisy doesn't know about this, but I want to break this bond."

Byron should have expected that much at least from Victorija. "So you can go back to your normal life, whilst keeping your word not to harm a Brassard?"

"You should know there's no breaking this bond. I went to see the Reaper in Paris, and I consulted with the Grand Duchess in spirit. They both confirmed there is no way to break it, or to gain forgiveness for past misdeeds. If I want both of those things, then I must walk willingly into death, and I knew coming here—after everything I've done to the

Debrek clan—that you would take my head and my heart. Then Daisy will be released from her blood obligation, and I will face what I have to on the other side."

Byron sat forward in her seat. "This is either an elaborate trick, or Daisy has really changed you."

"She changed me. She made me believe I could still be the person I was before I became a born vampire."

Byron was hugely sceptical. She wanted to believe it, but she found it difficult. Her mobile phone rang, and she stood quickly when she saw an unknown number. It had to be Anka. She accepted the call. "Byron Debrek."

Torija looked on as Byron paced up and down.

Byron said, "You better not harm her." Byron cut off the call. "Fucking Anka."

"What's happening?"

"Nothing of your concern," Byron said.

"Anything to do with Anka is my concern. She stole my clan, wants Daisy dead, and turned my Duca against me."

"Drasas?" Byron said.

Torija nodded. "She's driven by power. That's how she became my Duca—she killed all her rivals." Byron was silent for a few moments, and Torija filled the gap. "Tell me. You have me locked up—what difference would telling me make?"

"It was Anka's associate Asha. Anka wants a born vampire. It was meant to be you, but since they no longer have you, they took Sera, so I would give myself up to Anka."

"Of course, she gets a sniff of getting the most powerful born vampire, and she's taking it."

"It's not like you to admit I'm the strongest vampire," Byron said.

"Well, I'm becoming a different vampire, it seems." She watched Byron rub her forehead, considering what to do. "What are you thinking?" Torija asked.

"When I give myself up and meet my end...Amelia is pregnant. I'll never see them again, and I won't be there to protect her."

Torija walked over to Byron. "You will be, because I'm going to go."

"What? No. This is not going to be an opportunity for you to rejoin your friends."

"They are not my friends, they want Daisy dead, and I can't allow that to happen. I will take Sera's place. I can make up for some of the hurt I caused, break the blood bond so that Daisy can have a normal life, and I will be able to face those I've hurt along the way."

Byron shook her head in disbelief. "Victorija Dred wouldn't do that."

"No, she wouldn't do that, but Torija would. Let me do this. It's important for me to do this. Besides, I am the senior in the family here."

Byron considered her offer silently.

"Let me do this, Byron, please?" It took a lot for Torija to beg her former enemy, but her whole world had been turned upside down and shaken about.

"If you do this and Sera is freed, then you will die a Debrek, not a Dred."

"Thank you." This felt like how her life as Victorija Dred was meant to end.

"You give me your word?" Byron asked.

"Listen, Anka needs a born vampire, and I'm it. You need to look after the descendants and make sure Daisy is okay, and Sera. It should be me—it was meant to be me. I'm going to continue to get sick—Sybil says I'm like the Celtic Green Man. I need to walk into death for forgiveness. Let me do one good thing in my life. Remember I'm your great-aunt."

"That you are. Daisy believes in you. You've made quite the impression on her."

Torija smiled. "She sees me through romantic eyes, and too much good in me. I tried to come here alone, so that you would take my head and my heart, but she saw me trying to leave, and I couldn't say no to her."

"I never thought I'd see the day," Byron said. "It wasn't too long ago you were referring to humans as portable lunch boxes."

Torija looked down in shame. "I know what I did and said. It haunts me. That's why it's so important I break this bond. Daisy has this unshakable belief in me that I'll keep following the light. But I think you understand better than most what it's like to have darkness inside you. Given time, it might grow, and I couldn't bear to hurt Daisy. She deserves so much more in life."

"The last time we met, in Monaco, you said we are not dissimilar," Byron said. "You're right, I have darkness in me, and if I had been brought up by Gilbert, I could well have been in your position."

There was noise down the hallway, shouting and scuffling. "I want to see her. I won't let you hurt her."

"It's Daisy."

Byron stood and took the seat back to its original position. "Determined woman, isn't she?"

"Determined, stubborn, single-minded, nobody can tell Daisy MacDougall what to do." She started to hammer on the door. "You see?" Torija said.

Byron said, "Indeed I do."

"Let me see her now, Alexis."

"You are insane if you think Victorija Dred has changed."

Daisy took a breath. As angry as she was for being kept away from Torija, she understood Alexis's particular history and tried to be understanding, but she was just so worried about what Byron would do.

"I know what you've been through, Alexis, but she is trying to change and to find redemption."

"There is no redemption for that much blood on her hands."

Before she could respond, Byron opened the door and said, "Calm down, both of you. Daisy, Victorija wants to talk to you, and Alexis, Bhal, I'd like a word upstairs."

Alexis turned to the guards by the door and said, "Only Daisy can come out of there. Are we clear?"

"Yes, Duca."

Byron said to Daisy, "Just ask the guards to let you out, or if you need anything."

"Thank you."

Daisy went inside and threw herself into Torija's arms. "I was so worried about you."

Torija squeezed her tightly and rubbed her back. "Don't worry about me. I'm a born vampire. Come and sit down."

Daisy looked at the small sleeping area, the toilet facilities, and despaired that this was how their journey would end. She sat on the bed but kept a tight hold on Torija's hand. "What did Byron say?"

"She listened, mainly. I told her of our journey to get here, and of course Byron can't imagine that I'd changed, which I don't blame her for."

"And?"

"And she explained how Sera had been abducted by Anka."

Daisy rubbed her forehead. The tension was giving her a headache. "Yeah, Amelia was telling me."

"Anka wants an exchange for Sera. She wants a strong born vampire. Since they couldn't find me to use for their plan, Anka set her sights on Byron."

"There must be a way out. Byron can't hand herself over to Anka," Daisy said.

Torija lifted her hand and kissed it. "There is. Me."

Daisy gasped and stood up. "No way, no chance you're doing that. That's to be your punishment? Sacrificed like a lamb to the slaughter? I know how powerful Byron is, but I'm going to tell her to forget it." Daisy was feeling a mixture of anger and fear, which wasn't a good combination.

Torija got up from the bed and walked over to her. "This wasn't Byron's suggestion. It was mine." Torija took her hands. "It was always meant to be me, cherie. Anka wanted me from the start, and to be honest this was what I planned, with a few slight differences."

Daisy was confused. "What do you mean?"

"Our bond, it's not what I want for your life," Torija said.

Daisy felt the anger balled up in her chest, and it was about to blow. "You don't get to choose for me. I want this bond for my life because I love you."

"I love you, and that's why I don't want this for your life. But just let me explain." Torija rubbed her chin and tried to decide how best to explain. "Getting to know you, having this journey together, has been the best time of my life. Discovering love again, being capable of it again, is something I couldn't have imagined possible, but my grandmother, Angele, and you all believed in me."

"I know, and we wanted you to have a better life," Daisy said.

"I have had a better life, but I know Lucia wanted my redemption more than anything else. Lucia, the Reaper, and Sybil all told me that to gain forgiveness, I had to walk willingly into death. That's the cure for the green poison. The Green Man has to face the people he has wronged, killed, or caused pain to."

Daisy went back to the bed and sat down. She covered her face with her hands, then said, "That's why you were trying to leave without me last night, weren't you?"

"Yes, I was going to hand myself in to Byron, and after all I had done, I expected her to take my head and my heart. A born vampire's death. But I didn't want to hurt you, didn't want you to see it."

"I don't want you to go. I've only just found you." Tears started to fall from Daisy's eyes.

Torija sat down with her. "I don't want to leave you either, but I'll never be the Torija you fell in love with or leave Victorija behind unless I face my past. You and Amelia are the descendants. You have an important job to do against the coming darkness, and I'll be waiting for you on the other side."

Daisy couldn't find the words to express her emotions right now.

Torija put her arm around Daisy's shoulders. "Deep down you know it's the right thing to do. I'm putting others ahead of myself, which is what you taught me."

"Will you just hold me tight?"

Torija lay down on her side on the bed, and Daisy lay in front of her. Torija wrapped her arms around Daisy and kissed just behind her ear. "I love you."

Daisy took Torija's hand and placed it between her breasts. "You are the only one I will ever love."

In Byron's office tensions were high. Alexis and Bhal were disagreeing over their next move.

"Alexis, I know what she's done to you and to so many others during her long life, but we have to get Sera back."

"Of course we do. I'm the Duca to the Debrek clan, and I have pledged myself to them. I would die for Sera, but trusting Victorija is completely ridiculous. She wouldn't give herself up for anyone. It's a trick, an elaborate plot that Daisy has been unknowingly pulled in to."

"And I wouldn't? I would give anything to save Sera." Bhal was showing much more emotion than she normally did.

"But what are we supposed to do? Risk Byron's life and leave the Principessa a widow, and their child without a parent?"

Byron was getting more frustrated by the second. She slammed her hand down on the desk. "Enough! Both of you. The decision's been made. I trust the Grand Duchess and Sybil and Daisy. We are taking Victorija Dred's offer, and if Anka does not accept that, then I will exchange myself for Sera. If the worst happens, I will need you both, working in sync and securing this clan. Amelia must be protected at all costs, she holds the future of this clan, and Sera would become Principe. She will need you, Alexis, and especially you, Bhal, to guide her and teach her about leadership. Do I have your word?"

"Yes, Principe," they both said at once.

Byron stood. "Now I'm going to speak to the Principessa, and it's not going to be easy."

Byron knew where Amelia would be, where she always went in times of stress. She opened the door next to their own and found Amelia folding baby clothes into a chest of drawers. The baby's nursery had just finished being decorated, but only the furniture, like chests of drawers and chairs, had been assembled. The cot, mobile, and toys were all still in their packaging. Even though Byron assured her that vampire babies were strong and rarely had any problems, Amelia still didn't want to tempt fate by having everything set up perfectly, at this stage of the pregnancy.

One thing Amelia did allow herself was to buy baby clothes, and folding them away was therapeutic to her. Byron found her wife here often, making a little nest for their baby, and it warmed Byron's heart. But tomorrow, her spirit might only be able to watch from the other side. It would kill her to leave Amelia's side.

"Mia cara?"

"Byron. How did it go with Victorija?"

"Why don't we have a seat." Byron brought a wooden chair over to the nursing chair Amelia sat in.

"This sounds ominous."

"No, just a bit of a gamble, and I hope you think I'm doing the right thing," Byron said.

"Okay, tell me."

Byron launched into an explanation of what Victorija offered. "Alexis thinks I'm insane to trust her, and I suppose I am, but even after all she's done, my gut tells me that this is the right thing to do."

"No, you're not insane. Far from it. When Victorija took me out to dinner, do you remember?"

"How could I forget?" Byron said with some anger in her voice.

"I saw something in her eyes when she talked about the pain she had endured. There was something, some emotion left inside her, and after what Lucia said, I think the risk is worth it."

"This all hangs on the notion that Anka will accept Victorija. If not, I will have to—"

"Don't say that—don't even think it. How can she keep Sera locked up, anyway? She's a born vampire."

"I know. Anka is a slippery, extremely clever character, and powerful with it. Bhal says she has access to a very ancient power," Byron said.

"So what's the plan?"

"Anka wants us to meet at Stonehenge at quarter to midnight."

Amelia rolled her eyes. "She likes to be dramatic, then."

Now came the difficult part. Byron rubbed her hands together, and just as she was about to open her mouth, Amelia said, "Magda called. She said she would like to be there to help in any way she could."

Byron cleared her throat. "She is a very powerful witch, sweetheart."

Amelia must have taken her hesitancy as lack of enthusiasm. "No, of course she is. I'll be grateful for her backup. It wasn't that, it's—"

"Oh no." Amelia narrowed her eyes, and unfortunately for Byron her wife could read her like a book. "Don't even think about it. There is no chance you're leaving me here."

"It's too dangerous. We have too much to lose," Byron said.

"I am one of the descendants, Byron. Daisy and I are supposed to show the paranormal world how well everyone can work together against the darkness of our world. I can't not turn up to our first big challenge."

"I can't lose you, mia cara." Byron's voice cracked with emotion. Amelia took her hand. "Byron, everything is as it's meant to be. This is our destiny, and I have to be part of it."

Byron felt true fear inside, but it was Amelia's choice when it came down to it. "You better stay right at the back," Byron warned her.

"Don't worry, we are a team, and we're going to get Sera back. I promise."

CHAPTER NINETEEN

Drasas came striding into the front room of the farmhouse they had commandeered. Both Anka and Asha were sitting in front of the fire, poring over some ancient books. They stopped their conversation immediately when she entered the room.

That made Drasas both uneasy and angry. One minute she felt powerful and in control, and the next sidelined for Asha. Was she the new Principe of this clan or not?

"Can I help you, Drasas?"

"I'd like a word, Madam."

Anka looked to Asha and said, "Would you excuse us, Asha?"

"Of course, Madam."

Asha walked past her with an arrogant smile. Drasas was developing a hatred for Asha. A hatred fuelled by jealousy. When Asha was around, she always felt there was something she wasn't being told.

"Did you get rid of the bodies?" Anka asked.

"Yes." Drasas was told to get rid of the bodies of the humans they had killed when taking over the farmhouse.

"And Serenity?"

"Leo is watching her with some of our best vampires."

Anka smiled. "Good, now, what can I help you with?"

Now that she was face to face with Anka, all the complaints she had in her head, and her comebacks, felt that much harder to say.

"Spit it out, Drasas."

"Am I the new Principe of the Dred clan?"

"Of course you are, my little Drasas."

"If that's the case, then why am I getting rid of bodies and keeping watch over Serenity, and not being involved in your meetings like this one? You seem to rely on Asha more than me."

"Come and sit down, Drasas."

She took a seat and experienced a tingle all over her body at her close proximity to Anka.

"I ask you to do things like getting rid of the bodies because I trust you, and I would not believe it was being done properly unless you were taking charge."

"Oh, I see," Drasas said. That sounded better. "But what about meeting with Asha?"

"I was going over my plans and books of witchcraft. Asha understands magic and is a good sounding board. Tomorrow is your day, Drasas, the day you are to become an equal to all the born vampires who have looked down upon you. And the humans who once spat at you by the side of the road? They will be less than a bug under your boot. Tomorrow, Drasas, you will get everything you deserve."

"Thank you, Madam."

Drasas couldn't wait to stride with purpose amongst both vampire and human, and she felt strong.

"Now, send Asha back in."

"Yes, thank you, Madam Anka."

Torija never moved from her bunk, her arms holding Daisy close, all night. Last night Byron and Amelia came down to check on them. They tried to get Daisy to go upstairs and have dinner with them, but she said she'd only leave if Torija could get out of the cell, too.

She had told Daisy to leave it, but of course she didn't listen. Byron denied Daisy's request, which was exactly right. Byron was giving her chance enough to try to redeem herself, when so many wouldn't.

Torija admitted to herself that she would have done the same in Byron's position, and in fact she probably would have killed her on sight as soon as she saw her. But when Daisy stubbornly declined to join the Debreks at dinner, Amelia had two trays of food sent down.

It had been their last night together, and all Torija wanted to do was hold Daisy close. Daisy was emotional at various times in the night, and so Torija stroked her hair and soothed her any way she could. Now she felt Daisy start to waken.

She stretched and then turned around into Torija's arms. "Hi," Daisy said.

"Hello, cherie."

"I'm going to lose you today," Daisy said.

"No, you're not. You saved me, cherie."

Daisy caressed Torija's cheek. She remembered when Torija used *cherie* as a way to annoy her, but at some point, and Daisy couldn't remember when, it changed to a proper term of endearment. "I saved you so you could die."

"No, you saved me so I could save one of my family and walk into death, so I can come face to face with those I have wronged. If I didn't sacrifice myself, I wouldn't be Torija. I would still be Victorija."

"Why do you have to be so noble just as I've fallen in love with you?"

"Because I was waiting for someone to die for, and you're it, Daisy MacDougall."

Tears started to roll down Daisy's face. "It's not fair."

Torija cupped Daisy's face and wiped her tears away with her thumbs. "Cherie, I have been treated more fairly than anyone else who has done the things I've done would have been. I've been given the chance to love again, if only briefly, and a chance to say sorry to all the ones I have injured. Angele said she was my beginning, and you would be my end, and you are. This is what she meant."

Daisy gave her the deepest, sweetest kiss imaginable and said, "I'm never going to love again."

The night had finally come, and Anka was about to fulfil the plan that she and her god, Balor, had planned for some time. Drasas, Asha, Serenity, and the rest of her guards were over at the north of the henge, while she walked around and prepared each stone.

She stopped at the first stone and placed her hand in a container of human blood held by Zane, the boy that lured Serenity. Drasas had put him under a compulsion to follow any orders he got from them. Her fingers now dripped with thick, dark blood. Anka closed her eyes and spoke in an ancient language. "Balor, bless these stones with the blood of the innocents."

Anka smeared the blood on the stone, and then moved on to the next, and the next, until every stone was covered.

"Take this back to Asha," Anka said to Zane. He walked off, and Anka made her way to the centre of the Stonehenge circle. She did a quick spell to conceal them and anything that went on in the circle, so they wouldn't have any inquisitive humans popping over to see what was going on. Then she held her hands in the air, her skin covered in dried blood, and rubbed them together as if building up a charge. Anka then released her hands, and a bolt of energy flew from her fingers. It went from stone to stone, lighting up the bloodstains with a bright red glow, lighting up the night.

"The time has come, Balor."

She walked back to her people at the north end of the circle. "All is ready, Asha."

"Excellent, Madam."

Drasas was standing to the side looking worried. Anka could feel her doubt gathering. She moved to her. "Drasas, are you ready? This is your big moment."

"Are you sure it will work?"

Anka leaned forward and whispered, "Of course it will, and you will stand by my side as the world's greatest vampire." She ran her hand down Drasas's chest and heard her moan. "Don't you want to be the greatest? To have people fear you?"

"Yes, Madam. I want it."

"Good. Let us prepare, then."

Daisy held Torija's hand like a limpet for the whole two-and-a-half-hour journey to Stonehenge. She was dreading letting go, and the closer they came to their destination, the more dread she felt.

They turned into the car park and saw the bright glowing red marks on the stones.

"What is that?" Daisy asked.

"Dark magic."

Daisy's panic shot to the surface. "Don't do this, Tor, please. I've only just found you."

Alexis opened the door next to Torija and said, "Out, now."

Daisy nearly clambered over Torija to get to Alexis. "Don't you dare—"

Torija pulled her back and said to Alexis, "Can you give us a few minutes please, Alexis?"

Alexis never replied but slammed the door shut.

"I'm sick of the way she talks to you," Daisy fumed.

"Cherie, I turned her without her consent, then I ordered the attack that killed her girlfriend and her friends. This is why I have to do this. No matter what my grandmother said, or Angele, or you. I can never be redeemed, cherie. I've caused too much pain, destroyed lives, done to others like my father did to me. Why should I get a second chance at life?"

"Because I love you."

Torija smiled and caressed her cheek. "Alexis loved Anna, and my actions took that away from her. If you love me and want to redeem me as best you could, then let me do this. Victorija wouldn't walk into death, but through your love, Torija is part of me again. You were my May Queen, and I'm the Green Man." She pulled back her shirt and showed that the green vein of poison was inches from her heart. "You did what Angele asked you to do, and the path leads here."

All Daisy could muster was a nod as she wiped her tears away.

"Thank you. Let's go." Torija opened the door and got out. Everyone was staring at her, and all weapons were pointed at her.

"I'm being poisoned and am inches from death—do you really think the guns are necessary?"

Alexis got up close and pointed the muzzle into Torija's stomach. "For Victorija Dred? Very necessary."

Daisy ran around the car, pushed the muzzle of the gun away, and stood protectively in front of Torija. "She's going to die in exchange for Sera. Isn't that enough?"

"No, it will never be enough."

Byron came striding over to them. "Duca, lower the gun, now."

Alexis lowered it slowly.

Torija knew that before she met her end, she wanted to say a few words to Alexis. "I'm sorry I turned you. When I found you dying of your wounds on that battlefield, I thought, why not? Someone who has the courage to pass as a man to enter the army and protect their country should have the chance to live forever. It was like nothing to me, a whim, and until very recently, I didn't realize what that meant. But I understand you have had a long life serving my great-niece and now have love in your life. For your personal loss, I can offer no words and offer no justification. I only pray that I can beg Anna's forgiveness on the other side."

Alexis's eyes were a storm of emotion until Byron stepped in. "Victorija, follow me."

Daisy was close by Torija's side, as Amelia was by Byron's.

"Anka's certainly made the effort for our visit. Lit the stones blood red?" Torija said.

"Dark magic, like the kind I hoped I wouldn't see again for a long time. Anka said she would call with further instructions."

"Byron, will you look after Daisy for me?" Torija asked.

"Of course we will," Amelia said. "We are bonded like sisters."

When Byron's phone rang, Daisy jumped.

"Yes? I have brought Victorija Dred for you. Will you accept her in exchange for my sister?" Byron nodded and ended the call. "She will accept you, Victorija."

"Promise me this—can you ground your little sister, or something, for causing this much trouble?"

Byron actually gave her a small smile. "I will. You and I can move forward to the centre of the circle. Amelia and Daisy, stay close to Bhal and Alexis."

"May I have one last goodbye?"

Byron nodded.

Torija walked up to Daisy, slipped her hands on her waist, and leaned her forehead against Daisy's.

"Ah, cherie. It's been a grand adventure, hasn't it?"

She could see Daisy was trying to be brave. "Yeah, Vamp. It's been fun."

"You are going to have a good life and you'll find love again," Torija said.

Daisy's tears couldn't be held back any longer. "I told you, I'm never going to love again. I'm bonded to this powerful born vampire."

Torija felt her own tears well up. She kissed Daisy deeply, trying to convey every inch of love she had for her. "I'm dying for you. Thank you for leading me back to the light."

"Say hi to Angele for me," Daisy said.

"Cherie, Angele and I will be in very different places. I love you." Bhal, Alexis, and the rest of the guards stood just a few feet away. She spotted Magda the witch in the crowd. She nodded to her. "Goodbye, Debreks, one and all. It falls to me, Victorija Debrek, to win the day and save the damsel in distress. I take my leave of you." Torija gave a flourishing bow, and winked and blew a kiss to Daisy.

She then turned and joined Byron.

"Was the grand speech of goodbye and flourishing bow really needed?" Byron asked.

"I've lived my life with a flourish, and I see no reason to face death without."

"Let's go."

❖

Amelia lifted her hand and felt energy spark in the air. She turned to Magda. "What is this?"

Magda stepped forward and said, "The henge is like a huge casting circle. The most ancient kind."

Amelia remembered the casting circle she had entered in the New Forest. It had brought her the voices of her ancestors. She closed her eyes now and focused on the energy flying around the air like static. She heard wails and screams, and rain. Amelia tried to go deeper, and she started to hear the voices of her ancestors.

Amelia heard them and knew what to do. What every fibre of her being was telling her to do. She opened her eyes and turned to Daisy. "Do you trust me?"

"You don't have to ask me that," Daisy replied.

"Take my hand—we're going in. We have to run, or Bhal and Alexis will stop us. After three." Amelia counted out three, and they both ran as fast as they could. They got inside the circle, and Alexis and Bhal were prevented from following them by some kind of energy field.

"Come back, Principessa. You're in great danger," Bhal shouted.

But all Amelia could focus on was the swirling energy around them. She looked at Daisy, who was holding her hand up and marvelling at the sparks coming off her hand.

"Can you feel that?" Amelia asked her.

"Yeah, it's like my spidey sense on speed."

"Daisy? Look," Amelia said, pointing to the stones.

Daisy looked over at the spaces between the stones and saw spirits—miserable, grey spirits—all from different points in history.

"What's going on?" Amelia asked.

"The dead that haven't moved on. My Monster Hunters group did a video on Stonehenge. Archaeologists found burials all around the stones. It looks like they need the Reaper to help move on."

"Maybe it's to do with the stones," Amelia said. "The Reapers might not be able to enter the henge. Anyway, let's keep going. I'm being told to follow Byron and Victorija with you."

"I'm with you."

❖

As Torija and Byron approached the centre of the circle, Anka was coming to meet them along with Sera, and behind them, Drasas and Asha. Anka stopped and held up her hand.

"Send me Victorija, and Serenity will come to you."

Byron turned to Torija and said, "Good luck, Victorija. If you are truthfully helping us, then you die a Debrek, but if you are going to double-cross us, then—"

"You'll hunt me down and take my head and my heart, I know. I have a job to do. Goodbye, Byron."

Torija started to walk away from Byron, and as she did, Sera was coming from the other direction. When Sera was within earshot, she said to her, "Byron says you're grounded, young lady." Torija smiled. "Have a good life, Sera, and look out for Daisy."

Sera looked bemused. "You're handing yourself over for me?"

"Yes, my dear. Your old great-aunt is saving your little derriere, so go do something good with your immortal life."

Once they passed each other, Torija came into eye contact with Drasas, her Duca. Drasas looked away quickly, hopefully feeling shame for once in her life.

Anka welcomed her with a huge smile. "Victorija, we've missed you. Haven't we, Drasas?"

"Yes, Madam."

Yes, Madam? What had Anka done to her once proud vampire? "Well, here I am, reporting for duty, Anka. Now how is it you'd like to kill me?"

"By draining every ounce of life force from your body."

"Excellent, excellent. Good plan," Torija said sarcastically.

Anka walked a little closer and said, "My, my. You have got so much of your energy back. Your human blood donor must have quite an effect on you."

"Indeed, she is strong, a strong descendant, and she and Amelia will come for you and destroy you one day, and I will be laughing from the other side."

Anka laughed. "How sweet. Believe me, there will be no laughter where you're going. Watch her, Drasas."

Anka walked a few yards away and started to recite an incantation.

Drasas looked extremely uncomfortable beside her.

"Hello, Drasas. How have you been? Enjoying being Principe? One piece of advice I'd give you. Be careful who you choose as your Duca."

"I'm going to be the greatest vampire there's ever been or will be," Drasas spat back.

"That's what she promised you, did she?" Torija laughed.

"Listen—" Drasas started to respond angrily.

"Be quiet, both of you," Asha said

"Shut up, Asha. I—"

They were all distracted by a red light that zoomed from Anka's elaborate ring to each standing stone. It spun and spun, gaining speed with every rotation, until it seemed to have gained enough energy and shot into the centre of the circle, near where they were standing.

What Torija could only describe as a huge white portal opened.

Anka began to laugh. "Yes, Asha, it worked. After all this time, it worked."

"Your work is remarkable, Madam Anka," Asha said.

"Get them over here, Asha."

Torija leaned over to Drasas and said, "You're a *them* now, Drasas. Did you hear that?"

"I will destroy you," Drasas said.

"Ooh. You are confident. Good. That's what I like to hear. Asha? Where would you like us?" Torija could tell that she was getting to Drasas, and she liked it. She had decided that she would face death with the same cocky assuredness that she had lived her entire life by. No matter how much she had changed, there was still a part of her that would always be Victorija Dred.

They arrived at the portal beside Anka.

"Drasas, you know what to do." Anka handed over a ring.

Torija looked at Drasas and saw how unsure and frightened she was. All she could do was nod.

"Very good," Anka said. "Victorija, your time on this earth is over. Walk with Drasas to the other side."

"I walk willingly unto death. Keep up, Drasas."

"Will I return unharmed, Madam?"

"You will be as good as new, now go."

With one last look back to Daisy, Torija walked into the portal, and when she emerged, she was standing on a grassy bank near the edge of a cliff. The rain was hammering down, and there was the sound of thunder in the distance.

Drasas was beside her within a few seconds.

"So this is what death looks like," Torija said. "I always wondered."

"I'm not dead. I'll be going back," Drasas said.

"You just keep thinking that, Drasas. A woman like Anka uses people and disposes of them. You'll be next."

Drasas launched herself at Torija. Torija caught her arms and started to feel her energy draining. "What's happening?"

"What's happening is I am becoming the most powerful vampire in the world." Torija's energy was depleting through her arms, surging down Drasas's arms and into the glowing ring on her finger. She fell to her knees and Drasas taunted her. "You thought I was a joke."

Drasas punched Torija, and she felt the world spinning. There was virtually nothing left inside her. Then Drasas kicked her in the mouth. Torija spat blood onto the grass.

"You said I was being used and too stupid to know about it," Drasas said.

Torija lay on the wet grass and watched Drasas's anger spill out of her. With every moment her anger was building, the louder the thunder got. Her vision was getting slightly hazy, but she saw the black storm clouds gather and start to head this way.

Drasas spat, "I'm going to rule that world out there, the way you couldn't, and I'm going to kill your sweet Daisy."

Torija couldn't even summon the power to lift up her hand or form any words. Drasas's attention was suddenly turned to the growing black clouds, which appeared to be headed towards her.

"What is this?" she shouted.

Then the darkness came shooting forward into Drasas's chest. Drasas was knocked flat on the ground and started to shake. One minute later a figure was thrown out of her, onto the grass. It was Drasas's soul.

"What's happening?"

Shadowy hands reached from below the edge of the cliff and grasped Drasas's legs. "No, no. Help me, Principe, please?" High-pitched screams of the dead rang out from below the cliff. Drasas was terrified. "Victorija, help me."

But Torija couldn't help her even if she wanted to, which she didn't. The last Torija saw was Drasas's hands, trying to grab into nothingness. Drasas fell to her fate below, screaming as she went.

It comforted Torija to know that Drasas would spend eternity along with her, in the place dark souls go. She, at least, was resigned to the certainty of her death.

The last ounces of her energy were seeping away. As her vision deteriorated, she saw a ball of energy knock Drasas's body through the portal.

Torija's eyes were shutting. Her long immortal life was ending. Just before her lids shut for the very last time, she heard a voice say, "Look up, Torija." She would remember that voice forever, but she couldn't lift her head. Then Torija felt someone touching her head.

"Stand up."

She felt a surge through her, and then her body felt light as a feather. Torija managed to look up and saw the shining face of Angele.

"Angele?"

Angele held out her hand and was smiling. "Come with me, Torija."

Torija stood and was shocked to see her body left behind her, unconscious or dead.

Angele smiled. "You found your way back, then?"

This was so strange. "With your help."

"And Daisy's help."

It was a strange feeling, talking to your first love about the woman you loved now.

"You love her?" Angele asked.

"Yes, I do." Torija felt terrible saying that, as if she was betraying Angele's memory.

Angele's smile never faltered. "Don't feel bad. I told you both that I was your beginning, and Daisy was your end. We both had our destinies."

Torija remembered what she had done since Angele last saw her, and shame rushed through her. "I'm sorry, Angele. I turned to darkness. I've done so many bad things and killed so many more."

"The Grand Duchess and Sybil told you that you had to walk willingly into death and face those you have hurt and killed, yes?"

"Yes," Torija said.

"This is your chance to choose. You can come with me on the lighter path, and face those souls, or you can go where Drasas did and never have to look them in the eye."

There was no contest. She hadn't come this far to do the wrong thing.

"I wish to face them, Angele."

"Then follow me."

Torija followed her to the cliff edge but saw nothing beneath where they would be walking.

"Angele, there's no walkway."

"There is if you trust me. Take my hand, look towards the light, and walk with me," Angele told her.

Torija tried to summon her courage and believe in Angele. She took her first step and didn't drop.

"Thank you for trusting me," Angele said.

"I always will."

Angele encouraged her to walk, and she followed her into the light.

CHAPTER TWENTY

Daisy saw Drasas's unconscious body blown back through the portal.

"Did you see that?" Amelia said.

Byron was standing with her arms around both Amelia and her sister.

"I'm really sorry. I should have handled this much better. Some leader, eh?" Sera said.

"It's not your fault. We can talk about it later."

"Why does Drasas get to come back, and Tor doesn't?" Daisy said.

She wasn't having it. Daisy started to run as fast as she could towards the portal.

"Byron, stop her," Amelia said.

Byron sighed. She zipped with her supernatural speed and was able to grab Daisy just a few yards away from Anka.

"Let me go, Byron."

"No, she'll kill you."

Anka shot a blast of red energy at Byron's back. Byron dropped to her knees, and Daisy was able to run at the portal.

But just as she got near, Anka closed it. "Too late, Ms. MacDougall. She's gone forever."

Daisy dove onto Anka, and a struggle ensued.

Anka pushed Daisy onto her back and laughed. "Now I'm going to destroy you."

Daisy tried to push Anka's face away from her, but when her hand touched Anka's cheek, Anka screamed, as her skin sizzled and burned.

Daisy was as surprised as she was. Anka rolled off her, and there was a deeply burned handprint on her face.

"Drasas! Drasas!"

Anka stumbled to her feet.

Asha hurried over. "Madam, are you all right?"

"Don't worry about me—bring Drasas's body. Now."

Byron recovered and was by Daisy's side in a millisecond. "What happened?"

Daisy looked at her hand in astonishment. There wasn't a mark on it. "I really don't know."

Amelia reached them. "Byron, Daisy—are you okay?"

"Yes, we're safe."

"She closed the portal out of spite. I wanted to go find Torija," Daisy cried.

"Daisy, come with me," Amelia said as she marched to the middle of the circle.

"Amelia, what are you doing?" Byron shouted.

"Just trust me. Daisy, let's hold hands and close our eyes. Can you feel it?"

"Yes." Daisy experienced an incredible force travelling the circuit between their two arms. The more she concentrated, the faster the power raced around the circuit of their arms. The wind started to whip around them. "Amelia, what's happening?"

"Just keep concentrating."

Chapter Twenty-one

Torija stepped on an island between the cliff edge and the abyss below. Lots and lots of spirits were waiting for her. She recognized some of the faces. "It's them."

"Yes," Angele said, "the souls you killed or had killed. You must face them if you want to seek their forgiveness."

"How can I be forgiven?"

"It depends on the sincerity of your apology and the grace of those to whom your apology is directed."

Torija looked up and saw her grandmother, the Grand Duchess, walking with the aid of her stick.

She immediately dropped to her knees. "Grandmother, I don't know how to say—"

"You don't have to say, little Victorija. We neglected one of our own. Byron's father and I should have come and helped you and your mother, but we were ignorant of what you were going through. But Angele showed me everything, as well as your very own Brassard."

Daisy. Torija's heart ached.

"Come talk to us all, and tell us what's in your heart."

Torija was frightened. She was never frightened of anything, apart from her father.

"Come, my dear," Lucia said.

Torija thought of Daisy and her courage in handing herself over to the Dred vampires, just so she could try to redeem her. The thought made her move forward. As she stood on the island of rock, she followed her instincts and bowed down on one knee.

The spirits encircled her, just as in her nightmares, but this time she didn't scream.

The spirits spoke as one voice. "You wished to speak."

"My name is Victorija Dred. It should have been Debrek, but my father took my mother and me away from them when I was young. This is not to make excuses. The things I have done are some of the worst crimes you could commit, and every one of you knows that. All I ask is that you hear my testament."

Torija told them everything, the very worst she had done, and named some of the spirits as she went.

"I don't apologize, because how do you apologize for such great harm and evil? I only tell you my story from beginning to end, to show how far I have come, with three such astonishing women influencing me—Angele Brassard, Lucia Debrek, and Daisy MacDougall. Please know that I look on my actions with utter shame. That's all I can say."

She watched the spirits huddle together, and she could hear a murmur. Then they started fading away into the light, all except one, a beautiful young woman in eighteenth-century clothing.

"Stand up, Victorija."

She looked to Lucia and then Angele and stood, and from somewhere deep inside she just knew who this was. "You're Alexis's Anna, aren't you?"

To her utter surprise the woman smiled. "I am Anna, and I've been asked to convey the judgement of the group."

All Torija wanted to do was say sorry, but she was too ashamed to get the words out.

Anna held her hand up. "You don't have to speak any more. You didn't ask for forgiveness because you thought your crimes were too great, but your testament touched us, as did your bravery to let love into your heart again and protect Daisy against your very own clan. So, as I say, you didn't ask it, but you will receive our forgiveness."

"You're joking." Torija was absolutely gobsmacked.

"No, we don't joke about forgiveness, but there are conditions. You must dedicate your life to protecting Daisy and Amelia, the descendants, with Byron. We have no other chance against the great evil that is to come."

"But I am dead. How can I protect them?"

Anna smiled and said, "Tell Alexis to let go of the past. I'm so happy that she has found Katie. They are a perfect match." Then she just faded into the light. Behind her the portal opened back up.

"Grandmother? Angele?"

"You're going back," Lucia said.

"What?"

Angele took her hand. "You have passed every test given to you. You chose loyalty to an oath taken so long ago, you turned your back on your clan to save one human, you were the Green Man who met her May Queen and faced your past misdeeds when she asked you to."

Lucia stepped closer. "You came to those you hurt with humility, and most important of all, you put the needs of your family and the woman you love above your own life. You died for love."

"As you did, Grandmother. You died for me. You opened up my emotions and set me on this path, didn't you?"

Lucia shrugged. "It was my destiny. Your children and grand-children always come first. Now, go."

Torija turned to Angele. "Thank you for everything you have done for Daisy and me."

"I was your beginning, and she was your end—and new beginning. Be good to each other."

"How do I get back?"

"Just run at the portal, and your body will catch up, but hurry—they can't hold it much longer."

Torija nodded and gave a flourishing bow. "Thank you, ladies."

She ran as fast as she could and jumped into the void.

❖

Amelia and Daisy could only see each other as a typhoon of energy whirled around them. It was so hard to keep it together.

Daisy kept feeling her hands slipping, and then Amelia would shout, "Hold it! Hold it just a little longer."

Just when she thought she couldn't hold any longer, a body hurled through the portal and landed heavily on the ground. It was Torija.

Daisy broke the circuit and ran for her. "Tor!" She slid onto her knees and gently shook her. "Tor? Are you okay?"

"Ah...that was a hard landing," Torija said.

"You're alive!"

Daisy kissed her hard on the lips and peppered her face with kisses. "Yes, what a welcome. I should die more often."

Daisy smiled and gave her a playful hit to the arm. "No, you're not to die, ever."

"I just want it put on record that I died for you, so that should make up for some missteps I make in our relationship. Since I've never had a long-term relationship before, I'm sure the missteps will be many."

Daisy had never been happier in her life. She'd fought for Torija's soul, and she'd won.

Amelia and Byron came running over. "Is she okay?" Amelia asked.

"I'm fine."

"Wait, what about the poison?" Daisy pulled open her shirt.

"I appreciate you want to get me naked, but there's a time and a place."

"I can see you didn't lose your arrogant streak on the other side, but look at your chest. The green poison is gone," Daisy said.

Torija touched her chest and looked up and down her arm. "I'm as good as new."

Byron reached down and offered her hand. "You kept your word."

"I said I would." Torija took her hand and jumped to her feet.

"How did you know, Amelia?" Daisy asked.

"Angele. She let me know."

"You met her again?" Daisy smiled.

"Yes, she wished us a happy life."

One other person joined the group. Sera was looking sheepish. "Aunt Victorija…um…thanks for what you did."

"Something I've learned too late in the day—you risk everything for the one you love and your family."

"For family." Byron smiled at her.

Everyone went back to the Debrek house. Byron wanted everyone together, so they could take stock of everything that happened.

"This feels strange," Torija said.

"What does?" Daisy asked.

"Sitting in Byron's house as a guest, with an arm around my blood bond, who I love more than anything in the world." Torija gave her a quick kiss.

Everyone was here in the drawing room, waiting for Byron to return from her office.

Torija felt a presence beside her. She looked up and saw Alexis standing there with Katie. "Alexis?"

"I just want to know one thing. Did you see Anna on the other side?"

Torija nodded. "I did. She spoke to me and said that you should let go of the past, and that she is so happy for you and Katie. That you were a perfect match."

"Thank you," Alexis said. Then she walked away, holding Katie's hand.

"That was the most civil conversation I have ever had with Alexis," Torija said.

"You see, I told you now was the time to build bridges."

Byron walked back into the room, and Amelia joined her by the fireplace. "Everyone, Brogan has just informed me that Anka is back in Paris with her people. So we have some breathing room ahead, but believe me, we have a dark, difficult path to walk. The whole paranormal world could be torn apart. Not to mention the horrific toll it will take to win this coming war. But we have one advantage—a member of the family, returning to the fold. My great-aunt Victorija, or Torija, as she wishes to be called."

Byron kissed Amelia's hand and then walked over to Torija. Torija felt Daisy's hand clasp hers a bit harder.

"Torija, you walked into death for family, for the people you love, and we are eternally grateful for your courage. Will you take the hand of friendship and return to your family?"

"Yes." Torija took Byron's hand and shook it.

Byron smiled and said, "Welcome back to the family, Torija Debrek."

Everyone clapped except Alexis, but Torija could understand her feelings.

Daisy must have known her thoughts, because Daisy said, "It'll just take time. I love you, Vamp."

Torija smiled brightly. "And I love you with everything that I am. Thank you for having such faith in me."

"Thank you for trusting me and letting me in," Daisy said happily.

One of the staff came around with an array of drinks on silver platters.

"To mark this moment, I'd like to propose a toast. *Et sanguinem familiae*—blood and family."

Everyone, especially Torija, replied enthusiastically, "Blood and family."

EPILOGUE

Anka walked into the catacombs beneath her Paris home.
From behind the ritual area, Drasas walked out into the main part of Anka's worship space. Anka watched her look down at her body and then say, "I suppose if I can't have my own body, this one will serve me well."

Anka bowed her head in respect. "Welcome, emissary. Welcome, Gilbert Dred."

Gilbert gave her a smile, rubbed her hands together, and said, "Shall we take over the world, Madam?"

About the Author

Jenny Frame (www.jennyframe.com) is from the small town of Motherwell in Scotland, where she lives with her partner, Lou, and their well-loved and very spoiled dog.

She has a diverse range of qualifications, including a BA in public management and a diploma in acting and performance. Nowadays she likes to put her creative energies into writing rather than treading the boards.

When not writing or reading, Jenny loves cheering on her local football team, cooking, and spending time with her family.

Books Available From Bold Strokes Books

Business of the Heart by Claire Forsythe. When a hopeless romantic meets a tough-as-nails cynic, they'll need to overcome the wounds of the past to discover that their hearts are the most important business of all. (978-1-63679-167-8)

Dying for You by Jenny Frame. Can Victorija Dred keep an age-old vow and fight the need to take blood from Daisy Macdougall? (978-1-63679-073-2)

Exclusive by Melissa Brayden. Skylar Ruiz lands the TV reporting job of a lifetime, but is she willing to sacrifice it all for the love of her longtime crush, anchorwoman Carolyn McNamara? (978-1-63679-112-8)

Her Duchess to Desire by Jane Walsh. An up-and-coming interior designer seeks to create a happily ever after with an intriguing duchess, proving that love never goes out of fashion. (978-1-63679-065-7)

Take Her Down by Lauren Emily Whalen. Stakes are cutthroat, scheming is creative, and loyalty is ever-changing in this queer, female-driven YA retelling of Shakespeare's Julius Caesar. (978-1-63679-089-3)

The Game by Jan Gayle. Ryan Gibbs is a talented golfer, but her guilt means she may never leave her small town, even if Katherine Reese tempts her with competition and passion. (978-1-63679-126-5)

Whereabouts Unknown by Meredith Doench. While homicide detective Theodora Madsen recovers from a potentially career-ending injury, she scrambles to solve the cases of two missing sixteen-year-old girls from Ohio. (978-1-63555-647-6)

Deadly Secrets by VK Powell. Corporate criminals want whistleblower Jana Elliott permanently silenced, but Rafe Silva will risk everything to keep the woman she loves safe. (978-1-63679-087-9)

Enchanted Autumn by Ursula Klein. When Elizabeth comes to Salem, Massachusetts, to study the witch trials, she never expects to find love—or an actual witch...and Hazel might just turn out to be both. (978-1-63679-104-3)

Escorted by Renee Roman. When fantasy meets reality, will escort Ryan Lewis be able to walk away from a chance at forever with her new client Dani? (978-1-63679-039-8)

Her Heart's Desire by Anne Shade. Two women. One choice. Will Eve and Lynette be able to overcome their doubts and fears to embrace their deepest desire? (978-1-63679-102-9)

My Secret Valentine by Julie Cannon, Erin Dutton & Anne Shade. Winning the heart of your secret Valentine? These award-winning authors agree, there is no better way to fall in love. (978-1-63679-071-8)

Perilous Obsession by Carsen Taite. When reporter Macy Moran becomes consumed with solving a cold case, will her quest for the truth bring her closer to Detective Beck Ramsey or will her obsession with finding a murderer rob her of a chance at true love? (978-1-63679-009-1)

Reading Her by Amanda Radley. Lauren and Allegra learn love and happiness are right where they least expect it. There's just one problem: Lauren has a secret she cannot tell anyone, and Allegra knows she's hiding something. (978-1-63679-075-6)

The Willing by Lyn Hemphill. Kitty Wilson doesn't know how, but she can bring people back from the dead as long as someone is willing to take their place and keep the universe in balance. (978-1-63679-083-1)

Watching Over Her by Ronica Black. As they face the snowstorm of the century, and the looming threat of a stalker, Riley and Zoey just might find love in the most unexpected of places. (978-1-63679-100-5)

Always by Kris Bryant. When a pushy American private investigator shows up demanding to meet the woman in Camila's artwork, instead of introducing her to her great-grandmother, Camila decides to lead her on a wild goose chase all over Italy. (978-1-63679-027-5)

Exes and O's by Joy Argento. Ali and Madison really only have one thing in common. The girl who broke their heart may be the only one who can put it back together. (978-1-63679-017-6)

Paris Rules by Jaime Maddox. Carly Becker has been searching for the perfect woman all her life, but no one ever seems to be just right until Paige Waterford checks all her boxes, except the most important one—she's married. (978-1-63679-077-0)

Shadow Dancers by Suzie Clarke. In this third and final book in the Moon Shadow series, Rachel must find a way to become the hunter and not the hunted, and this time she will meet Eshee Yumiko head-on. (978-1-63555-829-6)

The Kiss by C.A. Popovich. When her wife refuses their divorce and begins to stalk her, threatening her life, Kate realizes to protect her new love, Leslie, she has to let her go, even if it breaks her heart. (978-1-63679-079-4)

The Wedding Setup by Charlotte Greene. When Ryann, a big-time New York executive, goes to Colorado to help out with her best friend's wedding, she never expects to fall for the maid of honor. (978-1-63679-033-6)

Velocity by Gun Brooke. Holly and Claire work toward an uncertain future preparing for an alien space mission, and only one thing is certain—they will have to risk their lives, and their hearts, to discover the truth. (978-1-63555-983-5)

Wildflower Words by Sam Ledel. Lida Jones treks west with her father in search of a better life on the rapidly developing American frontier, but finds home when she meets Hazel Thompson. (978-1-63679-055-8)

A Fairer Tomorrow by Kathleen Knowles. For Maddie Weeks and Gerry Stern, the Second World War brought them together, but the end of the war might rip them apart. (978-1-63555-874-6)

Changing Majors by Ana Hartnett Reichardt. Beyond a love, beyond a coming-out, Bailey Sullivan discovers what lies beyond the shame and self-doubt imposed on her by traditional Southern ideals. (978-1-63679-081-7)

Highland Whirl by Anna Larner. Opposites attract in the Scottish Highlands, when feisty Alice Campbell falls for city girl about town Roxanne Barns. (978-1-63555-892-0)

Holiday Hearts by Diana Day-Admire and Lyn Cole. Opposites attract during Christmastime chaos in Kansas City. (978-1-63679-128-9)

Humbug by Amanda Radley. With the corporate Christmas party in jeopardy, CEO Rosalind Caldwell hires Christmas Girl Ellie Pearce as her personal assistant. The only problem is, Ellie isn't a PA, has never planned a party, and develops a ridiculous crush on her totally intimidating new boss. (978-1-63555-965-1)

On the Rocks by Georgia Beers. Schoolteacher Vanessa Martini makes no apologies for her dating checklist, and newly single mom Grace Chapman ticks all Vanessa's Do Not Date boxes. Of course, they're never going to fall in love. (978-1-63555-989-7)

Song of Serenity by Brey Willows. Arguing with the Muse of music and justice is complicated, falling in love with her even more so. (978-1-63679-015-2)

The Christmas Proposal by Lisa Moreau. Stranded together in a Christmas village on a snowy mountain, Grace and Bridget face their past and question their dreams for the future. (978-1-63555-648-3)

The Infinite Summer by Morgan Lee Miller. While spending the summer with her dad in a small beach town, Remi Brenner falls for Harper Hebert and accidentally finds herself tangled up in an intense restaurant rivalry between her famous stepmom and her first love. (978-1-63555-969-9)

Wisdom by Jesse J. Thoma. When Sophia and Reggie are chosen for the governor's new community design team and tasked with tackling substance abuse and mental health issues, battle lines are drawn even as sparks fly. (978-1-63555-886-9)